Heather
for a
Highlander

by

Gail MacMillan

Heather for a Highlander

Cover Art by *Debbie Taylor*

The Wild Rose Press, Inc.
PO Box 708
Adams Basin, NY 14410-0708
Visit us at www.thewildrosepress.com

Publishing History
First English Tea Rose Edition, 2014
Print ISBN 978-1-62830-346-9
Digital ISBN 978-1-62830-347-6

Published in the United States of America

"Oh, my God." Doctor William MacTavish sank onto a chair, dropped his head into his hands on the table, and moaned. "Oh, my God!" He couldn't believe the story his brother had just told him, definitely didn't want to believe it.

"Don't fret yourself, Will." Captain James MacTavish colored his words with a soft, soothing Scottish burr. "I've thought it through. No one at the inn knew who I was except Mistress Heather here. I was only some stranger from the roads, a highwayman perhaps. They'll not be searching the seaports for us. Have another wee dram. It'll still your nerves." He poured more whiskey into his brother's cup.

"Argh!" William pulled himself upright on his chair. "There's not enough whiskey in all of Scotland to still my nerves. You know what you've done, you daft creature, don't you?" He glared up at his brother. "You've fitted both our necks into nooses. Sweet Jesus, a lady and a murder suspect!"

"There's little to worry about." The one identified as Lady Julia Thomas tossed her tangled dark curls. "Anyone pursuing me will most likely have headed for Scotland."

"And why, pray tell, might they have done that?" Weary exasperation tainted his words.

"I left a note saying I'd run off to Scotland's Gretna Green with a highwayman from the Highlands. At the time I had no idea I'd be coming to a place that once had a similar name. Ironic, isn't it?"

Praise for Gail MacMillan

"Be prepared to be hooked on the first word of the first page and go on to the next with anticipation. Her stories will live in your heart long after the last page is read."

~Rebecca Melvin, Publisher, Double Edge Press

~*~

"Gail MacMillan's stories delight the senses and brighten the dark days of winter like a candle glowing on a windowsill. Best enjoyed while curled up in your favorite chair...with some hot cocoa and a faithful canine companion."

~Sue Owens Wright, author, newspaper columnist, and two-time Maxwell Medal recipient

~*~

"Gail MacMillan's stories place you in a well-worn comforting chair. She writes of deep-rooted rural customs and traditions, of her love of dogs and horses. She shows glimpses of truth in revelatory detail."

~Heather White, Editor, Saltscapes Magazine

Dedication

To my patient and professional editor, Nan Swanson.
She lights my way.

Chapter 1

"Ah, Will, not my horse! You'd not go taking a man's horse, lad!" The man stared down at the two hands of cards laid out on the plank table in front of him.

"You gambled and lost, Jamie." His opponent shrugged broad shoulders, pushed back his chair, and stood. "Let this be a lesson to you that it's time to stop wagering."

"You know that stallion means everything to me." The loser looked up at the winner, handsome face crinkled into pleading lines. "Name your price, you great stubborn Highlander, and I swear by all that's holy, I'll have it for you when next my ship comes to this port."

"I've got what I need, a fast mount to get me to my patients." Doctor William MacTavish picked up his tankard and headed for the bar. "That stallion you've so aptly named Wings will do nicely."

"Will, I'm a proud man." His companion followed him and stood beside him as he waited for the barmaid to replenish his drink. "But I'm begging you. Don't take Wings. Remember how I took you on a dozen years ago as ship's surgeon during that war with the Americans? You were fresh out of medical training in Edinburgh, with no experience and…"

"It's presently 1824, that war is history, and you, Captain, as a privateer, were lucky to have any kind of medical aid aboard." His tankard refilled, he turned back to the man with the midnight black hair curling beneath his ears, the epitome of a handsome swashbuckler. "I was and am a *doctor*, not a sawbones surgeon. Even ships of the British navy weren't so blessed. At any rate, that was over a decade ago, long past history."

"Verrae well." The other man drew himself up and faced his companion, blue eyes snapping outrage, Scottish burr dragging on his tongue. "Take the damned horse. I hope he throws you flat on your backside!"

He started to turn away, but the doctor's voice stopped him.

"There is one thing I'll trade for the stallion."

"And what might that be? Three wishes from the fairies?"

"No need to be nasty, Jamie, although my offer of a trade might lead you on an interesting quest the next time you drop anchor off merry old England." The doctor took a sip of ale, his eyes narrowing with challenge over the mug's rim. He walked slowly, deliberately back to their table.

"I might have known." Following him, the captain hailed the barmaid. "Meg, another ale. I have a feeling my brother and I are going to have a tankard's full of discussion ahead."

The two men resumed their seats, the younger glaring at the older.

The woman behind the bar tossed the captain a sly grin he failed to notice as she filled up a mug. Then she sauntered across the room, hips swaying. As she bent to

2

place the drink in front of Captain James MacTavish, she gave him a generous view of her ample bosom all but popping from the top of her gown.

"How much longer will you be in port, Captain?" She batted her eyelashes as she slowly straightened up.

"Not much longer, Meggie darlin', not much longer. Winter's fast approaching, and I have no desire to be frozen in here when there're all the delights of the Caribbean and London to be enjoyed. I've never been partial to snow and sleet."

"Huh!" With a disdainful grunt, she swung around and flounced back to the bar.

"Jamie, Jamie, you've been cavorting with Meg Whalen again." The doctor lowered his head, shaking it slowly.

"Ah, Will, she's but a bit of fun. She's not about to take me seriously…not like that other one…and a man needs a bit of…companionship…from time to time."

"I wish to God you'd find a good woman and settle down." William narrowed his eyes and glared over at his brother. "Someday you'll either get some nasty disease or end up shot or stabbed by a jealous wench or her man, or so deeply in debt you'll be bankrupt."

"By God, Will, I swear you've become a bone-chafing annoyance with your self-righteousness. I recall that during the war you were as big a rascal as you now accuse me of being."

"Aye, well, those days are behind me." His expression cleared. "To business. Here are the terms of my request."

****

"You want me to do what?" The captain banged his mug down on the table and stared across at his companion.

"I said I want you to find me an assistant."

"Aye, but what an assistant! Someone who will cook and clean, is able to read and write and cipher, clever enough to learn about medicines and caring for the sick, will help you with the farm work, and has a stomach strong enough to assist you in your medical procedures. In short, a creature I'm about as likely to encounter as a griffin."

"There you have it, Brother." Dr. William MacTavish leaned back in his chair, strong brown fingers playing with the handle of his tankard, his eyes narrowing. "I'm in desperate need of such a person, and none is to be found here in the colony. What say? Are you up to the challenge?"

"Damn you, Will." The man lowered his head, shaking it. "Sending St. George to slay a dragon had nothing on this."

"So you're saying you're not willing to give it a try? That you'll desert your favorite mount without so much as an attempt?"

The big man sucked in a deep breath and drew himself up. "You're a bastard, Will MacTavish, but I accept your challenge...with one condition. The minute I deliver this paragon into your care, I'll expect to take my horse back in perfect condition. I won't have you jumping him over windfalls and breaking his leg to get to a lad who's cut himself in a lumber camp, or racing his heart out so you can deliver a babe that is perfectly capable of finding its way into this world on its own. Understood?"

"Understood." The doctor got to his feet and held out a hand.

"Agreed." The captain followed suit and accepted his offer. "But what made you decide you wanted an assistant? I thought you were content to be the hermit healer, buried away in that great stone house of yours."

"Too many people in need are coming to me for help, now that I've managed to convince a goodly number of this valley's residents that the pagan cures of that old witch Hannah Rob don't work. You know I've been trying for years to convince the local people to come to me instead of to her for treatment. Well, while you were away on your last voyage, fate stepped in to give me a hand. A village family became ill with a fever. Hannah treated them with one of her weird cures, and six of the children died. I was downriver ministering to another family with a similar complaint at the time. They all survived. It appeared I'd performed a miracle, although it was simply sound medical practices. When I returned and news of my success and her failure spread through the community, almost everyone turned away from her and began coming to me for medical help.

"Now I'm overwhelmed with patients, and my farm is falling into neglect. I need someone capable of taking care of it, as well a person I can train to dispense basic drugs and do rudimentary medical treatments when I'm not available. Hence my need for an assistant."

"Ah-ha. So Mr. I-Do-Verrae-Well-On-My-Own has finally realized he needs help. Well, I'll see what I can do. Now we'd best be off. I have a ship loading at the wharf. If I don't check the details, God only knows what kind of a mess my crew will make of it. I'm sure you've got patients in need of your attention."

They started toward the door, but a ruckus at the end of the bar halted them. Two men were struggling, one obviously far gone in drink.

"Jack, I'm telling you, my brother, you've had enough! You'll not be fit to work for a week if you continue like this."

"Let me go!" The inebriated one tried to take a swing at the man attempting to pull him away from the bottle on the counter. "You're nothing but a damned, straight-laced..."

"I think Tom could use some help." Captain Jamie MacTavish glanced at his brother.

"Aye."

"Need a hand, Tom?" Jamie asked as they approached the struggling pair.

"I'd be obliged, Captain." The man named Tom ducked another swing and tried to pin his companion's arms behind him. "If you'll just help me get him onto the wagon..."

"Definitely." Together the MacTavishes dove into the fray. Within seconds, they'd floored the drunk. With the doctor holding his upper body and the captain his legs, they carried him, wriggling and cursing, out into the cold, grey November afternoon and flung him into the back of the waiting wagon. The minute Jack Glen hit the boards, he vomited down his front, then rolled to one side and passed out.

"You'll have no trouble with him on the drive home." Jamie MacTavish brushed off his hands and grinned at the man's sweating brother.

"Thank ye." Tom Glen drew a deep breath. "But when he comes to, it will be hell to pay. Especially after he discovers I've found his stash and dumped it."

"He needs help." The doctor stood with his hands on the board side of the wagon, looking down at the man lying in his own filth. "Tom, try to convince him before it's too late."

"You know I've done my best, Will." Tom Glen shook his head. "I was hoping to send for Annie this summer. We've been planning on getting married for four years now. When I left the Old Country, I said I'd send for her just as soon as Jack and I got a house and a bit of a farm. This past winter I've worked like a dog cutting timber to get extra money for her passage. Then, last week, Jack discovered where I'd hid the earnings, and he started up again. Now there's nothing left."

"I've been doing right good on my last few voyages." The captain moved to the man's side and put a hand on his shoulder. "I'd be glad to give your Annie free passage."

"Thank ye, Jamie, but I have my pride. I'm not about to go accepting charity...not even to have the dearest wish of my heart." He climbed onto the wagon seat. "I'll just have to try to sort this lad out and make some more money."

"Remember, we know the cure." Jamie slapped a hand against the tailboard of the conveyance. "You've seen it work."

"What? More heathen remedies?" A woman, scraggly grey hair flaring out from beneath her cap, her faded black cape writhing in the wind, appeared from behind the tavern. In the murky overcast of the late autumn afternoon, she appeared a witch descended from the charcoal clouds. "The devil's spawn, both of them, Tom Glen. Don't go trusting your brother to their care. One consorting with the heathen Indians and using their savage cures on his patients, the other a pirate with a heart as black as midnight, the seducer of innocent young girls. Good people of Pine"—she swung on passersby who'd paused to witness her dramatics— "punish them as they deserve."

"You're daft as a loon, Hannah Rob. Get out of the way." Tom Glen flapped the reins over the backs of his team and sent them trotting down the rutted road.

"Ah, Hannah, quit your caterwauling and go home." A barrel-chested man with a bristling beard spat tobacco into the dirt at her feet. "Just because Dr. MacTavish has taken away the people who once came to you for your weird cures and Captain James has seen fit not to wed that banshee you call your daughter, there's no need to go screaming in the street."

"They're evil, I tell you!" The woman circled the two men in a half crouch, weird light eyes burning with hatred. "Don't let this one who calls himself a doctor touch your family. Lock up your virgin daughters from the other, despoiler of maidens that he be. They're both pirates, fresh from the war, with evil in their hearts!"

"Begone, Hannah." The captain shoved her aside and strode off down the rutted street. "Will, Wings is in my stable," he called back over his shoulder. "You may take him when the spirit moves you."

"Tomorrow." He untied his gelding and swung into the saddle.

"Mark my words, Doctor MacTavish, evil will come to you." The old woman grasped his stirrup and glared up at him, her wrinkled face contorted with rage. "You'll pay for disclaiming my cures."

He nudged her off and turned his horse downriver, toward the farm he'd once called home.

"You murdered your wife and babe!" The words that followed him were a shriek. "Poor, innocent waifs. You brought death to both of them! A curse on you and your fornicating brother, William MacTavish! A curse on you both!"

Grinding his teeth, he put his heels to his horse's sides and urged it into a gallop. Miserable old hag!

****

"Move over, Bess." On April 1, 1825, in the cow barn behind her brother's tavern in England, nineteen-year-old Heather Grey tapped the gentle Jersey with her pitchfork. "Can't have you standing in your own leavings."

Turning large, brown eyes on the young woman issuing the request, the cow moved her haunches to the left and mooed softly.

"Good girl." Heather shoved her fork into the pile of manure behind the animal.

The big black dog chained beyond the cow stall muttered as he tried to stretch cramped muscles on the short length of leeway his tether allowed him.

"Ah, Midnight, 'tis a shame and a sin that my brother keeps you such a prisoner." She paused to pat the animal's matted dark curls. "If I ever find a means of escaping this miserable existence, I promise I'll take you with me."

"Bonny, where are you?"

"In the cow barn, your ladyship." Heather grinned as she recognized the voice of her friend. "Mind your pretty shoes and fancy flounces. I haven't finished cleaning."

"Bonny Lass, I declare, this is an outrage!" Standing in the doorway, silhouetted in the fading light of a grimly overcast late afternoon, Lady Julia Thomas held up the skirt of her green velvet riding habit. "Your brother should be ashamed to have you doing such work. You who can read and write and draw and speak French and…"

"And cook and clean and manage farm animals and a kitchen garden and serve the rabble that frequents my brother's establishment." Heather paused to lean on her pitchfork and grin at her friend. "I'm a tavern wench, Jewels. You knew that when your father took me to be educated with you in the manor house. You knew he only tolerated my presence because your governess said you'd profit from a schoolmate and because I was the least slovenly among the girls of your age on his estate. You knew that eventually I'd have to come back here. So let's forego the indignation of your coming upon me doing what I was born into."

"Well, rest assured this won't be your life, Bonny Lass." Her friend stepped gingerly toward her down the barn's corridor. "As soon as I'm married and have a place of my own, you'll come to me as companion." She paused a few feet from the cow and lifted one daintily booted foot. "Bloody hell! How can you tolerate such filthy animals!"

"Hardly language becoming a lady." Heather leaned against the wall and chuckled. "Seems I've taught you something, as well. And stop calling me 'Bonny Lass.' My mother may have been from the Highlands, but my father was English to the core."

"But she gave you a name as Scottish as the Highlands themselves. Furthermore, you are a bonny lass, pretty as a picture and with a figure many a fine lady would kill to have."

"Don't try flattery, Jewels. We know each other too well. Now what's this about as soon as you're settled in your place? Has that young Lord What's-His-Name been paying court already, and his father barely cold in the grave?"

"If you're talking about Lord Glendon Ferris, yes, indeed he has. And his father passed away three months ago. The current Lady Ferris is eager for him to marry so she can quit the duties of the manor house and retire to the dowager residence."

"Ah, so the dear young man has convinced you you'll be doing his family a great favor." Heather returned to her work, throwing manure into a waiting wheelbarrow. "What's stopping you?" She paused a moment to glance up at her friend before going back for another forkful.

"It's all so cut and dried, all so cold and emotionless. Remember how we used to read those romantic stories and dream of knights on silver stallions and…"

"And castles in the clouds. Jewels, this is real life. There are no heroes coming to rescue us, no romantic conclusions in our future. You'll marry his lordship as intended, and I'll go on helping Neil in his tavern. One day my brother will perhaps marry, and I'll be the maiden auntie who becomes a factotum around the place until she dies of old age or boredom."

"Indeed! Factotum to a man who in all likelihood doesn't have the education to know what the word means." Lady Julia Thomas plunked her bottom down on an overturned bucket and wrapped her arms around her knees. "Oh, Bonny, don't you wish we could both just run away? Maybe to the colonies, where we'd never be found, and could live as we wish, and marry who we want to marry, and…"

"And perhaps starve, or die of exposure, or be killed by wild animals or savages?" Heather grasped the handles of the wheelbarrow and pushed it outside. "Stop dreaming, milady."

"We can take care of ourselves. Have you forgotten the highwayman who accosted us that afternoon when we were out riding?" A chuckle issued from her ladyship's throat as she stood and followed her friend. "We sent him packing in short order."

"Jewels, he was hardly more than a lad." Heather dumped the wheelbarrow at the pile of manure a few yards from the barn entrance, then turned to give her friend an exasperated glance. "It was probably his first attempt at robbery."

"Still, we did give him quite a surprise when we turned on him."

"Yes, we did, rash though it was of us, armed with only riding quirts, to tackle a robber with a drawn sword." She returned the wheelbarrow to the barn, dusted her hands together, and gestured toward the tavern beside the highroad beyond. "Now, if you'll excuse me, I have to get back inside. There's a stew simmering on the hearth that needs tending, and probably customers Neil has been neglecting while he dallies over ale or cards, or both."

"Heather, where in God's name are you?" A big, burly young man with flushed face and a mop of curly red hair burst into the doorway.

"I'm right here, Liam. What's the matter?"

"There's a man come in off the road, hurt bad and bleedin'. Says his horse threw him a mile or so back.

12

He's needin' your skills."

"Why don't you send for Dr. Phillip?" She heaved an exasperated sigh. "I've been working since sunup, and there's still more to do."

"Dr. Phillip is gone to London. You're the only healer in miles. Move smart, girl." He caught her roughly by the arm. "Before the man bleeds to death...or your brother throws him out for making a mess of his floor."

"Now, just a minute, my good man..." Lady Julia stepped forward to intercede, years of aristocratic breeding gathered into her outlook.

"Jewels, no." Heather stopped her. "I'll be fine. You'd best get back to the manor before your father discovers you missing and raises a hue and cry," she called back over her shoulder as Liam dragged her out of the barn toward the back door of the tavern.

"I'll go." Lady Julia brushed a straw from her skirt. "But I'm not about to give up on our dream. And you, you great oaf, be careful how you treat my friend."

"Never fear, milady. She'll be treated in the fashion to which she's accustomed." His tone implied a sneer.

"Don't bandy words with me, Liam Jones." Lady Julia caught up her horse's reins and mounted. "Remember, your farm is part of my father's estate. You hold it at his pleasure."

She clucked to her mare, and the high-spirited animal leaped forward into a gallop.

"No lady, that one," Liam Jones muttered, watching her go. "As notorious as her mother, I'll wager. Needs a strapping good man to take the starch out of her pantaloons. Now come along, girl. Your brother's not a patient man, as you well know."

Julia's words came back to Heather as she stumbled through the rutted mud of the tavern yard, propelled by the oaf clutching her arm. "Our dream." Dreams had no place in her world of endless drudgery. She yanked free and paused to watch her friend gallop away on a high-bred chestnut hunter, elegant green velvet flapping in the wind of the darkening day. *And she wants to escape.* Sarcasm colored the thought as Liam Jones seized her again, jerked open the scarred plank door, and thrust her into the hot, sweat-laced ale-house air.

Chapter 2

"It's about time you got here." Her brother Neil, his face reddened from drink, confronted her as she joined him behind the bar. "Just look at the mess that bastard is making of my tavern. Get him fixed up, and be quick about, else I'll throw him out, injured or no."

Seated across the room in a dark corner, bent over a table and clutching his arm, a man looked up at her, his face contorted in agony…a startlingly handsome man with jet black curly hair. Blood soaked the left arm of his well-cut black coat and dripped onto the floor beside boots that even in the gloom she could recognize as being of excellent quality. A gentleman of means.

"Let me look at that." She crossed the room and sat on a chair beside him. "What happened?"

"Bloody gelding threw me." Blue eyes glowed with pain he struggled to keep out of his voice. "Hit a tree and cut myself deep. If I'd had my own stallion, it wouldn't have happened. Are you a healer?"

"Of sorts." She began to ease him from his coat. "Can you stand?"

"Aye." Gripping the edge of the table, he faltered to his feet, then weaved dangerously.

He's not only handsome of face but tall and broad of shoulder. And clean. Not like the usual stinking crowd that frequents this place. I wonder who he is and how he came to be in this area?

"Lean on me." Thrusting her thoughts aside, Heather finished removing his coat, laid it over her arm, and took a position beneath his right arm. "I'll get you upstairs before I examine your wound."

"Mind you don't let the bastard take advantage of you, girl." Liam Jones, the only other occupant of the inn's common room besides her brother, mocked. "Remember I've a healthy interest in you, and I don't plan on gettin' soiled goods."

"You're soaked in drink." Heather's words gushed out as the weight of the man fell upon her. "You're seeing visions."

Liam's guffaw followed her as she assisted the man to the narrow staircase and upwards, out of the sight of the pair leaning on the counter.

"Nasty piece of work." The man, feeling like a sack of stones against her shoulder, grunted with the comment as they reached the top step and she helped him through the first doorway on the right. "I hope he's not your intended." The last words came out with a grimace as she eased him onto the narrow bed in the austere room.

"Hardly. Now, let us remove your shirt and see how badly that horse injured you."

As she eased the linen garment from his body, she was conscious of his eyes scrutinizing her and wondered what he was thinking. *Tavern wench*, most likely. *Bit of highway trash.* Her shapeless grey dress and shabby boots did little to recommend her as anything else.

"Both your shirt and coat will need cleaning and mending," she said as she draped the pair over the back of the chair by the bedside. Together with a scarred washstand and narrow bed, it constituted the furnishings of the crude little room.

"And you'll see to all that, will you?"

"Yes, of course. Who else? Those two oafs in the room below?" The disgust she felt for the pair billowed out in her words.

"Ah, not great friends, I take it?" He bared a flash of even white teeth in a grin as she eased him back to lie on the bed. She admired his fortitude. The pain had to be intense.

"Definitely not, although one is my brother and the other an egotist who fancies himself a fitting husband."

This man does have a fine body. Broad-shouldered, hard and muscular about the chest, with not even the smallest roll of fat protruding above that wide belt at his waist. Who can he be?

"Egotist? Rather a fine word for a young lady who works in a tavern." Intense blue eyes met her green ones so piercingly she wondered if he could see right through to her soul.

"I was educated at the manor house two miles to the north." She dropped her gaze and took his arm in her hands to examine it more closely. "This will need cleansing and stitching." She headed for the door. "I'll be back directly. Lie on the bed and try to rest."

She hurried down the stairs and into the small room off the kitchen where she kept what passed for medical supplies…a pitcher and a small cloth bag that held bandages, clean rags, needles, thread, and a bottle of whiskey purloined from her brother's stock. She paused to fill the pitcher from a bucket, then headed back upstairs, hoping the men still at the counter wouldn't take any notice of her. When she heard dice rattling, she relaxed. Involved in a game of chance, they wouldn't pause to acknowledge her presence. Both were inveterate gamblers.

Back in the spartanly furnished room, she placed her materials on the washstand and opened the bottle of alcohol. She handed it to the man bracing himself in a sitting position against the headboard.

"Take as much of this as you can manage." She turned away to pour water into the basin and drop a clean rag into it.

"Lass, you know not what you're advising." Glancing over her shoulder, she caught a glint of teasing in his eyes. "My brother often warns I've too great a capacity for the stuff."

"Perhaps, on this occasion, being a man who can hold his liquor will be to your advantage." She came back to the bed, damp cloth in hand, and sat down on the edge of his bed. "I'll rely on you not to vomit while I work. I'll be needing to sew up that tear, you realize."

"Sew up?" He tried to bolt from the bed, but she pushed on his good shoulder and he fell back. "With a needle and thread? Are you sure you know what you're doing, lass?"

"I've pieced back together enough roisterers after fights downstairs to say that I do. Can I rely on you not to cast your last meal while I work?"

"Aye, that you can, lass." He flinched as she began to cleanse the ragged tear. "But that's not to say I wouldn't appreciate your being as gentle as possible." He put the bottle to his mouth and quaffed a swill of the whiskey. "Let's get to it."

****

As evening shadowed the land, Captain James MacTavish lay ensconced in the small room above the miserable little tavern somewhere in England. His breath came in short, hard spurts. Heather pulled the covers over his bare chest and looked down at him. His neatly bandaged arm lay atop the quilts.

"Lass." He stopped her, Scottish burr heavy on his tongue.

"Yes?"

"Thank ye."

"'Tis nothing, sir. I'd do as much for any wounded creature." She went to the open window and threw the contents of the basin's bloody water outside. Then she began to gather up her medical supplies.

"Ah, well, then." He dragged himself higher on the pillow to better face her in the gathering gloom. "You're a rare one, lassie, a rare one indeed, to be able to sew up a man's arm without a single hesitation." He paused and looked her up and down. "I don't suppose you can read and write, maybe cipher a bit? You did throw that big word at me and say you were educated at the manor house."

"That would be none of your concern, sir." Her bag clutched in her arms, she headed once more for the door, then paused, her hand on the latch. "But, if it will ease your mind to know, yes, I can. Now, I'd advise you to rest."

What a strange question. She pulled the door shut and paused a moment to consider it. Then, with a baffled shake of her head, she went down the narrow stairs and into the kitchen. The man must still be under the influence of all that whiskey he imbibed.

****

"A fine meal, indeed." Her patient leaned back against the pillows she'd place behind his shoulders to allow him to sit upright and eat the meal she'd brought up to his room. "Was it of your own making?"

"Of course." She bent forward to tap a napkin against his mouth and chin. "I'm my brother's servant in all things. Cooking, barn work, cleaning, washing, serving at the bar when he's too drunk…"

"And you heal and write and cipher." Blue eyes narrowed as they focused on her. In the light of the single candle burning on the washstand, her patient was a bewitchingly handsome man.

"Aye, yes, and draw and speak a smattering of French. I'm a genuine paragon." Sarcasm tinged her words as she removed the tray from the bed and placed it on the floor. "Is it an offer of marriage you're contemplating, sir, that you ask so many questions? If so, I must warn you my brother will not take kindly to any attempt to deprive him of his jack of all trades." She cast him a taunting glance.

"No, no, lass." He dragged himself higher on the pillows and winced. "I know of a doctor in the colony of New Brunswick, in British North America, who's looking for someone to assist him in his work. He has requested me to find someone while I was in England. His list of requirements is long and varied, and I've been despairing of ever finding such a remarkable human being. Then the fates brought me here to you. What do you say, lass? Fancy an escape to a bright future in a new land?"

"Are you mad!" *What was this stranger proposing?* "I know nothing about you. How do I know you have such an acquaintance? You could be a seducer

20

of young women, luring them from their homes and then…"

"Lass, lass, calm yourself." He caught her hand in his good one. "In my coat you'll find papers declaring me to be Captain James MacTavish, master of the good ship *Highland Lass*. You'll further find a paper from Dr. William MacTavish, my brother, authorizing me as his agent in finding him such an assistant as he describes. I beg you, look and satisfy yourself. It's all in the inner breast pocket. You must have noticed a packet there when you were fixing it."

She hesitated, hands clutching both sides of her gown, fingers rubbing the coarse grey wool between them.

"Go on, go on, lass." He leaned back, his words becoming relaxed and confident. "You'll also find more than sufficient funds to pay for my care, bed, and board in this elegant facility. Take what you think fair."

"How do you know that I haven't already helped myself both to your coin and your papers?" She couldn't help bitterness from coloring her words. After all, wasn't that what was expected of tavern wenches?

"I value myself a decent judge of character, lass." Those intense blue eyes brooked no denial as he looked up at her.

"Do you, sir?" She matched his gaze with what she hoped was an equally intense one, then bent and reached gingerly into the inner pocket of the well-cut coat. She drew out a packet of papers and a well-filled purse.

"Open them." He jerked a thumb at the papers. "Read…as you say you can."

****

"So what do you think?" She looked up from reading the documents he'd pressed upon her to see him regarding her intently. "Now do you believe me?"

"It would be difficult not to." She drew a deep breath and laid them on the washstand. "It appears you are indeed the agent for one Dr. MacTavish in the matter of finding him an assistant."

"So what's your answer? Will you come with me? Have you enough daring in your heart to give yourself a chance at the adventure of a lifetime, indeed at a whole new life?"

"Although Dr. MacTavish doesn't specify, I believe he's expecting you to bring a male person." She tried to belay the excitement rising within her at the prospect of escaping the tavern and the bleak years ahead.

"Aye, I don't doubt he is, lass, but I've searched this land for the past month, and nary a single man have I found that comes anywhere near meeting the good doctor's demands. If you're concerned about either him or myself making unwanted advances on you, let me still that worry once and for all. We're both gentlemen to the core. In fact, my brother has of recent years become somewhat of a prude…if such a term can be applied to a man. Respectability is his stock in trade to the point that he's become downright annoying to a happy-go-lucky lad like myself." She caught the roguish twinkle in his eyes and felt a smile tugging at her lips. *Stop it. Don't let this handsome rogue charm you, Heather Grey.*

"Is he your older brother or younger?" She resumed her questioning.

"Older. We were raised by a bachelor uncle after

our parents passed. Our uncle was a tradesman, quite well-to-do and determined to educate us both so that we might be capable of entering society one day as he'd never been able to. He sent William off to be educated as a doctor, but when it came my turn, I bolted. Went to sea and never regretted it for a moment. Will and I reunited during the war—the War of 1812, that is—and have kept in contact ever since."

"And just what kind of living conditions might this paragon of a doctor provide for his help? I'm not about to give up the roof I presently have over my head for a hovel in the wilderness."

"No worries on that score, mistress. My brother has a fine big stone house, one of the best residences in the Miramichi Valley, and an excellent farm. You'll find it a much better situation than this." He waved a hand disparagingly about the room. "And more than enough good food to satisfy even the most robust of appetites."

"Hmmm. That sounds very nice, but I'd also like to know a bit about the country itself. Is there a village near this farm? Has the doctor neighbors, or shall we be isolated miles from others of the human species? How long are the winters, and how much snow can be expected? Does the country abound with…snakes?" Her words stumbled over the last query, and the captain shot her a surprised look.

"Snakes?" The captain's astonishment raised his eyebrows. "You want to know about snakes, not about bears or wildcats or highwaymen or savages?"

"I have an aversion to them." She looked down at her clasped hands. "Anything else, I have no doubt I can abide." Bringing her gaze back to the man's face, she threw her shoulders back and straightened her spine. "Yes, rest assured, anything else I can abide."

"Very well, then, let me put your mind at rest. Aye, there are snakes in New Brunswick, but they're wee, timid creatures, harmless to human beings. They live hidden deep in swamps, in mortal fear of encountering a person. Why, in all my years, I've only ever seen one such little fellow, and he made haste to get far from my presence. Now, as to the rest…"

Heather listened as he told her of the village of Douglastown, a mere three or four miles from the doctor's farm, how indeed there was a good deal of snow in winter, but the river that flowed past the farm, frozen during the cold months, provided an excellent highway both to the settlement and to the river's mouth.

"As to the dangers I've mentioned, wild animals generally stay far back in the bush, having no more desire to encounter one of us than we have to meet up with them. Regarding highwaymen and savages, the former are few and far between, there being hardly any coaches or wealthy houses to plunder. The local savages, as you've termed them, were never all that savage to begin with. In fact, they've often helped both my brother and me when the need arose. They live in nomadic bands that travel to the river and seaside each spring and summer to catch fish, then move back into the forest in fall and winter for protection from the bitter winds and to find moose and the like that will provide their food, shelters, and clothing.

"My brother enjoys a particularly agreeable association with them." The captain adjusted himself in the bed. "He provides them with medical help, and they, in turn, have shared a number of their herbal and mystical remedies with him. So you see, young lady, you'll be in a far more secure position in New Brunswick than I suspect you are at the moment, what with drunks and highwaymen and all kinds of riffraff frequenting this regal establishment."

The man's proposal sounds better and better. But I mustn't make any rash decisions. I'm not Jewels.

"Let me sleep on your proposition, Captain." She counted out sufficient coin to pay his keep, returned purse and papers to his coat, and headed for the door. "I'll give you my decision in the morning."

Outside his room, she paused to lean back against the door and draw a deep breath. The possibility the man who identified himself as Captain James MacTavish had offered made her heart bump against her ribs. A chance to be free of this hellhole of drudgery, a chance for a new life in a new land, as a doctor's assistant. She wet her lips and swallowed. This, in all likelihood, would be her one opportunity to escape the slavery her brother had imposed upon her. All she needed was the courage to take it. And a friend to share the adventure.

Chapter 3

"Heather, where are you, girl?" her brother bellowed from the bottom of the stairs. "We've customers, and you tarry with that bastard who bled all over my floor and has yet to pay me for my trouble and his keep. Get down here and scrub up his mess. If I'm forced to fetch you, you'll be sorry."

With a sigh, she started down the worn steps, steps she'd swept and scrubbed more times than she cared to remember. *Do I want to spend the rest of my life in this wretched place? I've just been given the means of escape. Still, how do I know I can truly trust this man who calls himself a sea captain? Papers can be forged. It's such a big decision...*

****

"Damn you to hell, you bastard!" Flinging his cards across the table, Neil Grey jumped to his feet, yelling at Liam Jones. Heather glanced over her shoulder from where she was on her knees, scrubbing the last of Captain James MacTavish's blood from the floor. "You cheated!"

"Prove it." The big man rose to confront him. Several of his friends moved in to offer support, belligerent expressions on their faces.

"There's no way you could have come by such a hand honestly!"

26

"I said, prove it." Liam Jones leaned across the table, his stubbled face flushed with drink. "I've won her fair and square. Now I'll just be taking her and the coins from this table home with me."

Her? Nausea rose in her throat. *Surely not even a cur like Neil would gamble his own sister…*

"Come here, girl." The big man turned to leer down at her. "We've a small journey before us."

"We'll play again. I'll wager something else!" Neil looked at his sister, sweat coursing down his drink-reddened face.

"And what else might you have to wager? This pig sty of an inn? I've no interest. I have a farm I call home, and no desire to take on such a miserable venture. I wanted the girl, and now I've got her." He shoved back his chair with such violence it fell with a crash as he strode toward Heather.

"No!" Heather scrambled to her feet and fled behind the counter to grab a bottle from a shelf. Grasping it by its neck, she held it above her head. "Come one step closer, and I swear I'll crack this over your great, dumb skull!"

"Ah, spirit." He paused on his side of the bar and leered at her over brown teeth, his breath fouled with drink spouting out at her. "I like that. I'll enjoy taming it out of you, girl."

"Stay away!" She backed toward the door that led to the kitchen.

"Come here, girlie. You're mine now."

"No!" Neil Grey lunged and managed to topple Liam Jones off balance. "Run, Heather, run!" he yelled as the brute struggled to right himself.

She did. Through the kitchen and out into the night,

into the trees beyond the barn.

Where to go, where to go? Her heart hammering as she fled into the woods, she could think of only one safe haven. Burkley Manor. Jewels. Her best friend would hide her until she could find a way to escape Liam Jones. Turning to the left, she stumbled down to a trot, a stitch inhabiting her side. Yes, she'd go to Burkley Manor.

****

"Jewels, wake up!" At midnight Heather bent over her friend's sleeping form.

"What…?" Lady Julia Thomas slowly roused, then started violently, jerking away against her bed's headboard. "Who…"

"Jewels, it's Heather. Hush. You'll wake the entire house."

"Bonny." She pulled herself into a sitting position, rubbing sleep from her eyes. "What in God's name are you doing here at whatever hour this is? How did you get in?"

"Your cook." Heather stood in the shaft of moonlight flowing through the long bedroom window. "Mrs. Kitchen always had a soft spot for both of us. Remember how she'd let us lick the bowls in the kitchen?"

"But why? What could be so important…"

"Jewels, I've found a way for us to escape to America, a way to start having real adventures."

"What are you saying? Bonny, have you been partaking of your brother's whiskey?" Lady Julia stared at her.

"Most definitely not. I've been tending a most interesting man, a sea captain named James MacTavish, who came into the tavern wounded in a fall from his horse this afternoon. He's offered me a position, a job as a doctor's assistant, in the British North American colony of New Brunswick. If I accept, he'll take me to New Brunswick. As a part of the agreement, I'm going to insist that I bring along a friend."

"Oh, Bonny!" The two words came in an incredulous outward breath. "Do you think we might trust him?"

"I, at least, have no choice." She dropped down on the edge of the bed with a sigh and told her friend about her brother's wager.

"The filthy beast!" Lady Julia drew herself up like an indignant peahen. "I always knew Neil Grey lacked moral character, but this! It's worse than despicable, Bonny Lass. Of course we must take a chance on this man, this Captain James MacTavish."

"But, Jewels, are you sure? There will be no coming back."

"Do you think I'm too thick not to understand that condition, or that I'm too stupid not to realize that your proposition also offers me an escape from a man I loathe to marry? Heather, this is a gift, a very great gift, that is being offered to both of us. We'd be fools to turn it down. Yes! Of course, yes, yes, a thousand times yes!" Julia Thomas leaped from her bed, white nightgown billowing, a vision in the moonlight, waist-length raven curls cascading down her back as she danced about.

"Hush!" Heather silenced her ecstatic outburst. "If you bring the inhabitants of this house running, all will be lost. I'll tell the captain I'll be bringing a friend…a friend I'll lead him to believe is a stout farm lad. You'll need to disguise yourself as such. I plan to purloin lad's clothing from my brother's hodgepodge he calls his wardrobe. It will make our escape all the more possible if the captain is seen to be travelling with two lads. Can you secure an appropriate outfit?"

"Of course. Mrs. Kitchen, bless her, mends the stable lads' clothing out of the goodness of her heart. She has a pile of such garments in her sitting room. She'll not notice if I snatch a few…at least, not until it's too late."

"Perfect! Now if you'll allow me, I'll spend the hours until dawn here. At that time I plan to return to the tavern, tell the captain we're going with him, and snatch up my disguise and a few items I might need."

"Yes!" Even in the scant light provided by a waxing moon, Heather could see the excited gleam in her friend's eyes. "Oh, Bonny, what an adventure we're about to have! But," she continued more calmly, "you mentioned stealing some of your brother's clothing. Do you dare risk going back to the inn?"

"I have to inform the captain of my decision. My brother doesn't concern me. He'll not be expecting me to return. Furthermore, as tomorrow dawns, he'll be too ill from drinking to be aware of anything that happens in his establishment. It will be a simple task."

"And this Captain MacTavish?" Lady Julia pulled her friend down to sit beside her on the bed. "Is he an old man, middle-aged, tall, short, ugly…?"

"You ask a great many questions, ones I consider most unimportant to the scope of our expedition."

"Oh, Bonny, please, tell me." Lady Julia bounced impatiently. "It would so add to the flavor if he were tall, handsome, and fair, with wonderful blue eyes and a charming manner."

"Well, if you must know, he's all of those things...except for the fair part. His hair is a mass of curls as black as midnight. And his eyes..."

"Yes, yes! Bonny, what about his eyes?"

"They're as blue as the heather for which my mother chose to name me."

"He sounds perfect. And what of his brother? Are they perhaps as like as peas in a pod? Oh, Bonny, how wonderful for you if he is!"

"I somehow very much doubt it." Heather let a small sigh escape her lips. "The doctor is the captain's older brother. He didn't specify by how many years, but he's given me to understand the man is a prude, reeking of respectability. I'm imagining such a man to be a shriveled prune, small in mind and stature."

"Oh, dear, Bonny Lass." Lady Julia caught Heather's work-worn hands in her own soft ones. "I was so hoping he'd turn out to be your prince."

"One can't have everything, my lady." Heather let a small grin crack her lips. "At the moment, I'm simply grateful to have found a way out of the clutches of one brutish Liam Jones. I'm not in the least troubled by whatever gnomish appearance the doctor may present. So long as he's a decent man who respects other people, women in particular, I'll be content. You may have the handsome captain, for all I care."

****

"I've slept on your proposal and decided to accept." Heather spoke without preface as she eased into the captain's room through the window. A spring dawn was greying the sky.

"W..what?" He opened one eye, then the other, and

stared up at her. "Sweet Jesus, who…?"

"Heather Grey, and please lower your tone. I don't want to awaken my brother. I said I've decided to accept your offer. But I have a few conditions." She placed hands on her hips and assumed a determined stance.

"Ah, it's you, lass. Give me a minute to come into myself." He pulled himself up on the elbow of his good arm. "My brain is still befuddled from sleep."

"Very well. Let me jog your memory." She took a stride that brought her beside the bed and resumed her bold stance. "Yesterday you offered to take me to America to be an assistant to your doctor brother. I told you I'd sleep on the idea and let you know. Well, I did, and now I'm letting you know. Yes, I will go with you…under certain conditions."

"Aye, I remember now." He dragged himself up on the pillows, grimacing as his wounded arm touched the bed. "And what might these conditions be?"

"First, that we depart without my brother's knowledge. He and I had a…a falling-out last evening. I fled the inn to escape him. You mustn't let him know you've seen me this morning."

"Now, lass, that could be dangerous…for me." He ran his fingers through his tangled curls. "If we're caught, I could be charged with abduction or kidnapping."

"We won't be caught, not if you follow my instructions." She stared down at him, determined to the core to convince him now that she'd made her decision.

"Very well." He leaned back against the pillows. In the dim light she saw a hint of a grin quirk one corner of his mouth. "But you said you had conditions. What others are there?"

"That my best friend accompany us."

"Ah, I might have guessed. A fine, strapping farm lad to protect your virtue. Well, that can be arranged. I can always use another hand aboard the *Highland Lass*."

"Yes, I'm sure you could."

"Horses. We'll need two more horses."

"My friend will arrange for them. They'll be ready shortly after midnight tonight, in a grove a short distance behind this inn." She held out her hand. "Agreed?"

"Agreed. You're a resourceful lass, that you are. I've chosen well." He shook it, then slid back down into his bed with a sigh. "I must rest and get my strength back. I foresee hard riding ahead."

"Yes, rest." Heather went to the door and held a warning finger to her lips. "Now I have to get to my brother's room and find some clothing suitable for our excursion. I'll come back shortly to let myself out the way I came in."

****

"Will this do?"

Heather, clad in her brother's clothing, turned from where she'd been sitting at her friend's dressing table, toying with silver combs and brushes and bottles of scent, to find a very different Lady Julia Thomas standing outside her dressing room door. In lad's trousers and shirt, her glossy black ringlets shoved up under a cap, she stood grinning at her friend.

"You look almost perfect." Heather stood, the corners of her mouth quirking upward. "But those shiny riding boots will never do."

33

"But they're all I have. The stable lads prize their boots too highly to leave them anywhere they might be stolen. Unlike you, I've never needed to wear boys' boots to do farm work. Any other male footwear I might find around the manor will be too large."

"You'll have to scuff them, get them really dirty, and hope anyone who notices thinks they're something you stole."

"Really, Bonny. I had these especially made by an excellent shoemaker. They cost a small fortune. Scuff them…?"

"Fine. Don't tarnish them, and risk getting caught and being brought back here to marry your fiancé, probably within a fortnight before you can get involved with any more infamy."

"You're being a royal pain, Bonny Lass, but you're right. I'll change into my Lady Julia garb and take them down to the yard to beat the poor things into appropriate condition. What else do you suggest?"

"A bit of dirt rubbed on your face and a good washing to take off any of these exotic scents." Heather indicated the array on the dressing table. "No street urchin or farm boy would go about smelling so fine."

****

"Hush!" Heather, dressed in her brother's trousers, shirt, and boots, worked at the chain that had held Midnight a prisoner most of his life. "You're coming with us to a new land and freedom, my lad. Stay quiet for a few more moments."

When he was finally free, she slipped a rope loop around his neck to serve as a leash and re-tied him.

"I won't be but a minute," she reassured the dog looking up at her with hopeful eyes. "I want to take one last look into the tavern to make certain my brother is asleep and won't come pursuing us, at least not until tomorrow."

Moving stealthily through the shadows, she reached a window and peered inside. In the lamplight, the room appeared deserted. Where was her brother? Too miserly to leave even a single candle burning, he never went to bed without extinguishing the lights, no matter how inebriated he'd become.

Then she saw him. Neil Grey lay sprawled on the floor in front of the bar. A dark pool she recognized as blood puddled about his head.

She ran to the door and rushed inside.

"Neil, Neil!" She dropped on her knees beside him. His eyes staring blankly toward the ceiling declared him dead. "God in heaven, Neil!"

What her brother had done in gambling her away had been despicable, but he hadn't deserved to die. No, no, he hadn't deserved to die. Horrified, she staggered to her feet and gazed wildly about.

Liam Jones! Liam Jones had killed her brother. She knew it as surely as if she held his signed confession in her hands. And he'd be back...back for her.

What should she do? What else could she do? She was already late for the proposed rendezvous with Julia and the captain. After a final glance at her brother's lifeless form, she extinguished the lamp, stumbled out of the only home she'd ever known, and headed toward the dark silhouette that was the barn.

"Hush, Midnight." She quieted the dog as she entered. "Just a few more minutes."

Soothed by her words, he stopped dancing and stood, trembling with anticipation.

Going into the cow's stall, she freed the bovine and herded her out into the night. "We all deserve a chance at freedom," she said softly, watching the animal amble away. Liam Jones would no doubt come to claim everything that had been her brother's. She wasn't about to let gentle Bess fall easily into his brutal hands.

Returning to the dog, she untied his improvised leash from the iron ring in the wall, picked up the small bundle that held a change of her brother's clothes and the few personal items she called her own, and headed out into the shadowy darkness, the big canine trotting at her side. Her heart pounded a mixed tattoo of freedom and fear.

She paused a moment to look back at the black outline of inn and stable. *This is the last time, the very last time, I shall ever see it.* A deep breath, half sigh, half shudder, vibrated through her. Then she swung away and scurried into the trees and down an incline to the appointed meeting place, drawing the dog along with her. On the bank of the designated stream, she and Midnight found two people and three horses, barely perceptible in the shadows.

"Bonny!" Lady Julia Thomas hissed in a voice that could have been that of a young lad. "We thought you weren't coming." Standing beside Captain Jamie MacTavish, she held two of the horses while he stood beside the third.

"There was a development." Seeking strength in the prosaic task, she turned her attention to throwing her bag onto the back of the horse she'd frequently ridden at Burkley Manor and fastening it. "Someone killed my brother."

"Good God!" Lady Julia caught at her busy hands

and forced her to turn to her. "Killed? Who? Why?"

"I can only assume Liam Jones." She shrugged free and went back to her task. She wouldn't give in to the tears threatening to burst into a wellspring, to the lump congealing in her throat. Her brother had been a bastard who'd gambled her away. She had to hold fast to that notion. Still, he had been her brother, her only kin...

"What's this, what's this?" Captain James MacTavish stepped between them. "Someone killed your brother and now you're running away? I assume you were to inherit that pile of boards he called an inn?"

"What are you saying, Captain MacTavish?" Lady Julia whirled on the man. "Are you suggesting Bonny Lass had something to do with his death? Well, she didn't. But even if she did, I'd not blame her. Do you know the man lost her in a card game last evening to that brute Liam Jones?"

"Sweet Jesus!" He rounded on Heather. "Is this true, lass? Did the man who claims to be your brother do such a thing?"

"Yes." Heather swallowed hard and leaned her head against her horse's side. "I'm sure he didn't mean to do it. He was very drunk."

"Drunk or not, lass, there's no excuse for doing such a thing." Captain MacTavish swung onto his horse. "Now mount up. We must get away from here before whatever type of law enforcement oversees this area finds him and decides you're a major suspect."

"Murder suspect? Me!" Heather's words were a gasp of disbelief as she swung to face her friend.

"Yes." Lady Julia caught her by the shoulders and shook her. "Surely you must realize you'll be the obvious choice. We have to be on our way before we're traced, before anyone can put together our disappearances and your brother's death."

"Oh, and that great ball of fur won't give us away?" The captain jerked a thumb in the dog's direction.

"He's been my brother's prisoner since he was a pup." Heather drew herself up and glared over at the blustering captain. "I promised him that if I ever got a chance to escape he'd come with me."

"No doubt he understood every word." The words reeked of sarcasm, but Heather recognized a softening in the captain's tone. "And just what might this elegant creature be called?"

"Midnight. I named him. My brother never bothered to."

"Midnight?" The captain looked down at the black silhouette standing by her side, tail moving slowly. "Sweet Jesus, this is becoming a travelling circus. I only bargained for you and your lad, lass, not whatever that thing is. Two extra horses, which I hazard a guess might have been stolen, are bad enough, but now him, and you a murder suspect to boot... Damned if the end of this quest doesn't see me swinging from a rope."

"You knew we'd need horses." Heather held her ground. "How else could we make our escape? I had no way of knowing Neil was about to be killed when I made the agreement with you."

"Aye, but this lad informs me I'm to take these horses with us on the voyage. I'd thought of selling them in Portsmouth."

"How are we to travel about in this New Brunswick place without horses?" Lady Julia ran her hand affectionately up the nose of one of the animals and lowered her voice to sound like a lad. "And, if we do have to sell them, we'll get more for them in America than we would in Portsmouth. I understand good equines are scarce in the New World." Her attempted voice change cracked over the last sentence.

"How old are ye, lad?" The captain urged his mount closer to Julia and peered down into her face. "I see no evidence of a sprouting beard, and your words have yet to gain the depth of a man's."

"Old enough, sir." Julia moved back from him.

"But too young to be chasing after a woman of her age." With another jerk of his thumb he indicated Heather. "She must be all of nineteen, and I'll wager you've yet to see your sixteenth year."

In spite of her recent bereavement, Heather felt a chuckle brimming in her chest and had to stifle it with a hand to her mouth.

"Love knows no age boundaries." Again Lady Julia fought with her cracking voice.

"Aye, well, don't say I didn't warn you, if she loses interest in you, lad. It's happened to more than one ardent young fellow infatuated with an older woman. New Brunswick is teeming with randy bucks looking for wives. Women are a rare commodity. You'll have your work cut out for you, keeping her interest, I can tell you."

"Heather will never desert me. She's as true as the bonny blue heather for which she's named."

"I hope you're right." The captain adjusted himself more comfortably in the saddle. "I'm trusting you can both handle a good canter without being cast onto your backsides?"

"Not to worry, Captain." Julia swung into the saddle with a fluid motion. Putting her heels to her mount's sides, she whirled it about and raced a short distance down the stream's bank. Reining smoothly about, she headed back to the waiting pair.

"And Heather is just as good." She brought her mount to a half-rearing halt so close in front of the man his horse jolted backwards.

"Aye, aye. Bloody hell, what manner of farm lad are ye?"

"One who exercised milord's horses. Hurry up, Bonny Lass," she urged, turning her attention to her friend. "Get your gear strapped to the mare, and let's be off."

"Allow me a moment." Heather finished fastened her bundle to the saddle of the waiting horse. Although Julia Thomas could master a sidesaddle during a hunt better than most of the fine ladies in the land, she and Heather had preferred to ride astride when on their own. Now that skill would stand them in good stead. "We've a lifetime ahead of us to be wild and free."

****

"You are the shyest lad I ever did see." Jamie MacTavish refastened the front of his trousers and turned back to where Heather's young man was fumbling with the girth on his horse's saddle. "Boy, that kind of modesty won't serve you well on shipboard. Men don't blush when another makes water in their presence."

The sky was brightening with the promise of a fine day to come when they had finally paused to rest and the captain chose to relieve himself. Heather, involved in tending her own mount, overheard and suppressed a chuckle. Men relieving themselves publicly had been a common enough event around the tavern, but not in the refined world of Lady Julia Thomas.

"Sorry, sir." Heather's friend lowered her voice as best she could. "At home we do such things in private."

"Aye, well, you'll find little privacy aboard the *Highland Lass* once you've slung your hammock in the bow with the rest of my men." He turned and started back toward Heather. Passing close to Julia, he caught his foot on a root and stumbled into her. The cap flew from her head. A riot of glossy black curls tumbled around the smudged, dirty face and over her shoulders.

"Bloody hell!" Captain James MacTavish staggered backwards, staring. "Who…what..?"

"Meet my best friend, Lady Julia Thomas." Heather came forward, a saucy grin taunting the man. "She's coming with us."

"Lady…Bloody hell…again! A lady? Now the fat's in the fire for sure and certain. I've absconded with an aristocrat…not to mention a possible murder suspect…both riding mounts that have been stolen, I'll wager. All the king's horses and all the king's men will be hot on my trail. When they catch us, I'll have a noose around my neck quicker than you can say Lady Whatever."

"Lady Julia Thomas," she informed him, a sly smile creasing her soiled face. "We won't get caught, Captain. We're a clever pair. We know how to cover our tracks and ride hard. We'll be at your ship long before anyone can overtake us. Then it's up to you to set sail as fast as ever you can."

"And I'm guessing your father is Lord Robsport, Sir Robert Thomas. Bloody hell!"

"You've met my father?" She cast him a roguish glance.

"I've not had the experience, but I know of the man by reputation. He's a great favorite at court, I've been told. Bollocks! He'll have half the kingdom out looking for you."

"Ah-ha! Well, rest assured, you'll have no reason to meet with him on my account. I've cleverly left a false trail for him to follow. By now he's headed north as fast as his best horse will carry him." Gathering her cascade of dark curls back up under her cap, she tossed him a saucy glance.

"Bugger all!" He fell back against a tree, pulled a handkerchief from his pocket, and mopped his brow. "A ruddy aristocrat's daughter. What have I gotten myself into? And all because of that blasted stubborn Highlander."

"Let me assure you, we'll be perfectly safe if you do as we tell you." Julia drew herself up to her ladyship stance and faced him. "Now, mount up and lead the way to Portsmouth as fast as you can, my good man. Don't worry. We're both excellent riders. We won't lose you. And I'd appreciate it if you'd use more acceptable language. It shouldn't be all that difficult. I assume by now you've used up most of your supply of rude remarks."

"Aw, bloody hell!" He heaved himself into the saddle, the words sounding like a sigh of resignation. "Ha!" He slapped his reins over the horse's neck, kicked him in the ribs, and was off in a bound.

"Come on, Bonny!" Julia leaped her horse after him. "This is going to be fun!"

As Heather took up Midnight's lead, swung onto

her mount, and urged it in pursuit of the pair, major misgivings about the adventure wafted over her. Maybe she shouldn't have brought Jewels along. Like a filly released into pasture in the spring, her ladyship might prove too wild to manage.

****

When the sun had risen high in the cloudless spring morning sky, the captain halted the trio at an inn, purchased a sack of foodstuffs, and led his charges off the road several miles farther along, deep into a forest, where a stream provided water for both themselves and their mounts.

"We rest here until dusk," he said, dismounting. "We'll be less likely to be detected, travelling under cover of darkness." He placed the bag of food on the ground and led his horse toward the stream. "You can start setting out a meal, lads."

"Of all the arrogance!" Lady Julia swung her leg over her mare's rump and slid to the ground. "Who does he think we are…his servants?"

"For appearances and our safety, yes." Heather dismounted and gave her mount a pat on the neck. "Jewels, don't make an issue of it. We need him."

"I suppose." Julia gathered up the reins of both their mares and started off toward the stream. "But just as soon as we dock in New Brunswick, his dominion over us will cease."

Kneeling to set out their meal, Heather shook her head. Would they be able to make it across the Atlantic without Jewels inspiring the captain to throw them overboard?

****

"We'll have to pick up the pace tonight." Captain

43

James MacTavish emptied the last of the wine from the cup he'd purchased at the inn and reached for the bottle to replenish it. "I want to get to Portsmouth in time not only to check the loading of my ship but also to make a wee visit to the Hound and Harridan. A man needs a few hands of cards and a couple of drams of whiskey before embarking on a voyage where he must remain sober and not fraternize with his men."

"And no doubt visit a lady of the night?" Lady Julia took a dainty sip from her mug and looked with wide-eyed innocence over its rim at him.

"And so what if I do? I never said I was a blinkin' monk!" He downed a mouthful of wine.

"Gaming and whoring and excessive drinking can lead to nothing but ruin." Lady Julia Thomas drew herself up to meet his anger. "I've seen it happen all too often with friends of my father's acquaintance."

"Oh, aye. And that puts you in a position to judge all and sundry, does it?" He bolted to his feet, his face red from the warmth of the midday heat and anger. "You just mind your tongue, your ladyship, or I'll up and leave you and your friend high and dry here in jolly old England. Then you'll both be in a major pickle!"

Mug in hand, he strode off toward where the horses were grazing beside the stream.

"Jewels, please!" Heather caught her friend by an arm. "Don't make him angry. He's perfectly capable of doing what he's threatened."

"Not to worry." Lady Julia turned to her friend, a wicked smile lighting up her face. "He's not about to abandon us. Never you fear, before we see the last of the good captain, I'll have him eating out of my hand."

"Jewels, don't be mad. This is no country lad or

fawning aristocrat ready to drop on his knees to obtain your favors. Captain James MacTavish is a man of the world who's probably had more women than you can imagine. Even you aren't sufficiently clever to handle the likes of him. Getting involved with the man will only make you another in a long line of conquests."

"I beg to differ. Look." She gestured toward the stream, where the captain was hunkered down splashing water over his face. "Currently he's the one in need of cooling off."

The sly smile she turned on her friend made Heather wince. Here, indeed, was the beginning of a battle with a most uncertain outcome.

****

"Hold there!" In the shadowy evening twilight, four masked men leaped out of the trees onto the road in front of the trio. Three held drawn swords, the fourth a pistol. Heather and her companions reined their trotting mounts to a halt. Midnight, on his leash by his mistress's side, muttered a growl. "Dismount and hand over your valuables."

"Now hold on, lads." The captain halted his horse and vented his affable personality on the robbers. "We're but a trio of poor wayfarers on our way to emigrate to the New World. We've nothing but the clothes on our backs and a change of those in our saddle bags."

"You've three decent-looking horses." The one who'd spoken, the one with the pistol, advanced toward Julia. "This one is especially fine. It will fetch a good price. Get down." He nudged Julia's leg with the barrel.

"Certainly, sir. Don't shoot, sir. Just, please, if you will, back off a step so that I may get down." In a display of fear, Julia appeared ready to dismount when, in the split second he took to move away, she freed her boot from the stirrup beside him, kicked the gun from his hand, banged her mare's sides with her other foot, and pulled back on the animal's reins, sending it rearing into the highwayman. Knocked off balance, the man staggered and fell.

Taking their cue, Heather and the captain swung their startled horses on two of the astounded swordsmen while Midnight, whom Heather had released, leaped on the third. Moments later the three were galloping down the road, Midnight by their side, the highwaymen trying to recover in the dust behind them.

Once out of harm's way, Captain Jamie MacTavish, in the lead, reined his gelding to a halt and turned a laughing face to the pair stopping their mounts behind him.

"Now that was fair-to-middlin' fun," he said with a chuckle. "Haven't had a scuffle like that in a dog's age. Always a treat to get back in practice." He turned to Lady Julia. "But where, may I ask, did you attain such skills?"

"Bonny and I read adventure stories." She tossed her head as if what they'd just done was old hat. "Once we ran off a highwayman who sought to waylay us. You've not taken on two helpless females, Captain."

"No, no, I certainly haven't." Still chuckling, he turned his horse back down the road and urged him into a comfortable canter. "Portsmouth by morning, me hearties. Portsmouth by morning."

****

"I'm going out for a bit." The captain faced the pair in the room he'd rented for them in a Portsmouth inn.

"You two are to stay here with the door bolted until I return, is that understood? This town is no place for two women, even disguised as young lads, to be running about in at night."

"And what will you be doing, Captain?" Julia sauntered to stand mere inches in front of him. "Gaming and drinking and whoring, no doubt?"

"You're a rare excuse for a lady." A storm cloud of a frown descended over his handsome features. "Such language is only befitting…"

He broke off, glancing at Heather.

"Say it, Captain." Not about to be bested by her friend's bravery, Heather stepped forward. "Such language is only befitting a tavern wench. Well, maybe I did teach Jewels a few colorful phrases, but they'll come in handy in her disguise as a tough young lad."

"Aye, perhaps." With an exasperated sigh, he turned to open the door. "But mind what I said. We sail on the tide at first light. Get your rest. Since I don't believe either of you is an experienced sailor, you'll need it. Now I'm leaving, but I'll wait in the corridor until I hear you draw the bolt. Is that clear?"

"Perfectly." Lady Julia fluttered her eyelashes, then cast her gaze to her boots.

"Aye, well, then, good. As long as you understand and obey." His tone softened as he turned away and left the room.

Oh, dear Lord, she's got him believing her. Heather closed her eyes and prayed her friend wasn't planning any infamy that could cost them their passage to America.

"Drawing the bolt, Captain." Lady Julia made as much noise as possible as she obeyed his orders.

"Satisfied?"

A grunt from beyond the closed panel was his recognition of her compliance.

*****"

"Let's go." Lady Julia turned from the window, her eyes bright with excitement. "The captain just left the inn and paused to greet what appears to be an old friend. We mustn't waste a minute. He may continue on his way at any moment."

"What are you talking about? Jewels, you heard what he said. We're to bolt the door and not leave the room. We mustn't annoy the man. He's perfectly capable of leaving without us in the morning. Then what will we do?"

"This is our first time in a dog's age...sorry, Midnight"—she addressed the dog lying at Heather's feet—"that we've been on our own in a town of any size. We have to go out and explore."

"But this is a port with sailors and all kinds of unsavory types..."

"I have one of the captain's pistols." She pulled it from her bundle. "And we'll follow close behind him. If we get into any trouble, we've only to scream and he'll come running to our rescue."

"How did you get that?" Heather stared at the weapon.

"He has two, the one he carries on his person and another he keeps in his travelling bag. I took the second while he was outdoors using the privy and you were taking the dog to relieve itself. Now come on!" She stuffed the gun into the belt of her trousers, pulled her coat over it, and headed for the door. "Quickly! Before he gets out of sight."

"You went through the captain's personal belongings?" Heather could barely believe what she was hearing as Lady Julia caught her by a hand and dragged her toward the door.

"I wanted to make certain he was exactly as he represented himself to be. I only had your description of his papers. You've no experience at recognizing authentic documents." Lady Julia drew the bolt with her free hand and forced Heather out into the corridor. "Sorry, Midnight, we have to leave you here," she called back to the dog.

"Oh, and you do?"

"Well, I have helped my father manage our household and more since my mother died. He's not the wisest of men when it comes to financial affairs and proper documentation."

"And, pray tell, did you find all of the captain's documents to be in order?" They were at the top of the stairs, and Heather managed to bring her companion to a halt. "Is he well and truly a licensed master mariner and owner of an ocean-going vessel named the *Highland Lass*?"

"Most definitely." She paused and faced her friend, eyes sparkling. "And that letter from his doctor brother authorizing him to find him an assistant? As near as I can determine, also authentic. Now come on. Time is a-wasting."

Heather found herself stumbling down the steps, propelled by an effervescent Lady Julia.

****

"You'll be coming home with me now, Papa." Julia, in her lad's garb, stepped up to the captain watching his companion dealing cards at a table in the

Hound and Harridan. "Ma has sent us to fetch you. She says if you persist in gambling away money what's due your family, she'll be taking the frying pan to your head and her foot to your arse."

Standing near the door of the murky barroom, Heather's breath caught in her throat. *Jewels, you'll get us both abandoned by the man.* The thought made her stomach churn. Lady Julia Thomas might be able to go home and have all forgiven, but not Heather Grey, murder suspect.

"What?" Captain James MacTavish looked up at her, his face registering astonishment. "I thought I told you to stay at the…"

"At home, yes." Julia interrupted him before he could mention the Fox and Ferret. "But the triplets are unwell, and what with Ma having only two breasts, you're needed to sooth the third. It's not her fault she has an even dozen of young'uns, she said."

The bar girl who'd been standing beside Jamie, her arm lightly across his shoulders, jerked it away as if burned and stepped back.

"You have a wife and twelve children?" She stared down at him. "Good God, man! You must be poor as a church mouse. I thought from the cut of your clothes…"

"He'd spend his last coin on a fine shirt while me and my brothers and sisters go barefoot in winter." Julia stuck out her dirty chin and faced the startled woman. "So if you've been expecting a handsome income from him for whatever you have to offer, you can forget about it. He might be randy as a ram, but he's pauper poor."

"Now just a minute…!" The captain rose to his

feet, shoving his chair aside so violently it fell to the floor with a crash. "I'm not married, and this mudlark most definitely isn't my son!" He glared down at Julia. Heather held her breath.

"Never said you was married, Papa." Lady Julia cocked her head saucily. "Just said you and my ma have a pack of children together. And now that Ma's losing her shape from having all your brats, you're looking for fresh fields to sow."

"Man, you'd best be gettin' on home." His companion at the table shook his head sadly. "I've no desire to be taking money from a man who should be using it to put food in his babes' mouths."

"Come on, Harry, you know me." The captain turned to him. "You know I've no passel of children, no woman whose bed I've been sharing for over a dozen years."

"Jamie, I only know you as a boon drinking companion and an honest gambler. What you do beyond these four walls has always been your own business. But now this poor young lad, with his tale, well..." He stood. "I'll bid you goodnight and hope you see fit to honor your commitments."

He touched his forelock to the boy and walked off toward the bar.

"You conniving little...!" Captain James MacTavish caught Lady Julia by an arm and dragged her from the barroom so fast her feet bounced to keep up with him. Heather followed them, her heart hammering in her throat.

"Just what did you think you were doing in there?" In the light gleaming out from the tavern's windows, he loomed over her, his face contorted with anger.

"Whoring and drinking and gambling are bad for a man's body and soul." She tilted her head and smirked up at him. "I've just taken the first step in making an honest man from a rogue. And you are a rogue, Captain, make no mistake."

A gust of wind caught her coat and blew it open, revealing the pistol stuck in the belt of her trousers.

"My pistol!" he yanked it out and stood glowering down at her. "Stole it, did you? Bloody hell, what next?"

"I had to." She glared right back at him, unflinching. "It would hardly have been safe for us to be out in such a rowdy town without a weapon. I can assure you I know how to handle it."

For a moment he stared down at her, his jaw working with a tick, his lips drawn back into a thin, hard line. Heather's innards roiled. Had Jewels driven him to the breaking point? Then, to her utter astonishment, he burst out laughing.

"You are a handful, and that's for certain sure. Bold as brass, to boot. I think you might make a decent sailor after all, you young guttersnipe." He shoved the pistol into his own belt, took each of them by an arm, and turned toward the Fox and Ferret. "But dunnae ever try anything like that again, or I'll be forced to give you a good hiding, lady or no." He paused a moment and looked down at Lady Julia, a chuckle in his words. "Do you know, I believe you might be as big a rogue as me."

Chapter 4

Good God! Will this cursed ship never cease rolling like something possessed?

Heather leaned over the edge of the crude bed built into the ship's wall and retched into the bucket Julia had left for her. The dog Midnight lay beside her bunk and gazed at her with sad, confused eyes. He whined.

"Do you feel as ill as I do, laddy?" She reached out a hand and touched his rough coat. "Are you sorry I've brought you along on this mad escapade? Maybe Jewels is the only one of us fit for it." She fell onto her back and gazed up at the rocking beams above her, despair joining the nausea in her gut.

How can Jewels awaken each morning feeling frisky and fit, while I wallow in such misery? Am I cursed for being the instigator of this mad scheme?

She wiped her mouth on the sleeve of her shirt and pulled the rough blankets more snugly about her as a chill gushed up her body. At least Captain James MacTavish had seen fit to give them the privacy of this closet of a cabin, miserable as it was.

"I sometimes take a passenger," he'd explained as he showed them into the crude cubicle outside his cabin at the rear of the ship. "I've told the men you are such."

If I survive to get to land, I'll never again board one of these wretched things.

Weak as a kitten, she struggled to settle more comfortably among the rough wool of the blankets. Her life at the tavern might not have been pleasant, but this was a living hell. And what of this doctor for whom she'd promised to work? True, he was a brother to the handsome and (she had to admit) affable Captain James MacTavish, but that didn't assure that he would resemble him either physically or mentally.

Her mind, disheveled by illness, began to produce weird possibilities. Perhaps he was a cruel beggar, nasty to the core, with a heart as black as her dog's coat. Perhaps he was a wizened, foul-breathed creature who pored over weird concoctions and potions made from bat wings and snake skins. Perhaps…

"Bonny." Julia pulled aside the sacking that served as a door for their living quarters. Her face glowed with health and excitement. "You really must get yourself together and come on deck. It's a glorious day, fair winds and sunshine. Jamie says if we continue at this rate, we'll make near record time in the crossing."

"Jamie is it, now?" Heather caught the moniker and managed a weak grin. "I hope you and our captain haven't been doing anything I wouldn't sanction."

"For heaven's sake, Bonny, how could we? I sleep here with you each night, and outside of this space, everyone's life aboard this ship is an open book from sheer lack of privacy." She swung her bottom around and planted it on the edge of the bed. "But he is a handsome devil, don't you think? Did you know he and his brother were privateers during the war?"

"Pirates, you mean."

"Hardly. He volunteered his ship to protect British North America when it had no navy of its own. His brother signed on as ship's doctor. Letters of marque and bounty awards from the government authorized him to keep some of the spoils he captured during his defense endeavors. I'm guessing he became quite rich as a result."

"Yet he continues to roam the seas, carrying cargo and seeking out a servant for his doctor brother. Really, Jewels, I think you're imagining a great deal."

"He loves the sea, Bonny." She pushed Heather's tangled hair back from her face. "He's an adventurer. No matter how rich he might become, he'll always long for new places and new experiences."

"And now you're coming to love the sea as well. Take care, Jewels. I have a feeling Captain James MacTavish has had many a lady at his beck and call in any number of ports. Don't let your heart get involved in what may well be for him a mere dalliance."

"Don't you worry about me. I'm no romantic school girl. Now come along, Midnight." She picked up the looped bit of rope that served as a leash and slipped it over the dog's head. "Even if your mistress can't manage a walk on deck, you must. Can't have you fouling this hidey hole. It's nasty enough." Wrinkling her nose, she picked up the bucket that served as their facility and nudged aside the curtain. "This needs emptying and rinsing. Midnight and I will be back shortly. Try to manage with that tin cup until we return."

After she'd gone, Heather drew a deep breath and smiled. Jewels, with her never-failing *joie de vivre*, always brightened her day. The image of the gnomish, leering doctor slid away. Perhaps, just perhaps, this Doctor William MacTavish might at least vaguely resemble his brother.

****

"Heather, you really must bestir yourself!" Julia burst into their closet cabin, her face bright with excitement. "We're entering the bay that leads into the river that leads to the settlement of Douglastown, which is the nearest village to where your doctor lives. Come and see! The trees are beginning to leaf out, and everything is fresh and green with the essence of spring. It's beautiful and unspoiled and…"

"Very well." The thought of the end of the voyage gave Heather strength. Pulling herself to a sitting position, she eased her legs over the edge of the bed.

"Hurry! There's so much to see and enjoy!" Julia slipped an arm through hers and drew her to her feet. "Our adventure is beginning."

"I thought it began the moment I met Captain James MacTavish." She groaned. "Now I'm regretting it."

"Do stop complaining." Julia caught up Midnight's lead and helped her friend out into the passageway. "Are you saying you'd rather be back in jolly old England, the slave of either your brother or that great lout Liam Jones? Good heavens, Heather, you might even be facing a murder charge."

They hesitated while Julia waited for Heather to steady herself on the gentle rolling of the planks beneath her feet.

"No." The word came out slowly. "No, I wouldn't rather be in England. But I will be eternally grateful to get off this conveyance from Hell."

"Well, then, buck up, me hearty!" Julia urged her toward the steps at the end of the passage. "There's a whole new world awaiting us, and you can't meet it languishing in bed."

With what Heather deemed nearly the last of her strength, she struggled up to the deck, hoping her stomach would behave and she wouldn't disgrace herself before the captain and his crew.

Midnight scratched and clawed his way up the ladder after her, with Julia pushing him from the rear.

"I swear, Bonny, taking this animal on deck to relieve himself has been the worst part of the voyage for me," she puffed.

"I couldn't leave him, Jewels…" Heather's words trailed off as she arrived on deck and stepped out into sunshine and balmy breezes.

"Oh, good Lord!" The words burst from her as involuntarily as air from a punctured balloon. The vista took her breath away. Spread out beyond the dark waters that lapped softly against the sides of the ship, beneath a sky of most perfect blue, was a long line of bright, fresh green as unspoiled as anything she could imagine. Overhead, grey-and-white herring gulls swooped as they sent out their inane cries. *Paradise. Surely Paradise could not be any more beautiful.*

"Oh, Jewels, it's wonderful!" She turned to her friend, enthusiasm coursing through her as it hadn't during the weeks of the voyage. "We were right to come!"

"Most definitely, my Bonny Lass." Julia slipped an arm about her waist to give her a quick hug. "Six weeks ago we couldn't have imagined this in our wildest dreams."

"What ho, lads?" The captain came to join them, a broad grin on his weathered face. "Never thought you'd live to see this place, I'll wager, did you, my boy?" He slapped Heather on the back, all but knocking her off her feet in her weakened condition, and winked at Julia.

"I'll never get on another ship as long as I live." She clung to the rail and concentrated on the widening band of green across the water.

"Oh, how can you say that?" Julia looked at her scornfully. "I've never enjoyed anything so much in my life…unless perhaps it was a flat-out gallop across the moor."

"Ah, a lad after my own heart." Captain MacTavish gave her a swat on the backside, winked again, and ambled back to the wheel, whistling a bawdy tune Heather remembered all too well from her tavern days.

"Jewels, what have you been up to?" She hissed, turning to frown at her friend and catching the smug smile on her face. "Jewels, you and the captain…?"

"A mere dalliance, Peter, never fear." She used one of the two aliases they'd assumed for the voyage and nudged her playfully. "And do try to remember my name is Paul. The good captain will have to put a ring on my finger before he gets any further than a kiss and cuddle. He knows what he's up against. I've told him that while my father may have a family tree that reaches back to the Conquest, my mother was a notorious woman from the theatres of London, a woman who teased and tormented any number of suitors until she found the one she'd been seeking in the person of my wealthy, handsome, titled father."

"But she was reckless, Jewels. She died young when her hunter failed to make an impossible jump. Surely you don't want to follow in her footsteps."

"Ah, but she lived gloriously, Bonny. And I plan to be just like her."

Julia stuck out her chin and concentrated her gaze on the shoreline. Heather guessed her friend was remembering the beautiful, vibrant woman who'd died three years earlier. Heather felt a catch in her own throat as she recalled the woman who had been Julia's parent. She'd admired Lady Sophie and thought of her as a second mother.

"Jewels, you may well have managed such men…gentlemen…as you came into contact with on your estate in England, but this man, this Captain James MacTavish, and his brother were pirates, picaroons who made their money fighting and killing and God only knows what else. They're not to be trifled with."

"Don't be a prude, Peter." Julia put emphasis on the last word as a sailor approached. "We're reckless adventurers. We'll make the world dance to *our* tune now."

****

Under fair winds and clear skies the *Highland Lass* rocked gently into the mouth of a river and continued up the wide waterway, where each moment brought more delightful vistas to Heather Grey, former tavern girl. The wine called freedom intoxicated her and made her feel like dancing and singing. It had been a miracle the day Captain James MacTavish had stumbled, wounded, into that loathsome barroom. Even her innards had chosen to calm themselves to the occasional flutter.

"I'm going below to pack up our bundles," Julia said. "No, no," she stopped her friend as she turned to join her. "You're feeling better for the first time in

59

weeks. Revisiting the scene of your discomfort won't further your recovery. You need to be as fit as possible to meet your new master. Never fear. It won't take me long. God knows, we've few enough personal belongings."

As the ship glided up the river, Heather became enthralled with the pristine beauty of the greening wilderness. Only at long-spaced intervals was the forest broken by the sight of a log cabin or a small house and farm. It truly appeared to be a new land where people such as herself and Julia could make a fresh start.

Or die trying, a small, sinister voice inside her head suggested. Perhaps those beautifully green forests held hidden terrors…bloodthirsty animals, or savages, or huge snakes. Struggling to reassure herself, she sucked in a deep breath of the clear air lightly seasoned with sea salt as the ship slid away from ocean and bay.

The captain has assured you this is not the case, so ignore such thoughts, Heather Grey, just ignore them. Keep in mind the alternative of living out your life either in that slavery of a tavern or married to a great lout of a farmer like Liam Jones, who'd keep you worked to the bone and constantly pregnant. And I won't have to fight a murder charge here in this new country. No, I've made the right choice. New Brunswick will be my home. Furthermore, nothing on the face of this earth can induce me to once again cross that heaving ocean. And this man, this Doctor MacTavish. Surely he must have a drop of compassion in his soul, to have become a surgeon.

She rubbed the matted head of the dog by her side, and he wriggled with delight.

"Once I get settled in my new position, I'll see you

get a good wash and brush, my laddie." She smiled down at him. "I do believe that under that neglected coat you're quite a handsome chap."

Midnight whined excitedly, and she giggled, then stifled her mirth. She mustn't sound girlish, not now, with freedom so close.

"There's something I've been meanin' to speak to you about." Captain James MacTavish had come to stand beside her, a trace of a frown wrinkling his brow. "And I must do it before we dock."

"Yes?" A wave of apprehension washed over Heather, both the man's tone and expression warning of something unpleasant.

"It's about my brother." He gripped the bulwark and stared off across the water.

"Yes?"

"I should have told you afore now, but I didn't want to put you off." He turned to her, and she recognized that he was trying to lighten both his tone and his outlook. "You see, Will has not had an easy time of it where women are concerned. He's been a bit off them for a spell." He wet his lips. "He's become something of a hermit and can be a fair curmudgeon by times."

"That would have been useful information several weeks ago." Hiding the surprise his information had given her, she met his blue-eyed look steadily.

"Aye, and I was remiss in not telling you." His expression softened as he looked down at her. "I would have, except that you seemed so perfect for the position, and..."

"And?"

"And I felt sure and certain that you're the perfect

woman to bring him out of it…no shilly-shallying, no excuses, just a good, swift kick in the arse, figuratively speaking, when he needs it."

"You've left me scant opportunity to change my mind, haven't you, Captain?" She squinted up at him in the sun, eyes narrowing. "I'll just have to make the best of your brother and his cantankerous ways and hope we don't come to blows…literally speaking."

****

The ship drifted up against the wharf as Heather stared about at the scattering of small log and plank buildings back from the shore. A rutted, dusty street wound among them. Waterfront wharves were piled with sawn lumber, and, at several locations farther down river, seagoing ships in various stages of construction stood in slips.

Hardly a thriving metropolis, but what had she expected to find in this outpost? At least the surrounding forest and fields looked fresh and clean. There were even a few plowed areas that suggested the planting of crops.

"We'll survive, Midnight." She picked up the dog's leash as a gangplank was lowered. "We're strong and clever. We won't let a woman-hating hermit named Dr. William MacTavish ruin our chance at a new life."

"You'll never guess the former name of this village, Peter." Julia appeared at her side, their bundles clutched in her arms.

"Hardly, Paul. It could be called anything…perhaps an Indian name. I understand they're in wide use in this country. Like the river…Miramichi. What did the captain say it means?"

"I neither remember nor care." She leaned close

and spoke softly into her friend's ear. "Get back to the name of the village, Bonny. Its present name is Douglastown, named in honor of a provincial governor, but formerly it was called Gretna Green. Isn't that an amazing coincidence? In the note I left for my father I said I was running off with a highwayman to Gretna Green. Naturally he'll assume that infamous place of false marriages in Scotland. At the time, I had no idea I'd actually be going to a village that had once had the same name. So, you see, my Bonny Lass, I didn't really tell a lie." She stepped back and grinned at Heather.

"Don't look so smug, my friend." Heather kept her voice low as well. "Your father travelled a great deal during his life as a young man. He may know of this outpost."

"Hardly." Heather guffawed. "Look at the size of it...no more than a dozen log-and-board houses, a larger structure that looks like it might be a place of commerce, a church and manse up on the hill, and an establishment near the docks that is probably a tavern. I shall feel quite safe in this once-upon-a-time Gretna Green."

"Let us hope such is the case."

"Oh, look!" Julia pointed shoreward, toward the road leading into the village.

Out of the forest, a horse and rider had burst into view. The animal, a magnificent silver grey with flowing mane and tail and arched neck, loped with such graceful ease that it brought a gasp of admiration to Heather's lips. The dark-haired, broad-shouldered man on his back sat tall in the saddle, his white shirt open at the throat. His well cut black coat, tan trousers, and shining ebony knee-high boots branded him a man of means. Although his mount was performing perfectly with seemingly effortless ease, Heather knew enough about horses to spot a spirit that needed skillful management. Admiration for both horse and rider enveloped her.

The pair turned toward the wharf, the man slowing the grey to a prancing trot.

"Will!" Captain MacTavish strode down the gangplank. "Wings! Ah, I'm glad to see ya both."

Will? William? Could this handsome man who rode like the most accomplished of horsemen on a magnificent silver stallion be Doctor William MacTavish, her future employer, the ill-tempered, woman-hating oaf the captain had described?

"Bonny Lass!" Julia's words were a hiss of excitement as she joined Heather at the rail, their bundles clutched in her arms. "Do you think that can be your doctor?"

"Possibly, Jewels." Struggling to keep her tone even and disinterested, Heather replied without looking at her friend. "He does bear a resemblance to the captain."

The rider dismounted and turned the horse loose. With a snort, it broke into a canter and headed toward the captain as he reached the dock. Heather gasped. James MacTavish was about to be trampled!

To her relief, the stallion came to a sliding stop just short of the man, lowered its head, and whinnied softly. Gentle as a lamb, it nudged the captain, bringing a hearty peal of laughter from James MacTavish.

"Wings, ya great babe! Ye've not forgotten me, have ya?" He caught the bridle and stood back to look at the animal. "You appear in fine fettle. Apparently my brother has been treating you with half-decent care."

Heather's attention swung back to the man who'd dismounted and was walking toward the pair at the bottom of the gangplank. So this was her new master, this bold-riding, handsome creature. *Hmmmm.*

"Of course I've taken excellent care of him." The newcomer joined the captain. She could now see the resemblance was close, except that where James MacTavish's face wore an expression of warm affability, his brother's countenance mirrored one of cool reserve. "Would you think I'd do any less to a creature that means so much to you, brother? But he's not yours yet. I'm wanting to see this assistant you've promised."

"Very well." Jamie MacTavish turned back toward his ship and yelled to Heather and Julia, "You young lads there, come on down."

Heather's heartbeat quickened as she and her friend headed for the gangplank. She must look a wreck. She hadn't bathed or washed her hair in weeks. And she'd been ill. Julia had wiped her face from time to time, but she'd had no looking glass in which to check on the results. Now she was to meet this handsome, well dressed man who looked as cold as ice and even less welcoming.

Worse still, I stink. There's no hope for it. I'll disgust this man and he will turn me away. What then?

She glanced over at her companion swaggering at her side and tried to gather a bit of her boldness and courage. Julia looked robustly healthy and bright-eyed, ready for adventure. *God, give me strength. Let me bluff my way into this man's employ.*

"Good God, Jamie, what's the meaning of this?"

Dr. William MacTavish stared at the pair as they came to stand beside his brother on the dock. "I said I wanted an assistant, not a couple of filthy street urchins. What am I to do with these two? And what's that great ball of fur?" He indicated Midnight by Heather's side.

"We'll go to my house and I'll explain." The captain waved to a seaman who had brought their three saddled, prancing horses ashore. "Over here, Johnson. Mount up, lads."

"Jamie, don't be mad, man." The doctor looked at the horses, half wild after weeks of captivity in the hold. "You might remain on one of these beasts, but these lads…"

"Worry not, brother." James MacTavish caught up the reins of the wildest of the three animals and swung smoothly onto its back. "These *lads* are among the best riders I've ever encountered. Now mount up and enjoy your last ride on my beautiful Wings. And here." He bent down, grabbed the two bundles of belongings from Julia's arms, and tossed them at his brother. "The lads' personal effects. You can tie them to your saddle easier than we can, what with these poor creatures of ours half wild from weeks of being cramped aboard ship."

A chance to impress him. Heather took up the reins of one of the two remaining horses and swung into the saddle. The animal pranced and half reared, but she managed to bring the mare back into control as Julia mounted her animal and made similar adjustments.

Out of the corner of her eye, Heather caught a glimpse of Dr. William MacTavish watching them. *He's impressed. Yes, he is definitely impressed. Maybe I still have a chance.*

The doctor was holding the bundles with all the

disdain merited by something that carried a contagion. Finally, with a snort of derision, he turned and began to tie them to his stallion's saddle.

"There'd better not be lice or worse in them," he snapped at his brother.

"Ah, Will, stop bellyaching." The captain wheeled his snorting, pawing gelding around with perfect ease. "Mount up, brother, or we'll be leaving you in the dust."

He put his heels to his horse's sides and set off at full gallop down the road that led out of the village, Julia close behind him. Heather cast a final glance at the doctor before bringing her mare about and charging after them.

After weeks of confinement aboard ship, Heather welcomed the freedom of an all-out canter down the dusty road behind Julia and the captain. The fresh air and sunshine of the beautiful spring day revived her, awakened her appetite for adventure. Beyond the humble little village, the country appeared bursting with the invigorating freshness and renewal of spring. Everywhere along the trail, deciduous trees stood fuzzed with the green promise of leaves, grass boasted the color of emeralds, a fresh breeze caressed her cheeks, and a flawless blue sky offered the promise of good things to come. A happiness that was freedom sang in her blood as the doctor overtook her on the stallion, cast her a disparaging glance, then spurred his animal to a flat-out run to overtake his brother and Julia.

Let him have this small victory. It's not the time to challenge him. I'll find a way to please him, to convince him I'm the assistant he needs. My heart tells me this is where I belong, where I'll build a new life. No big, nasty—albeit handsome—Highlander will spoil my claim to it.

The trio ahead of her had turned into the dooryard of a small, neat house. The captain's home on the outskirts of Douglastown appeared well kept and decent. She remembered Jamie MacTavish's description of his brother's house as one of the finest in the valley and wondered how it would compare with this one.

Chapter 5

In the paddock attached to the small barn at the rear of the property, all four unsaddled their mounts and turned them loose to graze.

Will watched as the two young lads freed their mounts. At least they knew how to handle horses. Nevertheless, Jamie had once again proven himself unwise in purchasing such fine animals for these urchins. But then, his brother always had been rash with money. And there was something strange about the pair, something he couldn't yet label…

"Come along," the captain urged his guests as he headed for the house. "I've no doubt it's more than a tad dusty inside, but I've left a bottle of fine whiskey in the cupboard. We can all use a wee dram."

More than a tad dusty, the interior of the house was an outright mess. Will wasn't surprised. Neither he nor his brother excelled at housekeeping. Dust motes, disturbed by their entrance, swam in the shaft of sunlight issuing from the open door. The room into which they stepped served as parlor and kitchen. A door at the back led to the establishment's single bedroom. Dishes displaying the remains of the last meal the mariner had enjoyed in the house littered the table, dirt crunched beneath their boots on the floor, and flies buzzed at dirty windows.

"Think you can set all this to rights?" His brother grinned at the lad who appeared the more robust of the pair.

"Of course, sir." The words set off a warning bell in his mind. Why did they sound strange, unlike those that normally would have come from a young scallywag fresh from a London gutter? The urchin grasped a broom leaning against the wall near the door and began to sweep. His efforts raised a cloud of dust that set all residents of the room to choking.

"No need to start directly." The captain stilled the effort with strong hands on the broom. "We'll have a wee dram and see Will and his workmate on their way before we get to serious cleaning."

He went to the cupboard and took down a full bottle of whiskey. Selecting four mugs from a collection on the dresser beneath, he glanced inside each, blew into one to expel a bug, then proceeded to pour out generous servings.

"To our health." He raised his cup once everyone in the room had a tankard. "And success and happiness."

"Yes!" The bold one spoke again in that unusual inflection. "To a wonderful future!"

The lad took a swallow, stifled a choke, and grinned broadly. His companion took a more cautious sip.

"Now to business. Will, you'd best take a seat." Jamie indicated a dusty ladderback chair. "Lads, I'll be asking you to remove your caps."

As raven dark curls and gold brown ones tumbled over shoulders, Doctor William MacTavish choked on his whiskey.

Dear God, what insanity was this? Even Jamie couldn't be so daft as to...

"Women!" His voice returned with such vehemence it echoed up into the rafters of the small house. "You've brought me a pair of women!"

"Calm yourself, Will. This one"—the captain took Heather by a shoulder and drew her forward—"can read and write and cipher. She's also a first-rate healer who saved me from bleeding to death when I took a nasty spill from my horse. Furthermore, she's a dab hand at farm work and can cook with the best of them. She fills all your requirements. You'll recall you didn't specify gender."

The last was accompanied by a twinkle in the captain's eyes that only served to further exacerbate the doctor's outrage.

"Sweet Jesus, I thought that went without saying!" He banged his mug on the table and stood. "So you'll be taking this one"—he indicated Heather—"which was to be mine, back to where you found her. What you do with the other trollop is entirely your business."

"Trollop!" Julia Thomas snapped into full aristocratic mode as she drew herself to confront the doctor. "I'm Lady Julia Thomas, and this is my best friend and companion, Heather Grey, the successful landlady of a flourishing inn on the Burkley Highroad in England. Trollop, indeed!"

She gulped more whiskey, coughed, and swung away from him to bang her mug down on the plank table with a vehemence equal to his.

"No." His response was a barely audible wheeze of disbelief. "Jamie, tell me this wench is lying. Tell me now." Blood drained from his head, his limbs weakened.

"Well, perhaps a wee bit has the ring of truth." Jamie wet his lips. "You'd best sit down again, brother, and I'll give you the rights of our situation."

****

"Oh, my God." Doctor William MacTavish sank onto a chair, dropped his head into his hands on the table, and moaned. "Oh, my God!" He couldn't believe the story his brother had just told him, definitely didn't want to believe it.

"Don't fret yourself, Will." Captain James MacTavish colored his words with a soft, soothing Scottish burr. "I've thought it through. No one at the inn knew who I was except Mistress Heather here. I was only some stranger from the roads, a highwayman perhaps. They'll not be searching the seaports for us. Have another wee dram. It'll still your nerves." He poured more whiskey into his brother's cup.

"Argh!" William pulled himself upright on his chair. "There's not enough whiskey in all of Scotland to still my nerves. You know what you've done, you daft creature, don't you?" He glared up at his brother. "You've fitted both our necks into nooses. Sweet Jesus, a lady and a murder suspect!"

"There's little to worry about." The one identified as Lady Julia Thomas tossed her tangled dark curls. "Anyone pursuing me will most likely have headed for Scotland."

"And why, pray tell, might they have done that?" Weary exasperation tainted his words.

"I left a note saying I'd run off to Scotland's Gretna Green with a highwayman from the Highlands. At the time I had no idea I'd be coming to a place that once had a similar name. Ironic, isn't it?"

"No one in their right mind would believe such a wild tale." He accepted the replenished cup the captain held out to him.

"Aye, but I did just that." She cast a coy glance at Jamie. "Your brother is surely a rogue if ever there was one, and this place, serendipitously, was once called Gretna Green. So you see, the truth...a bit manipulated."

"Anyone who knows Jewels would believe her perfectly capable of such an escapade." The pale, thin one turned to face him. "She's not your typical ladyship."

"Satisfied?" The lady herself tilted her head to one side, favoring the doctor with a saucy glance.

"Since I don't yet know you but your friend here does, I suppose I will have to be. Well, come along, then, the pair of you." He quaffed the whiskey, grimaced, and stood. "I'll have to be settling you both in until my brother and I decide what's to be done with the pair of you."

"You don't have to worry about her ladyship, Will." Captain Jamie MacTavish cast a roguish grin at Julia. "Jewels will be staying with me."

"Staying with you? Man, have you gone completely daft?" He stared at his brother. "You've already done everything but fit both our necks into nooses. Don't go begging to get us drawn and quartered, as well! I'll not go leaving either of them in your charge."

"Jamie shan't be living with me in the way you may fancy, Doctor." Her ladyship cast him a sly smile. "I'm to be his servant. He's brought a lad for you. Why not one for himself? Anyway, I'm not certain drawing and quartering is still legal. Furthermore, we've been in his charge, as you put it, for weeks now and are as unscathed as the day we met him."

"Jamie? Jewels? Such intimate name calling and I'm expected to believe there's nothing between you except as master and servant?"

"Jewels is Heather's nickname for me. I've always liked it and chose to adopt it when we decided to embark on this adventure...so much more fascinating than Julia, don't you think? At any rate, I can't very well go by my real name. I know you two gentlemen are eager to keep my identity a secret."

"So I'm to get the skinny, pasty-faced one, am I?" Dr. MacTavish circled Heather, looking her up and down.

"Skinny, pasty-faced...!" He saw her hands knot into fists at her side. *Spirit...for better or worse.*

"She had a touch of seasickness on the voyage." The captain put a big, restraining hand on her shoulder. "Give her a chance, Will. You'll soon discover I've made a wise choice. A few days of sunshine, fresh air, and good food, and she'll turn out to be as fine a figure of a lass as this one." He cast Julia a lecherous grin and received a playfully remonstrating frown in return.

"And what is she called, pray tell? Precious? Seems a fitting name for the companion of one named Jewels." The bitterness he was feeling colored his words.

"Jewels' nickname for me will serve the purpose. You may call me Bonny...short for Bonny Lass." Heather squared her shoulders and faced him boldly. "And I'll thank you not to go insulting me with your uncalled-for observances."

"At the moment, all I can think to call you is a bonny mistake."

"Very well, and I shall call you Surgeon."

"I'm not a surgeon!" *Brazen hussy!* "I'm a doctor trained at the best of medical universities, in Edinburgh, Scotland. Surgeon, indeed."

"Will's a tad touchy on the subject of title." Jamie MacTavish winked at her. "Doctors and physicians are educated medical men. Surgeons are simply sawbones who lop off limbs. A doctor might sit at the finest tables in England, but not a surgeon."

"Ah, so a man proud of his own title even though he tends to scoff at mine." Her ladyship flashed him a saucy smirk. "A double standard, don't you agree, Bonny?" She threw the pale, skinny one a smug glance.

"A double standard indeed, Jewels. We'll have to set about teaching this man the leveling effect of this new land where, according to our good Captain MacTavish, titles mean nothing."

"I never said exactly that," James protested. "I said this new land makes all men equal, where it's survival of the fittest and…"

"And also makes all women equal, even to men?" her ladyship challenged.

"Enough. It's time you were taking your new assistant home, Will." James finished off his whiskey. "I've got to see to the unloading of my vessel. And you, Jewels, will be needing to get down to work. The dust lies thick about this place."

"Of course, my lord and master." She bobbed him a mocking curtsey, then wrinkled her nose. "And a good airing won't go astray, either."

"This one won't do, for sure and certain." William circled Heather. "She's far too thin and sickly to be any good for the work I'd require of her. You may keep her as well. She can serve as a bit of a chaperone."

He paused in front of her and something in those emerald eyes startled him, caught at his innards. Was it foiled hope? Despair? Pasty and thin as he'd nastily branded her in his outrage, the lass looked undernourished and downright unwell. The concerned doctor jolted to the surface. But just for a moment.

He brought himself up sharp. Let Jamie see to her. Probably all she needed was a few decent meals and a surface beneath her feet that didn't dip and sway. He couldn't go getting involved with her. He turned and strode out the door, letting it bang shut behind him.

"Now hold on just a damn minute, Will." Jamie caught up with him halfway to the stable. Grabbing him by an arm, he yanked the doctor about to face him. "We made a deal and, by God, you'll be living up to it. This girl can read and write and cipher, cook and clean, tend a stable, and take care of sick and wounded. She's clever and strong and willing. And you'll not find her like where courage is required. You should have seen her fighting off a band of highwaymen on our way to Portsmouth. I searched the length and breadth of England before I found her, and you'll not go tossing her aside…not without a fair trial."

"And you're eager to get your blessed horse back." William faced his brother, hands clenched at his sides. They hadn't come to fisticuffs since they were young lads, but he sensed a return of those moments drawing near. "Can't you get it through your thick head I wanted a lad…a strong farm lad who could help about the place when he wasn't needed to assist me. A brave lad who wouldn't faint at the sight of blood or vomit at an amputation. Worst of all, this girl…this girl is suspected of having done murder. She's probably not above killing me in my sleep."

"Now you're talking just plain crazy, Will. This girl, as you call her, acted as doctor to any as were ailing in her county. Jewels told me all about Mistress Heather during the voyage. Why, the lass has even delivered babes as her mother taught her before she died. She's no more a murderer than the Reverend Scott. Will, think. Where will you find such a helper? And she makes a most delicious stew." His words softened over the last sentence, and William caught the twinkle in his eyes.

"We made a deal. You were to bring me a decent assistant." William fought to keep from giving in to his brother's plea. He knew how persuasive Jamie could be, and not always to his own personal betterment. "Not some sickly female!"

"You dinnae specify sex, and Heather fills all the other requirements. When I was injured, she treated me as well as any doctor in the land. She'll not go letting you down, you great stubborn Highlander, if you give her half a chance."

"Worst of all, she's a tavern wench. I didn't think I had to specify no creatures of Meg Whalen's ilk. No doubt I'll find her bedding the local lads to make a few extra bits in no time at all!"

"Heather is not like that." James MacTavish stepped back to square off with the doctor eye to eye. "As you've reminded me many a time, I've had my share of such ladies. I can recognize one a mile away.

Heather Grey is no whore. I'll stake my life on it."

"Oh, you will, will you?" William found himself relenting. His brother spoke the truth. Jamie MacTavish had a skill for recognizing loose women.

"Aye. But let's make the wager a little less violent. I'll allow you to keep Wings for the present. If you discover Heather Grey exhibiting loose morals of any kind within the next two months, you may have that fine animal forever and no dispute. What do you say?"

William hesitated.

"Come on, Will. You know that stallion is my prized possession. You know I wouldn't risk losing him on anything less than a sure bet."

"You did once before."

"Aye, but then I thought my brother would never enforce the wager. Now I know he will."

"Ah, verrae well, brother. But if I catch the slightest hint of that girl playing the whore, you'll never ride your silver grey prize again."

"Verra well. Shake on it."

William hesitated only a moment before he accepted his brother's offer. That horse would mean a lot to his practice. Jamie put an arm about his brother's shoulders and turned him back toward the house.

"I trust you've brought my supplies?" The doctor stopped his brother at the door. "I'm running to the bottom of mine."

"Laudanum, whiskey, bandages, and a bunch of other bottles and packages, the contents of which I have no idea of their uses. I'll send them down to you as soon as I get my cargo unloaded and put in order."

"Good. I'll be waiting." The two men stepped inside. Both women once again wore their caps, hair neatly tucked out of sight beneath.

"We thought it wisest to resume our disguises in case one of the neighbors chanced by to welcome you home, Captain." Julia cast Jamie MacTavish a coy little grin.

"Aye, that's a good idea." Captain MacTavish shot his brother a look. "They're a clever pair, as you can see."

"I'll be needing more proof before I'm convinced. Come along, lass." William took the young woman standing by the table by an arm and found himself confronted by a snarling Midnight. "Keep that creature under control," he bellowed. "Or I'll not be further coerced into taking you with me. My brother has convinced me to give you a try, but it won't take much to make me recant that decision."

"Hush, Midnight." Heather spoke softly to the dog and the animal obeyed.

"We've a short ride ahead of us to my farm. I want to return as soon as possible in case any patients arrive. Furthermore, you look as if you must be fed or you'll collapse into a bit of dust." Drawing her behind him, he stepped back outside and headed for the paddock. The dog, trotting beside them, muttered his discontent.

"Wait!" Julia hurried after them.

The doctor paused long enough for her to catch up and gather Heather into a quick embrace.

"I'll see you soon, Bonny." She drew her friend out at arm's length to gaze into her face.

"Take care, Jewels. Remember you are a lady."

As her friend released her and stepped back, the pasty-faced one turned back to the astonished doctor, straightened her shoulders, and said, proud as a princess, "As am I, sir."

Arrogant little gutter snip...

"Oh, and Will," the captain called after him from the doorway as they started off again, "I congratulate you. Wings looks fit as a fiddle. See that he stays that way. Now come along, milady. You've a deal of cleaning to get to."

William watched as his brother drew the woman, waving farewell to his present companion, back into the house.

"Fit as a fiddle, indeed." The words were a disgruntled guffaw as he once more claimed Heather's arm and urged her toward the field behind the stable, where they'd left the horses. "I wish I'd never won that confounded horse, now that I see what I've gotten in trade."

"I've been taken in trade for a horse?" His companion froze to a stop and yanked free of his hold. "*A horse!*"

"Aye, a horse. Now come along, woman." The doctor pulled open the paddock gate and thrust her inside. "The deal's done, and we've got to make the best of it."

****

He checked the stallion's girth and watched out of the corner of his eye as she did the same with her mare. *At least she knows her way around horses.* He led Wings out of the enclosure and swung into the saddle. Manners required him to help a woman aboard her mount, but this one was a tavern wench. Nevertheless, he couldn't help admiring the smooth manner in which she swung up on her own, the way she straddled the animal as easily as a cavalry officer heading into battle, and the skill with which she swung the animal into position beside him.

"Ready, Doctor?" She cast him a sidelong glance that he recognized as a challenge.

"Ready. Which of these elegant travelling bags belongs to your friend?" He gestured to the two bundles still tied to his saddle. "I'll drop the other at the house as we ride past."

"The larger one."

"I might have guessed. Her ladyship had difficulty leaving all of the luxuries of her former life behind." He nudged the horse into a walk and headed toward the house. "For God's sake, pull that cap down further on your head. I'll not have anyone thinking I'm taking a woman home with me."

As soon as he'd thrown the bundle onto his brother's doorstep, he put his heels to the stallion's sides and bounded off. *I'll leave this blunder Jamie forced upon me to eat my dust.*

Good God! Seconds later she thundered up alongside him, bent over her mare's neck, urging the animal forward at a speed he could barely believe, the black dog racing beside them.

"Do we continue to follow this road, Doctor?" she yelled. "I must know in case your horse fails to keep apace with mine."

Hell and damnation! He yelled to Wings and felt a satisfaction as the big animal burst into a full gallop that left her behind. But he knew the truth. Only the fact that he had a bigger, much more powerful mount put him out in front.

The woman rides like the wind. What manner of female has Jamie brought me? Her cooking must taste like sawdust.

A half mile further along, when he slacked his pace to a trot to give Wings a chance to cool down, she once again rode up beside him. The dog, panting, slowed also.

"How much farther?" she asked calmly, as if they hadn't just indulged in a heart-rousing challenge.

"About two miles." He glanced over at her, her face partially hidden by the lad's cap. "You ride well." The last came out grudgingly.

"I have a good mount. This lady," she patted the mare's sweating neck. "came from the stables of Jewels' father. If you know anything of Sir Thomas, you'll be aware he's noted for having some of the best horses in England."

"Sweet Jesus!" He jerked to a halt and stared over at her. "You mean you and that...that so-called lady stole horses from Sir Thomas's stable? The list of crimes Jamie has drawn me into goes on and on."

"Jewels feels that they're part of her rightful inheritance." She stopped beside him and tossed her head. "They're both animals her father had given her for her own personal use."

"I always suspected my brother and his way of life would lead my neck into a noose," he muttered. "Now there's no doubt."

"And that's where your neck belongs!" Waving her arms, Hannah Rob burst out of the trees into the road in front of them. "Murderer! Warlock, with your filthy Indian cures!"

"Whoa!" As a startled Wings half reared and whirled, William had to be quick to bring his mount back into prancing control before the animal trampled the woman. *Just what I need, another woman, and this time a mad one.* Out of the corner of his eye, he saw the lass likewise calming her mare. *Curse the old woman! She could have gotten us both killed.*

"I've warned you before, Hannah, stay out of my way." He nudged his cavorting horse close enough to make her retreat a few steps. "If you or your daughter is in need of my assistance, I'm willing to help, but until such time, don't annoy me with any more of your foolishness."

"You, there, young lad." The woman advanced toward his companion and squinted up into Heather's face. "You'll rue the day you threw your lot in with this man. He's evil, evil, I tell you!"

"Come along, lad." William urged his horse around her and on down the trail. "Ignore the old witch. She's nothing but a great bag of wind."

"A curse on the pair of you!" Hannah Rob stood in the middle of the trail, shaking her fist after them as they rode off.

"Is she quite mad?" the lass asked when they were beyond her hearing.

"Quite." He urged his horse forward into a brisk trot, and she kept apace.

"So very sad," he heard her murmur.

Astonishing. The hag has just cursed us and this lass's only comment is a sympathetic one. What manner of female is she?

****

Three miles down the dusty trail, he turned to the right, toward his home, a large triple-story rectangular stone structure across a grassy expanse of field, about fifty yards above the river on a sloping rise. To the right were a large log barn and fenced pasture, to the left another log structure on the edge of the forest that looked like a modest house.

"My home." He paused at the entrance of the lane that led through wide fields to the house.

He heard her give a sharp intake of breath.

"What?" He glanced at her.

"I never expected anything so grand...not in this country." Her eyes widened as she stared.

"Aye, well, I made a spot of money during the war." He nudged his horse forward down the lane, a sinking feeling invading his gut. He'd never thought he'd be taking another woman into that house, not even a serving wench.

Chapter 6

"*That* is not coming inside." Doctor MacTavish pointed to Midnight, panting at her side as they halted near the kitchen door of the house. "At least not until he's been given a proper bath and I can feel reasonably confident he'll not be infesting my house with fleas."

"Very well." Heather slid from the saddle, took the improvised leash from her horse's saddle, slipped it about the dog's neck, and tied him to the hitching post by the door. "Shall I stable our horses... Oh, my." She gazed at the stone well near the back door. "How convenient. I thought I'd have to draw water from the river. And over there..." She dropped her mare's reins and scurried a few feet farther away. "Is this..." She placed a hand on a large stone fireplace. "Can this truly be a baking oven?"

"Aye, that it is." He didn't leave the stallion unattended as she'd done with her mount but followed her, leading the animal. "It pleases you, does it?"

"Oh, my, yes. So many things I can bake and cook without making the house over-warm on hot days. Now, if one of your neighbors will just give me a bit of starter..."

"Starter?" Not understanding, he stared at her.

"A bit of leavened dough." She looked up at him, surprised. "Surely you know about using bits of dough from previous batches of bread to make loaves rise. Once you're started, you just keep a bit back from each baking and use it in the next one. Thus the term 'starter.' "

"I've no such thing. A neighbor lady supplies me with bread. I've an ice house back in the trees." He pointed to the woods beyond the smaller house. "You'll find victuals there you may use. There's a root cellar under the kitchen. It's depleted at this time of year, but there's enough to see us through a few more months. I'll be planting soon, to replenish it for next winter. The barn"—he swung his arm to indicate the log-and-board structure about forty yards upriver from the house—"contains a milking cow, several laying hens, my saddle horse, and a Clydesdale gelding to do the heavy farm work. Along with Wings, here, and your mare, they'll be in your charge."

He stood only a few feet from her, a handsome, powerful creature holding the magnificent grey stallion. The expression in those piercing blue eyes, in the hard lines of his cleanly cut jaw, in the drawn lips, told her that her competence was deeply in doubt.

"I'm familiar with such chores." Refusing to back down before his stern countenance, she continued, "And perfectly capable of handling them."

"We'll see," he said, confirming her thoughts. "I'll release our horses into the pasture behind the barn, and then I'll show you the house."

"No." She stepped forward to take the stallion's reins from his hand. "I'll take care of our mounts."

"That may not be wise. Wings can be a handful, at the best of times." His words were proven as the stallion threw up his head with a rattling of his bridle.

"And with your mare in close proximity…"

"Never fear, sir. I know all about randy horses." She untied her bundle from the stallion's saddle, tossed it to the ground near the door, and started to lead the horse together with her mount toward the barn. A few steps off, she stopped and threw back her own words of warning. "And men."

As she marched off toward the stable, Wings in submission, the doctor's guffaw that followed her made a smile tug at her lips.

"Aye, I can handle you, Wings, my boy," she said softly as the horse nuzzled up to her. "And your master, as well."

****

"Now." She arrived back at the house, where he waited on a chair on the stoop outside the back door, and scooped up her bundle of belongings. "I'd like to see the kitchen." She knew she was even dirtier than when she'd disembarked from the *Highland Lass*, but she was not about to allow feelings of inferiority to further blemish her impression on this stern man who was to be her master.

He stood, advanced to the door, shoved it open, and moved aside for her to enter. *A bit of a gentleman, perhaps?* She preceded him and suppressed a gasp.

The room, although large and well furnished, was a pig sty. Dirty dishes littered the table and sideboards. The plank floor bore almost as much dried mud and dirt as the path leading up to the door through which they'd entered. Sunlight struggled to pierce the squalor of the room's two filthy windows. Flies buzzed over the remains of several meals.

"What do you think?" She caught the challenge in

his voice. *So he's hoping evidence of his filthy habits will send me scuttling, is he?* Squaring her shoulders, she smiled up at him.

"It needs a bit of sprucing up, but it's a big, well furnished room. I shall enjoy working in it."

"Aye, well, we'll see." The letdown her optimistic response had caused him gave her a small nudge of triumph. He hastened onward. "There are certain rules you must follow while in this house, and I'll brook no variance from them."

"And they are?" She locked her gaze on his cold blue eyes.

"You are to keep the house clean and neat, launder my clothes and bedding, have meals on the table at proper hours, and tend the horses, cow, and chickens in the barn back yonder."

"Of course. Captain MacTavish told me as much when he offered me the position."

"And those pistols," he gestured to a pair on the sideboard near the door. "are kept primed and ready in case of any emergency that may warrant their use. Do you know how to use such weapons?"

"Yes, my brother taught me."

"Good. There is more...and most important." His eyes narrowed as he stepped closer to tower over her.

"I'm listening." Her heartbeat hastened to a quicker rhythm, her bravado struggling to remain intact.

"There is a room at the top of the stairs in this house." His tone lowered to a growl. His jawline hardened and ticked. "Its door is closed. You are never, under any circumstance, to open it."

This time he succeeded in startling her. She'd never seen such vehemence reflected in a human face.

"Well, answer me, woman." The words thundered out at her. "I want your solemn promise."

"Certainly…yes…of course…if that's what you wish. This is your house." *Good God, was the man as mad as that harridan they'd encountered on the road?*

"Very well, then." He stepped back and turned away, his bellicose expression dissolving as quickly as it had appeared. "The servants' quarters are on the third floor, but you will find the summer heat too great up there. I suggest you establish yourself in the small bedroom at the end of the upstairs corridor. Mine is across from it. In here"—he led the way through a door at the side of the kitchen—"is the stairs to the upper floor." He pointed to indicate it before continuing on down a darkened corridor that she could see past him ended in an exterior entrance. He paused midway down its length and indicated a pair of doors, one on the left, the other on the right. "Behind these are a drawing room and a dining parlor. There will be no need for you to enter either. I never use them."

"May I see?" She started to move past him, hand extended toward the knob of the door to the right.

"No." He caught her arm in a grip so hard it brooked no argument. "The kitchen and your sleeping quarters will be your province. There will be no necessity of your wandering elsewhere in this house. Now let me show you the most important theatre of your work, my surgery. Leave your bundle here and follow me."

"Of course, sir." Obediently dropping her small bag of possessions at the foot of the stairs, she followed him out of the house and across the greening yard to the log building near the trees.

"I've chosen this location because it's distant from the house and barns," he said, pulling from beneath his shirt a key he was wearing on a chain about his neck. "It allows patients peace and quiet." He inserted it into the lock and pushed the door open.

And quite possibly keeps their screams of agony from disturbing other creatures in the vicinity. She knew the reality of severe injuries, devastating disease, and childbirth.

A spartanly bare room with a large plank table in its centre came into view. The stains upon it she recognized all too well. The wall to her right was lined with shelves above a wide dresser. These were filled with bottles, jugs, jars, and bowls…his medicines. Laid out upon the dresser were a number of surgical instruments, the uses of some of which she could guess, others she realized she would have to learn their functions.

Through a doorway at the rear, its curtain drawn back, she saw a crude bed built into the wall, its coverings rough woolen blankets twisted into a mass. A ladderback chair and a washstand beside it were the only other furnishings.

"If anyone arrives in my absence suffering to the extent of needing a couch, you will put them in there." He indicated the room. "Under no circumstance are you to attempt to treat them."

"But of what value will I be?" She looked up at him. "I came to work with you, Doctor, in the full expectation of being your helpmate."

"Aye, that you did." The admission came out in a sigh. "Verrae well. As soon as I have time, I'll begin teaching you the basic medications that I prescribe for simple illnesses. Perhaps you'll be capable of dealing with them until I can decide what to do with you."

"I'm sure I shall." She walked confidently into the recovery room. "But first I will do something about this bed." She pulled aside the blankets to reveal a covering of spruce boughs. "No patient can be expected to rest comfortably on such as this."

"It's readily replaceable." He threw her a scathing glance. "Often times it becomes necessary to dispose of bedding after a patient fouls it. I've no time to go washing sheets and changing the mattress."

"Of course you don't." Moderating her tone to a soothing one, she returned to stand in front of him. "But with a helper, it will be possible. I've no objection to scrubbing bedding or refilling a mattress with fresh fodder from the barn. Believe me, Doctor, I'm no stranger to cleaning up messes."

She saw him wince. Apparently being reminded of her tavern background didn't sit well with him.

"It's not for you to go making judgments about how I maintain my property." His words were hard and cold. "You are a servant here. I'll thank you to remember it."

"As you wish, sir." She bobbed him a curtsy. "Now, if you'll excuse me, I'll put my things in the room you've indicated. Then I'll see to the livestock and the making of your supper."

"No need to provide food for me this evening." He headed for the door. "I have patients to visit. I will not return before dark."

"Nevertheless, I'll do up the barn work and have a meal ready."

Without warning, the room began to swirl around

her, and she caught at a sideboard for support. The next moment, strong arms were about her and she was being carried out of the surgery, across the yard, and into the kitchen to be placed on a chair.

"I'm fine," she protested, struggling to get to her feet as he knelt beside the chair, his face tinged with concern. "A moment of weariness, nothing more."

"A bit more than that, I'll wager. When last did you manage to keep nourishment in your stomach? Were you seasick the entire voyage?" Chafing her wrists, he peered into her face.

She started to deny his assumption, then, as weakness threatened to overwhelm her again, nodded.

"Verrae well." He stood. "Easily remedied. Stay as you are. I'll get food."

****

Twenty minutes later Heather felt strength returning to her limbs as she swallowed the last of the food from a plate of cold ham, cheese, and bread, then picked up a mug to finish her third cup of hot, sweet tea. When it was empty she replaced it on the table and glanced across to where he sat watching her.

"Thank you." She mustered a smile.

"No reason to thank me, lass." His outlook had changed to one of compassionate concern. *The doctor coming to the surface.* "I was a great oaf not to have realized you must have been running on your nerves these past hours. I let my annoyance at what that lummox of a brother had done take precedence over my duties as a physician."

"I can understand your chagrin." Avoiding looking at him, she toyed with the mug's handle. "It must have come as a great shock when you saw who he'd brought…and both of us with a trail of trouble behind us."

"Still." He stood. "No excuse for a doctor not to recognize illness and treat it. Now I have patients I must visit. Do you feel strong enough to stay alone?"

"Of course. I'll clean the kitchen and…" She started to rise, but he waved her back to her chair.

"This place has been a pig sty for a goodly length of time. Another day won't hurt. Rest."

He picked up a black bag from the corner of a cupboard and strode out of the house, leaving her to wonder about a man who could exhibit such ire one moment and become a dedicated physician the next.

After he'd left, she got to her feet and stood for a moment to assure herself she wasn't about to collapse again. As the sound of a horse galloping from the yard told her the doctor had left on his rounds, curiosity crept over her. He hadn't said not to enter the two rooms along the first floor corridor, only that they wouldn't be used. Making certain her legs weren't about to once again desert her, she headed into the dark hallway. Her heart beating at the back of her throat, she opened the one to her right.

At first she could discern little in a room darkened by tightly closed shutters. When her eyes did become accustomed to the gloom, she saw a large, elegantly furnished parlor complete with an ornate fireplace, fine wall coverings, and richly carpeted floor. A layer of dust filmed everything; the air held the cold pall of having been undisturbed for a long time.

Going to the other door, she discovered another securely shuttered room that was a large dining parlor with a long table, chairs for over a dozen people, an ornate sideboard, and a door at the far end which she guessed opened into the kitchen. This dark room also smacked of having been frozen in time. What had happened in this house? What was in the forbidden room at the top of the stairs?

A shudder wafted over her. Who was the weird woman on the road who'd branded her master evil and thrown curses after both of them? He used Indian cures, she'd barked. But what kind, and why? Was Doctor William MacTavish more conjuring warlock than scientific physician?

Well, I'm here now, and I must make the best of it. She closed the door and proceeded up the stairs. The food had brought strength back to mind and body, and the house, although a long way from Burkley Manor, was astonishingly civilized for such a pioneer countryside.

She should have been delighted to discover her new home was such a dwelling, but as she walked up the shadowy steps to the second floor she couldn't escape the feeling of emptiness that filled it, the feeling that some kind of tragedy had occurred within its walls. In spite of the warmth of the spring day, the house exuded a bone-chilling ambience that branded it devoid of life and love.

What had she expected? She tried to shrug off the feeling. The man was a bachelor, probably away from home in his work most of the time. Men alone never managed to make a house a warm and welcoming place.

At the top of the stairs she faced the door to which she assumed he'd been referring. What secret lurked behind it? Why was it so important she had to vow never to enter it?

An adventure. Jewels and I decided to have an adventure. If a mysterious room is part of it, so be it. Maybe someday, after he comes to trust me, he'll see fit to let me in on his secret.

With a shrug she tried to dismiss her misgivings as she continued on to her room at the end of the corridor. Its door, too, was shut, but not the one across from it, the one he'd declared to be his own. Glancing inside, she grimaced.

Clothing littered the floor, and the bed looked as if it hadn't been made up with fresh covers for ages. A large spider's web hung over the window that faced out from the back of the house toward the forest and road— probably, she guessed, so that he could see approaching patients. In the web, a trapped fly buzzed. She felt a sudden kinship with the insect. Crossing the room, she brushed aside the cloying grey mass, opened the window, freed the fly, and sent it off into the spring air.

I wish it were that simple for me. She turned back to the untidy room with a sigh. *Oh, well, first things first. Wash Midnight...and myself. The river will do nicely for the moment.*

Heaving a sigh, she opened the door of the room designated as hers to find a dusty, pristine little space with a neatly made up bed, a washstand, and a chest of drawers. The same sense of abandonment that had engulfed dining room and parlor hung over it. This was a house that life had deserted.

You're getting as fanciful as Jewels. With an effort she thrust her imaginings aside.

She placed her bundle on the end of the bed, then went to open the shutters and window to look out over the river. Warm, sweet air wafted in, accompanied by a shaft of sunlight. The little room struggled back to life. She smiled and drew a deep breath. Sleeping with the window open on a warm summer night would be wonderful. But perhaps not tonight. She revised her thoughts as thunder rumbled in the distance. With an effort, she pushed all negative thoughts from her mind. She and Jewels had been right in setting out on this adventure. She'd ignore the man's mysterious room at the top of the stairs and his skepticism about her ability to do the job. She'd show him she was not only trustworthy but capable, as well.

Looking downriver, she frowned. Black clouds were moving toward the farm, blotting out the sunshine that had colored the earlier part of her first day in this new country. She hurried downstairs and outside to take up Midnight's leash and head for the river.

"A quick bath before the storm hits," she told the dog. "We need to get that chore done before our lord and master arrives home. He won't allow you into the house in your present condition, and I'm not going to leave you outdoors in a deluge."

****

The last of the storm clouds had scudded from the night sky, allowing a thin sickle of a new moon and a few shy stars to appear above him as Dr. William MacTavish rode back to his farm. Beneath him, Wings moved restlessly, eager for a gallop after hours of waiting for his rider to complete his rounds, but Will wasn't in the mood to exert the energy a hard pace on such a powerful, spirited animal would require. It had been a long day of difficult cases, and now he had to go home to that woman his brother, in his lack of discretion, had foisted upon him.

He rolled his shoulders to relieve some tension. Even though her untidy appearance denied the probability, she might make a decent housemaid. Lord knew he needed one. The shirt he was wearing was stained with sweat, and it smelled. His house hadn't been cleaned in ages, and the last time he'd had a decent meal it had been received from the grateful wife of one of his patients. If, on the other hand, this girl who called herself Bonny turned out to be a slattern, he'd have Jamie take her back to England on his next voyage, he'd gain an excellent mount, and that would be the end of it.

A vision of hopeful green eyes in a pale face wasted from the sickness caused by a long sea voyage loomed up in his mind. The rush of empathy he always experienced when confronted with a suffering creature enveloped him.

Dunnae weaken, man. Stick to your resolve. You need a strong, clever person to assist you in your work, and unless, which I very much doubt, this lass proves to be such, you'll have no choice but to send her on her way.

As he rode into the farmyard, he saw a light burning in the kitchen. Was she still up? He'd been hoping to avoid another confrontation until morning. At the barn, he dismounted and led the restless stallion into its dark interior. As he opened the door of the animal's box stall at the end of the corridor, the horse snorted and surged ahead.

"Whoa!" he ordered. Then he recognized the reason for the stallion's behavior. In a shaft of moonlight streaming in a window, he saw the manger filled with hay and a bucket of water in the far corner. As he removed the stallion's bridle to allow him to eat and drink, surprise washed over him. Had she...? She must have. Who else?

After he'd settled Wings for the night, he made a circuit of the barn, observing as best he could, in the moonlight, the condition of the other animals and his hens. Her mare, the Clydesdale, his gelding, and the cow all appeared to have been fed and their stalls cleaned. His hens shut in their coop, safe from night predators, clucked contentedly as they pecked at grain in their trough.

"Huh." He stepped out into the damp freshness left after the thunderstorm, barred the barn door behind him, and headed toward the light beckoning from the kitchen window. She might be worth her keep after all. Just to have his barn work done when he returned, weary from a long day's work, was a boon. Now if she could only cook and clean...

As he approached the house, barking erupted from within.

Damnation, she's taken that filthy animal inside. After I specifically told her—not until he was clean.

He tried the door and it opened. She'd failed again. It should have been barred against the night. This valley was raw, with any number of reprobates roaming the forest and fields.

"Doctor." Her voice startled him as she arose from a rocking chair in a dark corner of the room lighted only by a fire on the hearth. In her right hand she held one of the pistols he kept near the door. The dog, brushed and damp, stood by her side, a growl muttering from his throat. "Perhaps next time you should identify yourself. I am a decent shot. Quiet, Midnight," she settled the dog. "It's but our lord and master returned."

Good God, what has she done to herself? A tangle of damp golden brown curls fell about her shoulders, her formerly dirty face had been washed, and she wore a clean (albeit still a lad's) shirt. *She's comely, pretty, even...hard to tell for certain in this light, but still...*

"Perhaps you should put that weapon back on the sideboard." Struggling to overcome his surprise, he advanced into the room, one hand raised in a defensive gesture. "I've told you I keep it primed. And," he continued as his amazement lessened, "what do you mean, letting your hair down and looking womanly? What if someone arrived and saw you?"

"If it were a friend or neighbor, I assume they'd have the good manners to knock and give me time to replace my cap." She pointed to it on the sideboard, stuck out her chin, and tilted her head. "If it weren't, if it was someone intent on violating your home, I'd have shot him and the very least of his concerns would be seeing your serving lad with long hair before he went to meet his Maker. Now sit. I reckon you're hungry and thirsty after your long day." She put the pistol on the sideboard and indicated a place set at the table. "It's not a repast fit for a king, but it will get you through the night. Tomorrow I'll prepare decent victuals."

She'd laid out cheese, butter, and ham she must have gotten from his ice house back in the trees. Several slices of bread rested on a plate. On the hob, a blackened pot suggested hot tea.

And the kitchen. From what he could see in the fire's light, she'd cleaned away most of the filth. The table upon which the food waited appeared freshly scrubbed, the sideboards and shelves put in order. The barn, now this. He suppressed a sigh of gratitude. He couldn't let the wench see she was pleasing him. At least not yet. Not until he knew more about her.

"The bread is a bit stale, but it was all I could find in the box on the shelf," she said as he sat down and she went to fetch the teapot.

"As I've told you, a neighbor woman makes it for me. It's still two days before she'll send me more."

"Ah, well, there'll be no need for her to do so any longer. I can make bread. That oven outside cries out to be filled with a fine batch. If I can just get a bit of starter..."

"I'll not go cancelling her baking just yet." He struggled to get back to the gruff, unpleasant persona he wanted to maintain in her presence. "I'll wait until I taste those fruits of your labors."

"Very well. Tomorrow we'll have stew and dumplings...you've sufficient beef and vegetables for such. I've investigated your ice house and ventured into your root cellar. You're a bit lacking in sugar, flour, salt, and tea." She poured out a cup of amber liquid, and its well steeped aroma warmed him to the core. He'd never learned how to brew the drink decently.

"That meat in the ice house...it's not beef," he tried to throw another barb her way as she returned to the hearth. "It's moose. We have few enough cattle to provide milk and butter in this country without killing them for the pot."

"Ah, well, then moose stew it shall be." She rounded on him, a defiant glint in those beautiful emerald eyes. "I've never tasted such, but I'm sure it will be every bit as satisfying as beef."

"Argh!"

Too weary to exchange words with the wily little witch, he turned his attention to the food and ate in silence while she moved quietly about, involved in more cleaning and tidying. He began to relax and enjoy the improved ambience, at the same time trying to keep his eyes from those freshly washed curls and the curve of hips that even in a lad's patched trousers bespoke of the woman beneath.

No, no, no! She's not that alluring. It's only because I've been celibate too long. Because it's been years since a woman graced this house. Years since anyone has taken care of me...and my farm. Don't get seduced by tended animals and a bit of food.

"Midnight and I took advantage of your absence to refresh ourselves with a bath in your beautiful river," she said when he'd finished and she came to clear the table. "I used one of the horse brushes from the barn to make him presentable."

"And yourself?" He spoke without thinking. "How did you make your own tresses beautiful?"

The last word was out before he could stop it. Damn! Her food, the clean house, the barn work done—it was mellowing him, making him careless.

"Although I travelled as a lad with only suitable clothing to maintain the ruse, I did bring along hair brushes. I could not entirely abandon my womanhood." He felt something soft and round he fancied was a breast brush against him as she bent past him to pour more tea into his cup. He swallowed hard.

Dear Lord, save me from the urges this woman is forcing through my man's body.

"Now, Doctor, you must be weary." She faced him,

hands on her hips. "Off to bed with you. I'll finish up here. And worry not. I'll be sure to bar the door before I go to my room."

"Very well." He stood, scraping back the chair with more than necessary vehemence. "I wish you good night, lass."

"And you as well, sir." She bobbed a quick curtsey, then returned to her chores. He glanced once more at those shapely hips in the lad's pants as she turned to her tasks, bit his lower lip, and headed for the stairs.

He didn't bother to take a light. He knew this house, board and nail. When he stepped into his room, however, even in the moonlight he barely recognized it. Clothes had been removed from the floor and hung on pegs along the wall, and the bed had been freshly made. The window was open to let in the reviving essence of after-the-storm freshness. He pulled off his dirty, sweat-stained clothes and, for the first time in months, hung them over a chair back. Naked, he fell into the bed and let the songs of frogs and night birds lull him sleep.

****

He awoke the next morning, stretched languidly, and wondered why he felt so good. Then he remembered. Fresh bedding, barn work done, a clean house, and food on the table. Ah, yes. The lass. He sat up on the edge of the bed and recalled the previous day. Perhaps Jamie hadn't made such a disastrous choice. Perhaps...

Stop it, man. Just because she can cook and clean and tend animals is no reason to start believing she's fit for what you need most...someone who can assist in your medical practice. And remember who she is...a tavern wench.

He stood and stretched again. Then he noticed the change in the room. His soiled clothing had disappeared. A single outfit of pants, shirt, and drawers, possibly the least soiled of his lot, hung on the pegs. She must have come into the room while he slept and taken the rest. Damnation, he hoped he hadn't been lying as he'd awakened, with the covers thrust off in the warmth of the spring morning, his nakedness exposed. A hotness gushed up his body.

The blessed woman has me blushing like a timid virgin, for God's sake!

Pulling on the clothing, he glanced out the window. Another fine day. After yesterday's rain, his plowed fields would be ready for planting, but when would he get the time? Today he had a long list of patients, spread out over several miles. He'd take Wings. He might not have many more opportunities...unless he won that infamous wager. For the first time in his life, he found himself wishing he'd come out the loser. The thought of her with some other man sent a sick feeling coursing through his gut.

Downstairs, he found the kitchen clean but empty. Beside the fire a bowl of porridge sat keeping warm, while the teapot hung on the hob. From outside came the sound of a female voice singing something about her love being like a red, red rose.

Going to the open door, he paused to watch her, dressed in her boy's attire, hair tucked under that ugly cap, sleeves rolled, rubbing clothing vigorously in a tub of water. Already a long string of bedding and garments flapped merrily in the breeze coming up from the river. She was using the old clothesline he'd put up years ago and which in the past few years had seen no use.

"Good morning." He caught her attention with the greeting. She paused and turned to face him.

"Good morning to you, sir. Your breakfast is on the fire. Would you like me to serve? I've been busy. You have a deal of laundry to be done. Such fine linen garments and household items shouldn't be left dirty to stain."

"I take it to a neighbor lady...when I find the time and have the inclination." A hot flush of embarrassment flooded up his body. His clothing and household linen were a disgrace, but exposing his lack of its care to this saucy little wench shamed him. "I'll serve myself. You're gainfully employed." He turned away and went back into the kitchen. One thing of which he could not accuse her, as yet, was laziness.

****

He'd barely finished his meal when the sound of an approaching wagon drew his attention. As he rose from the table, he saw Arthur Weatherspoon, a farmer from a few miles upriver, drive into the yard.

"Good morning to you, Arthur." He stepped outside to meet the man with a hearty greeting. With decent food in his belly and his house set in order, he felt better than he had in ages. "What can I do for you?"

"I'm in need of your services, Doctor." The man wound his horses' reins around the whipstand and lowered himself gingerly to the ground.

"You arrived just in time. I was about to ride out to visit patients downriver. Come over to the surgery, and I'll see if I can help. Peter," he called to the woman who'd paused in her washing to look over at the men. "Come along. I may be needing your assistance."

Give her a good dose of what this job is all about.

Hopefully Arthur has a boil on his backside.

"Will, I don't think you'll be needing the lad." The man shifted uneasily. "It's...ah...a bit of a private matter."

"Not to worry." William put an arm around the other man's shoulders and headed him toward the small log cabin on the edge of the trees. "Peter is my apprentice. He needs to learn how to treat anyone who comes along in my absence."

"Well, if you're really training the lad up, I guess it will do no harm for him to hear of my complaint." By now the two men had reached the cabin, with Heather following. William paused to draw the key from beneath his shirt and unlock the door.

"Now, Arthur, what is it?" he asked with alacrity once all three were inside and the door closed behind them. "A boil on your bottom? An itch in a private part?"

He glanced at Heather, struggling to keep a malicious gleam from his eyes. She'd proven so adept at each chore, he needed to see her chagrined, to prove he'd been correct about the mistake Jamie had made in bringing her to him.

"No, Will, nothing like that. It's my bowels. I've got the trots something fierce. Argh!" He turned and rushed out.

"A common enough complaint in springtime, is it not, Doctor?" She canted her head to one side to cast him an amused glance. "Too many fresh greens in the diet, perhaps?"

"Ah, well, yes." Annoyance chafed him as he caught the humor dancing in those beautiful green eyes. "Easily remedied."

"Oh, aye, I daresay. No problem for a doctor such as yourself." She placed emphasis on his title.

He went to a shelf filled with flasks and covered bowls. "This will settle his problem." He selected one. "A mixture of rhubarb, magnesia, and laudanum, the last of my stock. I'll need to mix more. The proportions for all my drugs are kept in this book." He reached up to a high shelf and took down a worn, leather-bound volume. "You can read and cipher?"

"Of course." Heather cleared her throat and spoke in her lad's voice. "If you wish, I'll do it this very morning. We must have more of this magic elixir in case another patient arrives with the same complaint." The ill-suppressed humor in her voice rankled him.

"I think not." He faced her squarely, struggling not to be put off by her teasing. "I'm out of laudanum. I trust Jamie has brought a fresh supply, but it's still aboard the *Highland Lass*. I'll have to wait until he delivers it. I'm not about to let you go mixing medicines."

The farmer, red-faced, reappeared at the surgery door. "Sorry, Doctor, but nature waits for no man."

"Understood. Here, this should help." He handed him the small flask.

"Now another small problem, Will." The man wet his lips as he accepted it. "I've no money at the moment. Will you take one of my laying hens in payment?"

"No, but I will take some of that fine rhubarb that grows so well on the south side of your house, if you've a mind to share it with me. Mine is terrible slow, and I need the juice to make more of my drugs."

"Of course, of course, Will." The man's face lit up

with relief. "I'll send one of my boys with an armful directly as I return home." He pulled the stopper from the bottle and took a long drink.

"Take it easy, man," William admonished. "A little at a time or you'll be too sleepy to drive your team home."

"Don't worry, Will." The man wiped his mouth with the back of his hand and rammed the cork back into the flask. "They know the way. Now, thank you. And a very good morning to you both." He tipped his battered hat first to William and then to Heather before hurrying off toward his wagon.

"Don't forget to return the bottle," William called after him.

"Rhubarb in payment?" She slanted him a grin. "You'll never get rich that way, Doctor."

"The man has eight children. He can't afford to part with a single hen. Now go back to your washing. Arthur, let me know how you make out," he called out as the farmer drove out of the yard.

"For certain, Will. And thank you again." He flapped the reins over the backs of his team, sending them forward at a shambling trot.

Chapter 7

Heather watched a half hour later as Doctor MacTavish mounted the prancing stallion and galloped up the lane to the road, medical bag secured behind his saddle. He'd said he wouldn't be back until late in the evening, and that suited her just fine. She had more than enough work to keep her occupied. A small chuckle rose in her throat as she remembered their encounter with the farmer. The flush that had risen up the doctor's face when he'd learned the nature of his patient's illness had done her heart good. Humming softly, she returned to her chores.

She'd finished her washing, set the kitchen to rights, and was in the barn beginning her work there when a shadow fell across the straw-strewn floor between her and the door. Her breath caught in her throat as she turned to see a tall, broad-shouldered man in buckskins, straight black hair caught back into a queue, arms crossed on his chest, feet planted firmly apart, facing her. Partially blinded by the sunlight after working in the shadows of the barn, she could only see him in outline, but as her vision settled, she saw his high cheekbones and dark skin, his brown eyes perusing her with penetrating scrutiny. A native, one of the indigenous people she'd heard termed Indians by the sailors aboard the *Highland Lass*. A savage.

"Good morning." The man astonished her by addressing her in perfect English. "You're new here."

"Yes." She gripped the hay fork she was holding in both hands. *What did he want? Was he dangerous?*

"I'm Benjamin Two Rivers, a friend of Dr. MacTavish's." He advanced toward her, right hand extended, a smile brightening his features. "And you would be?"

"Peter…Peter Grey." In her surprise, she almost forgot she was supposed to be a lad as she accepted his introduction. "I've come to work for the doctor."

"Ah." He nodded, the welcoming smile turning into an amused grin, his gaze roaming up and down her body. "Peter, is it?"

"Yes." The word snapped out defiantly even as she stood frozen in place. *Good Lord, the way he's looking at me… Does he suspect? How can he?*

"I've brought herbs for William." He removed the packsack from his back. "Will you see that he gets them?" He held it out to her.

"Of course." She accepted it.

"Good. I'll be going." He turned and strode to the barn door. There he swung back to face her, that disturbing grin in place. "Tell William I'm glad he's found help…and companionship."

Then he was gone, as noiselessly as he'd come. Heather was left holding the sack, confused by the well-spoken, mannerly native who seemed to have seen through her disguise with uncanny ease.

****

A half hour later Heather turned from where she'd been cleaning a corner of the kitchen as she heard a conveyance rattling down the lane toward the farm.

Going to the door, she saw Captain Jamie MacTavish seated on the high seat of a truck wagon headed for the surgery. She watched as the captain halted the team, wound the reins around the whipstand, and jumped to the ground.

"Hi, you there, Peter," he called out to her. "Summon your lord and master and tell him I need the key to his place of business and a hand unloading his supplies."

"He's not here at the moment." She headed across the expanse of bright green between house and surgery. The captain wasn't taking any chances on calling her by her name when he couldn't be certain no one else was within hearing distance. "He had patients to tend. He took the stallion on his rounds. He had many patients to see, and Wings is fast, and…"

"Bloody hell, I'll kick his arse… Excuse my language, but the man is enough to exasperate the devil. I can't believe you've had time to run amuck, and yet here he is, already treating the animal as his own."

"Run amuck? What are you talking about, Captain? Am I the centre of yet another wager between you two?" Hands on her hips, Heather faced him, annoyance rubbing through her body.

Is there no end to how men are ready to treat me as a chattel?

"Nothing, nothing," he muttered. "Now if you'll just unlock the place, you and I can unload that part of my burden."

"I don't have the key." She stopped a few feet away and looked at the big man rattling the surgery door. "Doctor MacTavish keeps it on a chain around his neck."

"Oh, aye." The captain stopped his efforts and turned to her, calmer, it appeared. "Yes, perhaps it is too early for him to trust you with such responsibility. Verrae well, lass," he returned to the head of his team and started to lead them toward the house. "We'll unload the whole kit and caboodle into his kitchen and let him sort through it."

"Where is Jewels?" she asked, as she fell into step beside him.

"Fast asleep when I left." He winked. "She was worn out."

"Captain MacTavish, you..." She whirled on him, eyes flashing green fire. "If you've taken advantage of Jewels..."

"Never fear, lassie." A slow grin curled the corners of his mouth. "She's not about to be taken in by the likes of me, and you're well aware of the fact. In truth, I'd be afeerd that if I tried, I might come out of the fray missing some vital body parts."

"You very well might, Captain." She quirked him an impish smile. "Now, I've tea and a bit of porridge left. You look like a man who's come from home without breakfast. Let me get you something to eat."

****

"That hit the spot, lass." Captain Jamie MacTavish leaned back in his chair and rubbed his belly. "I'm in a much better frame of mind. Never was any good on an empty stomach. I hope Jewels proves as good a cook and housekeeper as you." He glanced around the neat kitchen. Heather suppressed the bubble of mirth that rollicked inside at his words. The captain was in for one large surprise. Heather seriously doubted if Jewels knew how to boil water, much less get a fire started to do so. "This place looks a treat."

"Captain, do you know a man named Benjamin Two Rivers…a native?" She changed the subject.

"Of course. Good man. Good friend. What about him?"

"He came here this morning to bring a packsack of herbs for Doctor MacTavish." She indicated the bag in the corner, which she had brought up to the house to keep it safe from mice. "He was amazingly well spoken for an…"

"Indian? Indeed, he is. Full-blooded Mi'kmaq. Had a hard go, as a young lad. Got kidnapped by traders and taken to England as an amusement. There, a rich milord bought him, thought it would be a lark to see what the young savage could learn, and had him educated. After his lordship had proved the boy had a good head on his shoulders, he lost interest. Ben was thrown out into the streets of London with no money, no home, and no one who would employ someone of his skin as anything more than a common laborer.

"He stowed away on a ship headed for New Brunswick, returning at twenty years of age, educated as a white man but with the blood of his birth family strong in his veins. It wasn't easy for him. At first his band was suspicious of his white man's ways. Eventually they accepted him and became so impressed with his intelligence their shaman took him in and taught him many of the healing arts of their people. Later, Ben became friends with Will and, over time, began to show him some of these medicines. You can trust Ben, lass."

"Shaman?"

"Ah, you'd have no way of knowing, now, would

you. A shaman is a kind of priest who supposedly uses magic to cure the sick by entering the spirit world to capture the soul lost to illness and reintegrate it back into the body. In actual fact"—the captain quirked a corner of his mouth—"I believe they're simply clever men, skilled in the art of using herbs and plants. Ben has become one of the best."

"So he and Dr. MacTavish have learned to work together to help the sick and injured. A wise idea. More tea?" She picked up the pot as she asked the question.

"Tempting as the offer is, I must be on my way. Thank you again for the food and fine brew."

****

Captain Jamie MacTavish drove off, leaving Heather in a kitchen piled high with a collection of barrels and boxes beside the modest packsack of the man who'd identified himself as Benjamin Two Rivers. Doctor MacTavish had his medical larder replenished and much more.

Curious to discover some of the contents, she walked slowly round the heap. She'd been quick to put the canisters of tea into metal boxes on the shelves before mice could find their way into the precious commodity. Now she turned to the pile of dry goods heaped on the table. There were fine white linen shirts, stockings, breeches, undertrousers, two coats, and three pairs of fine boots, as well as several blankets and lengths of linen that could be cut to make bedding and drying cloths.

Not the purchases of a poor man, and yet he'd already demonstrated that his patients often were not forthcoming with payment in coin. That horrid old woman had called him a warlock. Was he indeed a sorcerer who could turn straw into gold?

Wake up, Mistress Heather Grey! You're falling back into those romantic tales you and Jewels were once wont to devour. This is reality. Even if Captain MacTavish has declared Benjamin Two Rivers a shaman, he's been quick to attribute the man's success to normal, earthly cures. There are no such things as warlocks and sorcerers or actual shamans. Jewels has already discovered the MacTavish brothers were privateers during the war. Those adventures could have left them wealthy men indeed. And if the doctor was shrewd with his prizes...

****

Late in the day, Midnight's bark drew her to the window in time to see the doctor ride up to the barn and dismount. He paused long enough to greet the dog with a not-unkind look, if not a pat. *Getting to like my boy.* She smiled smugly.

As he led the stallion inside in the twilight of the spring evening, she recognized weariness in the man's movements. Returning her attention to the hearth, she was glad she'd been able to prepare a hearty meal.

She cast a final glance around the neat, clean kitchen and took pride in her work. That room and the two bedrooms they occupied upstairs had benefited from her diligence.

She watched a few minutes later as he came out of the barn and headed for the house. At the door, he paused to stare at the washstand beside it. She'd supplied it with clean water, a piece of soap, and a bit of toweling. On a peg above hung a clean shirt.

"I thought you might like to wash after your long day." She stepped out to indicate the setup.

"Aye, that I would. And perhaps a bit of privacy to do so?" He looked at her, blue eyes brooking no refusal.

"Oh, aye." She gave him a saucy glance before turning and sauntering back into the house.

But she couldn't resist peeking a moment later, when he pulled his soiled shirt over his head and began to wash a broad, hard-muscled chest and flat belly. Doctor William MacTavish was a fine figure of a man, and no mistaking.

A small grin tickled her lips as she remembered how she found him lying naked on his bed when she'd slipped in to get his laundry.

Oh, my, yes, he is a fine figure of a man.
****

"You milked the cow and fed the stock." Wearing the fresh shirt, he came into the kitchen, his hair damp and slicked back, the dog at his heels. "And I see Jamie has been here." He strode over to the stack of supplies neatly placed against the back wall. "I assume he was not a happy man." He picked up a snow-white shirt from the collection and spoke without turning back to her as he examined the garment.

"No, that he was not, sir. He would have much preferred to put some of the supplies in the surgery. And I believe he wants his horse back. He mentioned…" She couldn't continue. The thought of her being bartered between these two charismatic men stuck in her throat.

"Just exactly what did he mention?" He rounded on her, blue eyes so intense they brooked no refusal to reply.

"He mentioned my running amuck having something to do with your transaction." She swung back toward the hearth. She couldn't bear to have him see the chagrin in her face.

"Oh, aye, did he now? I can see keeping an agreement strictly between gentlemen doesn't apply to my dear brother."

She heard a chair scrape back and knew he'd seated himself at the table. "Bring on whatever victuals you've made for supper, lass. If it pleases this weary doctor, the good captain may just have more of a struggle on his hands than he's foreseen."

Heartened, she went to the sideboard and removed the cloth from the centre cut of freshly poached salmon cooling there. She carried it to the table and placed it before him, then went to the hearth to scoop a bowl of greens and a hearty serving of potatoes from a pair of pots and bring them to him.

"What is this?" The surprise in his voice did not quite mask the pleasure as he looked at the meal.

"I saw a fisherman unloading his nets in the river in front of the farm this morning. When I called out to wish him good day, he brought me this fine fish. I offered him fresh eggs or milk in return, but he'd have none of it. He said you'd had no pay for delivering his last child and the salmon was small enough recompense. He also showed me how to pick fiddleheads—which I believe these greens are called— down by the river. I hope they will not give you any digestive troubles, Doctor." She couldn't resist teasing him in remembrance of the farmer's visit.

"Well, well, this is a fine meal, I must say." Weary and hungry, he reached for the fish to serve himself as she hurried back to the sideboard. "And never fear. Jamie has brought the means of making another batch of the cure for such an ailment. I'm perfectly capable of dosing myself. if need be."

"Ah, well, then, good. Physician, cure thyself. Is it not the saying?" She went back to the sideboard.

"What's all this?" he asked, when she returned with a bowl of dry oatmeal and a piece of butter.

"My mother was a Highlander," she said. "She loved her potatoes rolled in butter and oatmeal. I fancied you might, as well."

"It's been years since I've had such a dish…and served with salmon." The words came slowly, as if he were lost in thought. "So your mother was a Highlander, was she?" He was tucking into the meal as he spoke. His obvious enjoyment gave Heather hope, hope that in pleasing him she might somehow have convinced him to keep her on.

"Your care of the stock has measured up," he said, as he finished his second plate of salmon, fiddleheads, and oatmeal-wrapped potatoes and pushed it back from his place. "The house and its contents are coming along nicely. Perhaps you'll do…as a maid servant."

"Only a small part of my duties, as I understand them, sir. Now, would you like a wee dram?" She indicated one of the whiskey bottles on a top shelf.

"A cup of cold well water, if you please." He drew himself up. "A dram, no matter how wee, after such fare and a hard day's work, would see me fall fast asleep too soon. I was fair to middlin' hungry."

"Don't the families of any of your patients offer you food?" She stepped back, placed her hands on her hips, and looked down at him.

"I don't eat at the homes of my patients. Most are poor folk. In their houses, every spoonful counts."

"A thoughtful gesture, Doctor. I'm hoping your patients appreciate it."

"Aye, well, at the moment I'd appreciate that cold drink." He leaned back in his chair, his taciturn tone returning. "And don't go trying to flatter me in the hopes I'll not send you packing."

"Oh, I'd never, never try to do that." She turned and went out to fetch the water, feeling that she was in no small way working her way into the doctor's world.

****

"I'll give you this, lass. You can make a decent repast." He polished off the mug of cold water and stood.

"Thank you, sir." She began to clear the dishes. "I try my best. Is there anything you would like me to do tomorrow? I trust you'll once more be off tending patients?"

"Not if I can help it." He walked to the window to gaze down toward the river. "Tomorrow I should begin planting my crops, but with the newly arrived supplies, I've medicines to mix. It isn't easy being both a doctor and a farmer, but in this country a man must have more than one way of making a living."

"The plowed field beyond the barn... What will you plant there?" She busied herself cleaning up the meal without looking at him.

"Potatoes. A staple. The field back of the orchard is also plowed. That's the kitchen garden."

"You've planned well. I saw that fine collection of fruit trees you've established near the ice house. Vegetables, fruit, and no doubt you have hay fields not far off."

"Aye, that I do, but they'll require no tending until

it's cutting time, in July."

"Well, then, tomorrow, it's planting I'll do." She turned back to him. "I had a small garden that supplied our family needs back home. I know what it's about. You can get on with mixing your potions."

"Planting and tending a small garden patch is a long way from doing the same on a working farm that must provide food for a long winter." He looked at her doubtfully. "Although the ground has already been harrowed, there's still a lot of work to be done. You'd best leave it to me. Tomorrow I'll begin teaching you about my medicines. Since I now have a decent supply of ingredients to work with, it's an excellent time. Farming will have to wait. Now good night to you, lass."

He went out of the kitchen and up the stairs.

****

"Do you know anything at all about medicines?" He faced her squarely as they stood in his surgery before the counter and shelves lined with bottles and jars. With her help, he'd carried the supplies brought by Ben Two Rivers and his brother into the building and organized them in rows on the operating table.

"I know that laudanum"—she picked up a bottle containing a reddish brown liquid—"can put one to sleep quickly. And"—she turned him to him with a bright smile—"that a piece of clove placed in an aching tooth will kill the pain. Wet horseradish leaves applied to a throbbing head may give a person ease."

"Verrae good." His amazed look made her brave, and she hastened to continue. "I've also heard it said that rheumatism can be eased by sleeping with potatoes in your bed, and that wrapping dirty socks around a sore throat can cure it."

"Dear God, woman!" His expression of surprised pleasure vanished and a scowl clouded over his features. "I hope you haven't inflicted any such ludicrous treatments on anyone suffering from either malady."

"No, of course I haven't." She stuck out her chin and cast him what she hoped was a withering look. "I simply said I've heard of such cures."

"Well, then, rinse such medieval treatments from your mind. I've no desire to work with someone who has such ridiculous ideas of medicine. Next you'll be telling me you're in agreement with that wicked old wives' cure for measles...a brew made from hard sheep droppings."

"I'd never suggest such a disgusting treatment." She glared at him. "Now are you going to teach me how to make and dispense your cures and potions, or are you simply going to spend the rest of the morning demeaning whatever I have to say?"

"Argh!" He swung back to the counter and took up a bottle. "Poppy seeds. Excellent for quelling pain, and when mixed with milk, a cure for insomnia." He picked up another and thrust it at her. "Mercury, believed to be effective in treating syphilis, but I have serious doubts. The best defense against the disease is the same as it always has been...stay away from whores."

"And rogues." She shot him a defiant glance.

He hesitated. Then she saw a slackening of his stern expression and what she thought might have been the slightest twitching of a grin at his lips. "Aye, and rogues."

"And this?" She picked up a canister of white

powder.

"Borax, useful in treating wounds. But dunnae confuse it with this." He picked up another container. "This is Peruvian Bark, used in cases of malaria. I've never encountered one here in the colonies, but I've kept it on, in the event that I do. And now to the books." He took down one of the thick volumes on a high shelf. "If you want to be my assistant, I will expect you to study each and every one of these."

"Oh, aye, of course, sir." Overwhelmed by this requirement, Heather struggled to hide her chagrin and accept his instruction calmly. "If you'll point out the one with which you'd prefer that I begin, and the sequence thereafter, I will start reading at my first free moment."

"You may begin with this one on anatomy." He handed the book to her. "Some of the most common injuries I'm confronted with involve broken bones. It would be helpful if my assistant knows what is attached to what, the proper name of each, and how they affect movement."

"Very well. It will be my first reading."

"Good. I'll be questioning you on its contents, to make certain you've made a decent effort."

By the time they left the surgery, Heather felt her head stuffed with medical information and was praying she'd gotten it all straight and would retain most of it. Her future depended upon it.

"Do you know that old hag Hannah Rob advocates a person suffering from asthma eat field mice fried in butter?" he said as they walked back toward the house. His mood had mellowed. Having spent the last two hours absorbed in discussing medicine with an ardent listener most likely had been the cause, Heather speculated. Perhaps, too, he'd been pleased with her ability and willingness to learn. She could only hope.

"And to cure warts, rub them with a potato, bury it in the ground, and when it rots, the warts will disappear." He shook his head in apparent dismay as they continued across the yard. "Utter nonsense."

"Have you tried either?" The thick volume on anatomy clutched beneath her arm, she kept her outlook serious but couldn't resist the tease.

"Fortunately I've never been afflicted with either, and if I were, the last person on the face of this earth I'd allow to treat me is Hannah Rob. Now, let us get on with the day. There's farm work to be done."

"Aye, sir." Her jest having fallen on unresponsive ears, Heather squared her shoulders and picked up her pace.

****

Hoofbeats pounding into the dooryard at high speed caused both Heather and the doctor to turn from their meal toward the open door through which midday sunlight flooded the room. A moment later, a distraught young man burst into the room.

"Doctor, you must come at once!" Sweat beaded the teenager's face. "Father's been gored by our bull! He's bleedin' something fierce!"

"Is your horse near winded?" William bolted to his feet and strode across the room to grab his black bag. "If he isn't, I'll take him and save the time of saddling my own."

"She's an old mare, Doctor." The lad wiped perspiration from his red face with the back of his hand. "I fear she'd drop beneath you if you tried to run her back to our farm."

"Verrae well." Medical bag in hand, the doctor headed for the door. "I'll take Wings. Get this young lad a cup of strong, sweet tea." He yelled back the order as he strode off toward the barn. "He looks fit to drop."

****

Dr. William MacTavish rode into his farmyard, reined his horse to a halt, and gazed around his property. His harrowed fields, both kitchen garden and potato patch, looked very much as if they had been planted. His body, weary from long hours of fighting for the life of the injured farmer, pulled out of its slouch in surprise.

She couldn't have… But who else? Holy Mother…

"You've arrived just in time for supper." Wiping her hands on her apron, she came out onto the back step. "It's not much, I'm afraid, just cold salmon and tea. Still, it will take away the hunger."

"Did you do…all this?" He waved an arm to indicate the planting.

"Yes. That's why there'll be no fresh meal tonight." She came down the steps. "But it had to be done. The moon is right, and I've been given to understand the growing season here is short."

"But planting such a large area… How did you know where to find the seeds?"

"I assumed a canny farmer such as yourself would keep them somewhere in the house to prevent their freezing over the winter. I searched the cupboards until I found them. Seed for the potatoes I made from those left in the root cellar. Now, enough questioning." She took his horse's bridle. "You get on up to the house and wash for supper. You look spent. I'll see to Wings."

"The plowing... You didn't use Charlie, my Clydesdale? You couldn't have. He's a huge beastie."

"Charlie, is that his name? He's a most obliging, gentle soul." She grinned up at him. "Lowered his head like a perfect gentleman that I might get his collar on. I had to climb up the side of his stall to get the harness in place, but once again he behaved wonderfully."

"By all that's holy, woman..."

"Oh, come now, Doctor. It's not such a great feat. Women have been plowing and sowing and harvesting since biblical times. Dismount and let me see to the needs of this poor animal, who is probably hungry and thirsty."

In stunned amazement, he swung to the ground. "There's no need," he started to protest as she turned the animal toward the barn.

"Oh, yes, there is, sir." She kept going. "You wanted to hire a jack of all trades, and such I will prove to be. Now get yourself to the washbasin I've left ready for you. You'll find a clean shirt beside it and the table laid for our meal. I'll be in directly."

****

Probably because of the chill in the evening air, she'd moved the washstand inside the door of the house. With a weary sigh, he pulled his sweat-and-blood-stained shirt over his head and began to wash.

Sweet Jesus. She's heated the water. Was there nothing this woman didn't think to do?

It should have annoyed him that she was etching her way so comfortably into his life, but the pleasure of the moment held such feelings at bay. Letting the warmth of the water soothe away his exhaustion, he washed his face, neck, and upper body. He was pulling the freshly laundered shirt over his head when she entered the cabin and went to add a log to the fire on the hearth.

"It might be the month of May, but the chill of winter seems to delight in lingering in this country," she said, moving to empty the water he'd used into a bucket and refill the basin with fresh liquid. "Wings is safely stabled." She washed her hands, dried them, then returned to the hearth to fetch the pot of tea keeping hot there. "Sit." She indicated his place at the table. "Everything is ready."

There seemed nothing he could do but comply as she filled his cup, then took his plate to the sideboard to fill it with cold salmon and potatoes.

Astonishing. The woman was utterly astonishing. If only she hadn't brought the fear of the noose along with her, if only she weren't a tavern wench...

He gave himself a sharp mental reprimand. He had to get rid of her and whatever pursuers she'd inspired. The only doctor in miles, he wasn't about to let a chit of a girl, albeit a remarkable lassie, allow him to be taken prisoner and hanged. He was needed.

"And what of your patient? How is he faring?"

"Verrae well, I'm pleased to say. The wounds looked worse than they were, once they were cleaned and dressed. Nevertheless, I will watch closely for infection."

"Yes, indeed. And what further treatment did you prescribe? How often will you visit?" She sat down opposite him.

And suddenly he was discussing the case with her as he'd never been able to discuss one with another living soul since he'd left university. She had a decent knowledge of rudimentary medical care, and the bright interest in her expression as they talked led him to believe she thirsted for more. Her attention to his teachings that morning in the surgery indicated that not only was she willing to learn, but she was sufficiently clever to do so.

Perhaps Jamie hasn't made such a disastrous choice after all. He leaned back in his chair, cradling his tea cup in his hands, and continued to explain his plans for the farmer's future treatment.

When he'd finished, she gathered up his dishes, placed them on the sideboard, and turned to smile at him. "It appears we've both had a full day, Doctor. If you'll excuse me, I'll retire."

"Yes, of course." He caught himself rising as he would if a proper lady were about to retire from the room, then reseated himself abruptly. "I'll bar the door and be up directly. Good night, lass."

"Good night, sir." She left the room and went out to the stairs, her footfalls light on the steps, the dog at her heels.

For a few minutes he sat quietly, enjoying the order of his house, the frogs chorusing from the brook beyond the barn, and the pleasurable ambience of the spring evening. A sense of peace settled over him, and he heaved a soft sigh. This woman, this lass, was making his life better than he could have hoped, and yet, much as he fought to stifle them, the words "tavern wench" echoed in his mind.

Dunnae be a fool, William MacTavish. Dunnae get yourself involved with such a woman. You're not your brother.

He heaved himself out of his chair, weariness

returning, and went to bar the door. After throwing a small log onto the dying fire, he made his way out of the kitchen and up the stairs. A slight shaft of light coming from under her door made him pause. Surely, after the day she'd put in, she'd fallen asleep. He'd have to check. It wasn't wise to leave a candle burning. He eased open the door and stopped short. Propped up in bed, she had fallen back against the headboard in sleep, the anatomy tome open in her lap.

Something warm and strong and elemental stirred inside him. She was so innocent, so downright beautiful in a simple white chemise (something that had been in the small bundle she'd brought with her, he assumed), golden brown hair falling over her shoulders. He felt his body react in a way that startled him, unnerved him to the core. An urge to go to her, to take her into his arms, to join her in that bed, flooded through him.

Get a grip, man. Sweet Jesus!

Forcing himself back to his mission, he blew out the candle guttering on the washstand by the bed and left, closing the door softly behind him.

As he stripped off his clothing in his own room, a sense of dissatisfaction raged through his body. It chafed his innards like a hair shirt. Why did she have to look so pure, so innocent, so angelic, with that blasted book on her lap? Why had she fallen asleep with a candle burning, so that he'd had to enter her room? Why, why, why…? The questions irritated him as he tried to fall asleep in a room that felt like a furnace even with the window open to let in the fresh country breeze.

****

"And what would you be up to this fine morning, brother? Get down and join me. This second chair has been waiting for you."

Heather had heard a rider approaching and now the doctor's greeting. She peeked out the partly open kitchen door to see Captain Jamie MacTavish drawing rein in front of his brother, who sat on the stoop enjoying a rare moment of leisure in the sun while he waited for her to finish the kitchen work. Today he'd said he would begin teaching her dosages.

She watched from the shadows as the captain dismounted with a grunt, tied his horse to the hitching post, and took the proffered seat. He slumped into the chair and stretched long legs out in front of him.

"Thought I'd pay a brief visit. Then I'm off downriver in search of a serving lass," he replied.

"What! Didn't you bring one from the Old Country?" Heather caught the taunting in the doctor's voice and grinned. "Can't milady do housework? Mine's a fair to middlin' hand. Am I to be thinking I got the best of the pair? Maybe taking the pasty-faced one wasn't such a bad bargain, eh?"

"Ah, now, there we could have a hearty argument." Astonished, Heather caught a jovial lightening of James MacTavish's tone. "While Jewels may not be able to boil water without burning it and knows not one end of a broom from the other, she does have other qualifications for which I'm most grateful."

"Sweet Jesus, Jamie…"

"Ah, no, not what you're thinking, brother. At least not yet. No, for now it's kisses and cuddles only, more's the shame of it. What I'm referring to is the woman's ability to keep track of cargo and cost and prices and the like. She can even speak French, so when I pull into such ports, she will be able to keep me informed and not cheated. And what a sailor! On the voyage here she was as good a mate as any man could want. She'll be coming with me when next I set sail. Hiring a serving girl is but a small inconvenience with such a woman to companion me."

Heather sucked in her breath. So Captain James MacTavish believed he'd found his mate, did he? She smirked. Perhaps the good captain had also found his match. He'd also said Jewels would be sailing away with him. Inside her, something sank like a stone.

"Lass, is there any more of that tea left from breakfast?" Doctor MacTavish bellowed. "It seems my brother might have come away from his house with not so much as burned water to comfort him on his ride."

"Aye, Doctor." Heather quickly filled two mugs and carried them out to the men. "Good morning, Captain." She bobbed a slight curtsey to their visitor. "I trust this morning finds both you and my friend well."

"More than well, mistress." He saluted her with the cup. "Hale and hearty, I'd say." He took a swallow of the tea. "My, my, you do brew a fine drink." He touched his forelock.

"Thank you, kind sir." She favored him with a smile. "Now, I must be getting back to my duties. There's more in the pot on the hearth."

She returned to her work in the kitchen, but she could still hear the two men's conversation.

The captain's voice came to her. "Will, I've been thinking."

"Oh, yes? And what about, pray tell? It seems that when you get to thinking we frequently find ourselves knee deep in trouble."

"Those days are past. I'm a reformed laddie now.

What I had in mind was a good deed that together we have the power to execute."

"Good deed? And how much will this be costing me?"

"Ah, Will, you purse-pinching Highlander. Not a penny. No, what I've in mind is our playing matchmaker for Tom Glen."

"Matchmaker? Don't be daft, man. That Lady Julia has softened your brain. Tom Glen can't bring his sweetheart to this country until he's got his brother under control, until their house can be made to look more like a place in which to live than a den for vermin."

"That's my point, brother." Jamie's voice rose with enthusiasm. "We have it within our power to do just that. We can cure Jack of his drunkenness, and once that's done I'll bring Tom's Annie back with me on my next voyage, free of charge."

"Don't talk nonsense, man. Jack Glen will not submit to be cured. I've talked to him. I've tried."

"Ah, but things have changed over the winter." The captain's voice softened. "Jack has become so ill he can barely crawl from his bed. He's spittin' blood and moaning for help. That crazy old Hannah has been trying to convince Tom to use some of her potions, but Tom, so far, has refused. If Jack's suffering is allowed to go on much longer, however, I'm not sure he won't give in."

"I haven't seen Tom in months, except for the day you most recently returned. He's been working in the woods. You're right, Jamie. We have to do something, and not just to act as matchmakers for Tom. If Jack doesn't get the cure, he'll die. Come on. We have to enlist Ben's help. We'll need to use his band's sweat lodge and all of his powers as shaman."

"Shaman? I thought he was an apprentice, of sorts."

"During your absence, the band's previous shaman died. Ben has taken his place. Now, come along. From what you've told me, there's no time to waste."

He strode back into the house for his black bag.

"Lass, I need you to do something verrae important." He paused beside her, and she looked up from where she'd been putting a pot of water over the fire to heat, to cover the fact that she'd been eavesdropping.

"Of course." She straightened and tried to look strong and capable. *Another test of my ability?*

"You're to saddle that little mare of yours and ride downriver three miles…until you come to a place where a stream crosses the road. Turn to your right and follow the path beside it to the riverbank. There you'll find an Indian encampment and, with luck, my friend Benjamin Two Rivers. Tell him Jamie and I will be bringing a man in need of his help. Ask him to prepare the sweat lodge."

"And if your friend is not in residence?" She called after him as he started toward the barn.

"Then, for God's sake, use your head, woman, and talk to any adult." Exasperation colored his words as he shrugged her off. "They'll know what to do. Just be quick about it. Come on, Jamie." He headed for the barn. "Help me saddle that fractious stallion of yours. We've no time to lose."

She shut Midnight in the house, then ran behind them to the barn to fetch her mare. The brothers made swift work of preparing the stallion and within minutes were galloping out of the farmyard.

She finished tightening the girth on her mare, then paused, watching them go, the pain of loneliness that had started earlier rising in her stomach. Alone. She would be alone. Jewels apparently had consented to sail away with Captain MacTavish.

Ah, well, no time to go feeling sorry for myself. I've been given work to do, and I must prove myself a worthy assistant. She swung into the saddle and sent the little mare loping up the lane to the road.

****

She halted her mount on the edge of the woods and looked at the dozen or more hide tents set on a promontory overlooking the river. What she estimated to be about twenty natives of various ages were working or, in the case of children, playing in the small settlement. When a woman noticed her, she nudged her companion, and both paused to stare at the newcomer. It set off a ripple effect. Soon all the buckskin-clad individuals' attentions were focused on her.

Forcing a smile, Heather dismounted and led her mare toward the group. Did they speak English? She hadn't thought to ask Doctor MacTavish. He'd given her scant opportunity for any inquiries.

"Good morning." She paused and spoke to the first woman she approached. "I'm Peter Grey, Doctor William MacTavish's...helper." She had to scramble to find a word she thought might be understood and accepted by these people. "The doctor has sent me to find your shaman, Benjamin Two Rivers, and ask for his help in preparing your sweat lodge. He and his brother will arrive shortly with a sick man."

A nearby tent flap opened, and Benjamin Two Rivers emerged. Tall and handsome, he embodied what Heather could best describe in words from one of the fanciful novels she and Jewels used to read...noble savage.

"Will has need of our sweat lodge?" He strode to stand close in front of her, towering over her, making her feel small and vulnerable. "Has his old trouble returned? Is it for himself?" His strong features crinkled with concern.

"No, no." She fought to keep from stuttering as the band of natives formed a circle around her. "It's for a friend who is ill." *What old trouble? What was the man talking about?*

"Ah, of course." Relief slackened Benjamin Two Rivers' features. "I might have guessed. Jack Glen, no doubt. He's mentioned his concern for that man. Very well." He turned to the assembled group and spoke in a tongue Heather assumed was their native language. Certain members turned away, possibly to do the shaman's bidding, but the rest remained staring at her.

Benjamin spoke again. With slow, wise grins beginning on the faces of the adults, they turned away, the children following.

"What did you tell them?" Alone with the man who was a friend of her master, her confidence returned.

"I told them you are Will's companion. You are just that, are you not?" Humor quirked one corner of his mouth and raised an eyebrow in a manner that reflected his years in England. "Now," he continued before she could protest, "ride back the way you came. If you meet Will and his patient, tell him all will be ready by the time he arrives."

Chapter 8

Glad to have completed her task, she remounted and turned her horse back up along the stream that led to the road. Surely, now, he'd see she was capable of being more than his servant, that she was worthy of being his medical assistant.

She had reached the road and was turning for the farm when she saw a wagon approaching, a tall, lean man she guessed was Tom Glen on the driver's seat. Riding close behind were the doctor and his brother. As she came up to them and halted, they did the same.

"Did you deliver my message?" Doctor MacTavish's face had lost none of its sternness.

"Yes. Benjamin Two Rivers said all will be ready by the time you arrive." Glancing into the back of the wagon, she saw another man, Jack Glen she presumed, lying in a tangle of bedding. He was writhing and moaning. "Do you think it will help?"

"It helped me. Move on, Tom. We've no time to lose." He nudged Wings past her. "I may not be back to the farm tonight...nor tomorrow, either. Do not go venturing away from the buildings on your own. Bears are fresh out of hibernation, and they're hungry and not particular about what they make their next meal."

"I'll take care." She watched as he walked his horse away from her.

Jamie touched his hat brim as he followed his brother. "Good morning to you, Peter." He winked at her. "And thank you."

She was left alone on the road to contemplate the doctor's remark. "It helped me." From what had he been suffering? And when?

****

Dawn was greying the sky as she struggled up on one elbow and shushed the dog. Someone was banging on the barred kitchen door.

"Lass, it's me." His voice came to her through her open window. "I'd be obliged if you'd hustle yourself down here and let me in."

"Immediately, Doctor." She scrambled out of bed, wrapped a quilt around her chemise, and scurried downstairs.

"Finally." He stepped into the kitchen, and even in the poor light of early morning she could see his sweat-stained shirt and the weariness in his face. "I'm right tuckered and need my bed."

"Was the cure successful for your friend?" she asked, as he bent to feel the teapot on the hook over the embers of the fire.

"Verrae. But then, I was sure it would be. It worked for me."

"You had trouble with drink?" The idea had come to her in the night. She moved to put fresh wood into the hearth and take the teapot to the sideboard for refreshing.

"Not that it's a concern of yours, but yes, I did. I went through a dark time in my life and was foolish enough to think I could find relief in a bottle. Only Jamie and Ben taking me to the sweat lodge of Ben's people saved me. Otherwise I would have lost my life to alcohol."

Although she longed to ask about the dark period in his life that had driven him to drink, she refrained. He was not ready to take her into his confidence, not about that part of his life, nor about the mysterious room at the top of the stairs.

The sound of a wagon racing into the yard made her drop the teapot.

"Doctor, come quick! He's dying!" A woman's voice screamed.

"Good God, what now?" He swung on her. "Get back to your room and dress. Don't forget your cap."

As she hurried toward the stairs, he flung open the kitchen door to admit a woman. Heather, pausing to glance back, saw her silhouetted against the river in the predawn light.

"Doctor, he's in the wagon." The newcomer flung an arm wide to indicate something beyond her. "He can't breathe!"

"Drive him on down to my surgery. Lad!" He turned to Heather. "As soon as you're dressed, come along. I will need you."

He strode off after the woman.

****

"Help me." At the surgery, the doctor waited for Heather beside the wagon. A gasping man lay on the flat bed of it, but when the woman moved to assist, the doctor shook his head. Heather saw the reason. She was well advanced into a pregnancy. "No, not you, Mrs. Johnson. You, there, Peter, give a lift. We need to get Richard inside."

He grasped the man under the arms, leaving

136

Heather to take his legs. His weight made her stagger, but together she and the doctor carried the man inside and laid him on the table.

"Now, you, Mrs. Johnson, go up to the house, stir up the hearth, and get some water on the boil," he ordered the woman who stood, mouth gaping in horror, as the first rays of sunlight illuminated the room. "Then take care of your team. We'll let you know when we've got things under control."

As she continued to stare, frozen in distress, Heather took her arm and guided her gently to the door.

"Dr. MacTavish is a fine physician," she said. "You can trust him to do the very best for your husband."

"I will, I will." The woman nodded and went out.

When Heather turned back to the patient and doctor, she saw William bending over the prostrate man, a tube of rolled paper in his hand, one end pressed to Johnson's bare chest, the other to his ear.

"Listening to his heartbeat," he explained, when Heather came to stand beside him. "A new technique discovered by a doctor in France."

"It actually works?" Heather leaned close.

"As well as can be expected, for such a rudimentary invention." He shrugged. "Perhaps someday someone will invent a device that will be much more efficient, but until then this will have to do."

"What do you deduce from what you've heard?"

"Nothing I didn't know previously. The man has a weak heart. He's had it for some time. I've been telling him he must take it easier, not work so hard, but this can be an unforgiving country. Only the strong survive.

He's got a son of sixteen, who is taking over a deal of the heavy work. I can only hope that will help."

"What about bloodletting? Dr. Phillips back home swears by it. He used to tell me that most diseases are related to tension in the blood vessels and that bloodletting can ease it."

"A theory I regard as ignorant and medieval." The doctor gave a sharp guffaw. "How often have you seen someone or something bleed to death? Isn't that proof that the body needs every drop it can keep? No, I'll be treating Richard as I have in the past, with the native remedy from the foxglove plant. Fetch me that third flask from the right. He's coming back to consciousness and can swallow a dose."

****

The sun was well up in the sky by the time Richard Johnson was able to sit up, clinging to the edge of the table for support.

"Thank ye once again, Doctor." His gaunt, weathered face still grey from the attack, the farmer looked up at William. "I thought I was a goner this time."

"Perhaps next time you will be, Richard, if you don't ease up on the work." Doctor MacTavish stood back from him, hands on his hips, and spoke with a harshness that startled her. "You must let your two oldest lads take over the heavy chores. And"—he drew a deep breath before continuing—"you and your good lady have enough children. She's getting worn down by all this childbearing, Richard, and not getting any younger."

"But Will…"

"I know, I know. Men have urges, and when a man

loves his wife… But, as I've told you, there's ways of enjoying the bed together without making another wee bairn. I can…"

Heather felt a hotness rushing up her body. She knew such talk could well be part of a doctor's advice; still, this was the first time she'd been present for it.

"Doctor, that's kind of ye, but we're Catholic. The priest…"

"The priest doesn't have to clothe and feed a great gaggle of babes!" William's bellow startled her. "Nor grieve the loss of a beloved wife and mother. For God's sake, man!"

"Well, there's only one cure for it, then…if you say Becky's in danger if she bears another babe." The man eased his gaunt body from the table and steadied himself on his feet. "I'll move to the barn. I'll not chance losing my darlin' just to satisfy my cravin's."

He started for the door, then staggered. William caught him on one side, Heather on the other, and together they helped him out into the early morning dew of another sunny day. His wife, waiting on the seat of the truck wagon, scrambled awkwardly to the ground and scurried to meet him. They embraced, and Heather saw such love and devotion in their reunion, her eyes smarted.

Catching the doctor looking down at her, she blinked the tears back and swallowed hard.

"Breakfast for four, Doctor?" She hoped there was no crack in her voice as she met his gaze.

"That would be nice, lad, that would be verrae nice." His words sounded gentle, kindly even. Was she gaining a small bit of respect?

****

His wagon was gone. Will stared at the place it had been sitting when he'd left to attend a patient two hours earlier. Surely no one would steal it. It wasn't such a desirable vehicle. He swung to the ground and led Wings toward its spot. Earth in the area where its shafts had rested had been churned up. A horse had been harnessed to it. He looked more closely. And from the size of the shoes, one particular horse.

"Lass!" Leading the horse at a pace that made it trot, he strode into the barn. "Lass!"

No answer, and Charlie's stall stood open and empty.

"Argh!" He headed back outside, the stallion's ears pricked from the excitement in his master's attitude, prancing behind him. "Whoa, damn it, whoa!" he ordered, as he swung back into the saddle. "We've got tracking to do. By God, I'll find her if it's the last thing I ever do!"

At the point where his farm lane merged into the public roadway, he halted and looked down at the ground. Fresh wagon and hoof prints turned toward the village. With a muttered oath, he put his heels to Wings, sending him bounding in pursuit.

He slowed his mount as he approached the village. During the ride he'd had time to master his reasoning. He didn't want to attract attention to either himself or her by creating a scene. But she'd have to learn she couldn't take his belongings without asking permission.

As he trotted his horse into the lower end of the village, he spotted his wagon, Charlie attached, outside the general mercantile halfway down the rutted street. The Clydesdale was tied to a hitching post, the wagon back holding two barrels and several smaller containers.

Good God, she'd gone shopping. With what? He'd given her no money.

My credit! She must be using my credit to buy God only knows what!

He stopped at the rear of the wagon, tied Wings to it, and strode into the mercantile with long, angry steps.

She stood at the counter, waiting while shopkeeper Benjamin Fowler tallied a list of items.

"What's the meaning of this?" The cool reasonableness he'd determined to affect dissolved.

"I'm purchasing a few much needed items." She turned to face him calmly. "Your larder is sadly depleted, Doctor."

"Sweet Jesus!" He swung the shopkeeper's slate toward him and looked at the total. "Are you daft, boy? Do you think me a lumber baron?"

"Come now, Will." Benjamin Fowler was quick to placate the man. "You're not a poor man. We all know it. Loosen those Scottish purse strings and let the lad have the means of making decent meals for you and your patients who have to remain in your care."

"I'll not have you judging my financial state." Will drew himself up angrily. "As for decent meals, we have those already."

"At this time of year, potatoes, with perhaps a bit of rabbit or partridge when you manage to get one." The shopkeeper's good humor was undiminished as he winked at Heather. "This lad says he can cook. Allow yourself the opportunity to see if he speaks the truth. He's only purchased staples…sugar, salt, molasses, and the like."

"Furthermore, it's already been loaded on the wagon, and I've signed for it." She tossed him a saucy, self-satisfied look. "You'd not go reneging on the transaction, now would you?"

"Argh!" He turned and strode toward the door. "Come along, lad. The sooner I get you and the spoils of this trip back to the farm, the further I'll be from becoming a pauper."

"Yes, sir." He heard her boots tripping along behind him and felt a snarl again rising in his throat. *Totally unrepentant of what she's done.*

"Watch where ye're goin', young lad." As they emerged from the store, a big, bearded man rammed into Heather, knocking her off her feet and against the storefront. Although she scrambled to prevent it, her cap toppled from her head.

Silence engulfed onlookers as golden brown curls tumbled around the shoulders of the rough shirt. *Sweet Jesus!* Heart pounding, Will snatched her hand and pulled her to her feet.

"Holy mother, it's a lass!" The man who'd collided with her stared down at her.

As a circle formed around the couple, Heather grabbed her cap from the dust, slapped it back onto her head and began to stuff her hair under it.

"No use, lass." The dirty, bearded man leered, over his missing front and eye teeth. "The good doctor's secret is out. He's not only got a helper, he's got himself a bit o' fun. And a fine-lookin' one, at that. Not many men have that kind of luck."

A snigger rose from the men in the crowd. Will drew himself to his full height, squared his shoulders and swiveled slowly to face them one by one.

"My apprentice is just that and nothing more." The words hung cold, like a January frost on a vine. "Her gender is not of importance. She's proven herself more than worthy of the position, and I'll thank you to treat her with the respect she deserves." Feet shuffled and eyes averted from the doctor's steely stare.

"Now, you'd best get on with what you were about." Will grasped Heather's arm. "My apprentice and I have purchases to take back to my farm. Purchases that will no doubt come in handy if any of you or your family members come seeking *our* services."

He propelled her toward the wagon, leaving a chagrined group to disperse in their wake.

****

"Greensleeves was my heart's delight." She sang in a pure, clear voice that on another occasion he might have been tempted to admire, but at the moment, hot with outrage at her highhanded use of his credit and the revelation of her gender, he could feel only gut-knotting annoyance.

"Stop that caterwauling," he snapped, flicking the reins over Charlie's back and sending him into a shambling trot. "I'm not in the mood for your ditties."

"What is chafing you most?" She swiveled on the wagon seat to face his sour countenance. "The fact that I left the farm without your permission, or that I purchased much needed supplies without your approbation?"

"Don't ya go throwing your fine words at me, woman." His jaw ticked as he clenched it. "I know what they all mean."

"Oh, my, yes." She swung away from him with a swish of her shining curls and flung her lad's cap up in the air to catch it a second later. "You are a doctor, a physician, not a mere surgeon or sawbones. And where were you educated, may I ask? At the famous medical in Edinburgh, did you say?"

"As a matter of fact, yes, that was it." He narrowed his eyes as he turned his head to face her. "If it's any concern of yours."

"Just thought I'd ask." She jutted out her chin and chest. The silhouette made him catch his breath. *She's a fine figure of a woman, and no mistake. But taking a man's horse and wagon and using his credit...*

"Now, if you've no further objection, milord, I'd like to continue my song. 'Tis a beautiful spring day, I'm thrilled to be free of that ugly cap, and my heart is light with the joy of it. Greensleeves is my heart's delight..."

"Go along there, Charlie. The sooner we get home, the sooner we'll be free of this noise the woman calls singing." But, despite his harsh words, her song was lightening his mood. By the time they turned into the farmyard, he had to suppress the urge to join in.

He wound the reins around the whipstand and jumped to the ground. He was heading to release Charlie from the wagon when her voice taunted him.

"Well, Doctor, since our secret is now out, don't you think you should start treating me as a woman?" She was standing in front of the seat, smiling coyly down at him.

"What do ye mean?" The Scottish accent that came unbidden into his voice whenever he was agitated colored his words. Squinting up at her in the sunlight, he screwed his features into what he hoped was the darkest of scowls.

"I think you might be lifting me down." She held

out her arms, hands ready to grip his shoulders when he reached up for her.

"Oh, you do, do you? Well, you're still wearing britches and a lad's shirt, and will be for some time, I assume, since those are the only garments you possess. You can hop down as easily as any young lad."

He released the Clydesdale from the wagon and started to lead him toward the barn. "Now, I'd be grateful if you'll begin to unload the wagon and get supper started. What happened in the village today in no way changes your duties or responsibilities."

Damn, damn, damn! He cursed silently as he unharnessed Charlie and led him into his stall. Now the fat was in the fire, sure and certain. People would draw the obvious conclusion, and he'd be seen as a fornicating bastard. Ever since the war, ever since he'd come to live in this valley, he'd prided himself on the respectability of his position. Even after he'd had his illness, he felt he'd been able to return to his status as a respected member of the community. Now here he was, appearing to all and sundry to be living in sin with a girl who'd been disguised as a young man. Sweet Jesus, what kind of two-faced bastard must people see him as?

Charlie nudged him gently with his nose and, against his will, he found his mood mellowing.

"So you like her, do you, lad?" He drew a deep breath and removed the horse's bridle. "She has a few good qualities, I suppose. But using my credit and letting herself be revealed as a lass…"

Charlie nuzzled him again, and this time he let a smile curl his lips. "You're right. She is a fine helper. Perhaps we'll have to try to make allowances for some of her shortcomings."

Chapter 9

With each pull of the teats, Will became more and more angry. Where had that chit of a girl gotten herself to this time? *Probably taken up with some young buck from the docks or timber camps now that all and sundry know she's a lass. Damn her!* Well, he'd sure as hell be taking possession of Wings permanently, if she had. But, damn it, no horse was worth the roiling outrage in his gut. The milk frothing into the pail reflected the feeling.

"Sorry, Molly." He excused himself to the patient cow as she jerked away from him. "Annoyance is making me rough. At least this time she saw fit to take her own mare and not Charlie."

Then he heard the steady trot of hooves in the barnyard and a female voice singing a ballad.

He turned on the stool but remained seated. A moment later she appeared on her mare, silhouetted against the sunset streaming in at the door.

"Good evening, Doctor." She slid to the ground and led the animal inside. "I apologize for my tardiness. As soon as I take care of my mare, I'll relieve you of that chore."

She led the animal into her stall, replaced her bridle with a halter, and returned to the barn corridor. As she reached for a water bucket, he stood, a mixture of anger and what he refused to recognize as relief burning his gut. Damn her, she'd left without his permission but…she'd come home.

"And just where have you been, mistress? This poor lass"—he gestured to the cow—"has been near bursting, not to mention the other chores left undone."

"I am sorry, but more urgent matters took precedence." She turned and headed for the door.

"What urgent matters might those be?" He followed her, self-righteous indignation making his strides long and hard.

"'Becky Johnson's baby." She reached the spring a few yards from the door and bent to fill the bucket with cold, clear water.

"Becky Johnson's baby? What are you talking about, girl? The woman isn't due for a good month."

"Not any more." She hefted the container, strode back into the barn, and into the mare's stall.

"What are you saying?" He caught her by an arm, as she returned to the corridor after placing the bucket before the thirsty animal, and swung her to face him.

"I'm saying she gave birth this afternoon to a pair of healthy twin boys." She faced him, a proud, defiant smile tipping her lips. "Mother and young lads are doing fine, thank you, Doctor."

"You didn't… You can't mean…" Her audacity garbled the words coming from his mouth.

"I delivered them." She shrugged away and headed out into the corridor to grasp a pitchfork. "Now, if you'll excuse me, I've hungry animals to feed."

"Not until you tell me exactly what you did, how all this came about." He blocked her path.

"Very well." With a sigh, she leaned the fork back

147

against the wall. "While you were gone, tending that boy who fell from his barn roof, Mr. Johnson arrived to say his wife had gone into labor. I think the scare she got when her husband had that heart attack brought it on. I knew you couldn't be spared from your present case, so I went."

"And just what would you know about birthing babies?" He glowered down at her.

"My mother acted as midwife in our district." She looked calmly up at him. "I accompanied her when there was no one else to help."

He sucked in a deep breath and tried to calm himself. Was there nothing to which this exasperating woman couldn't turn her hand?

"You should not have taken on the duties of a doctor." He let his tone moderate. Better that she'd gone to help, even with her limited knowledge, than that Becky Johnson had had no one with any medical skills at her bedside. "I will not have it happening again."

"That I won't promise." She looked up at him, green eyes as hard as emeralds. "You are only one person. You cannot be everywhere. If the need arises and you're not available, I shall do what I can to help anyone in distress. You must agree we cannot allow needless suffering. And to do that, you must give me more training…serious training."

"Argh!" He turned and went back to his milking. But as he filled the pail, he recognized the wisdom of her words. Until he found a way to rid himself of her, he'd be wise to teach her as best he could.

That evening he removed the key on the chain from about his neck and hung it on a peg at the foot of the stairs.

"There," he indicated it as they headed toward their bedrooms. "There, in case you need it."

"Thank you, Doctor." Her words were grave in the darkness. At least she had the good sense to recognize the importance of the concession he was making.

****

She finished washing the kitchen floor and paused to gaze out at the river glinting in the sunlight, the greenery of fields and forests. It had been two weeks since she'd delivered the Johnson twins. She and the doctor had been living in relative harmony. At night she struggled through medical books, and by day they each went about their assigned duties.

She sighed. There were animals to feed, a barn to clean, housework to do, more than enough to keep her occupied. Yet the beauty of the spring day beckoned. The trees in the orchard were in full bloom, the sky a most magnificent blue, and the grass a carpet of brightest green. The doctor had left early that morning to tend patients, with the remark that he would not be home until suppertime.

"Come on, Midnight," she called to the dog. "We'll take a few minutes to enjoy this beautiful day."

Setting off with the dog beside her, she headed into the orchard and down a path that led into the forest beyond it. The gurgle of brook water attracted her, and she turned to her left to find a pretty little stream bouncing over rocks as it headed to join the river.

"I wonder if there are any fish in it," she mused aloud to the dog. The animal's growl answered her. Whirling, she saw a huge black bear standing stone still beside a small pool a few yards upstream.

"Hush!" She admonished her companion that stood as still as the bear, staring back at it.

Hoping the beast would remain concentrated on his fishing and that the wind was blowing her and Midnight's scent away from it, she clutched the dog by the scruff of his neck and stayed frozen in place.

Movement would only serve to attract the creature, which remained staring down into the water. Hopefully the sound of gurgling water had drowned out the dog's initial growl.

Now I see the wisdom in the doctor's warning not to venture too far from the farm. I should have listened...and obeyed.

Suddenly, with amazing speed for such a large, awkward-looking creature, the bear shot out a massive paw. A second later a large fish flashed into view, writhing on the animal's claws. With a flip, the bear flung it onto the bank, into the trees, and lumbered in pursuit.

"A narrow escape, Midnight." Rising to her feet, Heather let out a huge sigh of relief. "We'd do well to heed the good doctor's advice from now on. And," she continued to the dog as they headed back to the farm, "we'll never, never mention this incident to him."

She emerged into the orchard to see a farm wagon pulled up to the surgery and a man in the rough homespun of a farmer pacing around, apparently looking for inhabitants.

"May I help you?" She wet her lips and tried to dispel the shakiness the encounter with the bear had induced.

"Ah, there you are." He turned to her and she saw it was Richard Johnson. "It took me a moment to recognize you…with your hair down." He tried not to look uncomfortable as he acknowledged the fact that had spread throughout the community like wildfire. "I've had a few twinges in my chest, and I was hoping the doctor would have a drop more of that Indian brew that does wonders to relieve it."

"Of course. Wait a moment until I fetch the key." She ran to the house and came back to open the surgery door. Glancing through the jars and bottles, she found the container of medicine made from the foxglove plant. Carefully she poured a small amount into a flask and handed it to the man. "I don't dare give you more without the doctor's permission," she said as he took a sip. "But if you'll come back tomorrow after I've had an opportunity to receive his instructions, I'll probably be allowed to give you a larger amount."

"This will hold me for now, thank you." Clutching the bottle, he climbed back onto his wagon.

"It's a blessing Will has seen to take you on. He's often from home and, on occasions like this, his absence doesn't bode well for such as me."

"How are Mrs. Johnson and the twins?" she asked, as he gathered up the reins.

"Flourishing, thanks to you. You did a fine job birthing them…miss."

"My name is Heather." She smiled up at him.

"Then I'll be thanking you again and wishing you a good day, Mistress Heather." He flapped the reins over his horses' backs and sent them shambling down the lane to the road.

"Well, Midnight, it seems as if we are becoming valuable to the good doctor even if he's a tad slow to admit it." She waved farewell to the farmer. "We must hope Mr. Johnson never has reason to mention our initial absence to that great stubborn Highlander."

****

"I've brought you a small present in thanks for what you did for Richard yesterday." Becky Johnson eased down from the wagon and reached up to remove a cloth-covered basket from the seat. "I'm sure you've more than enough to do, what with helping the doctor, and doing farm and house work, and being…"

The last came out without any ill intent, but once the woman realized her blunder, her face reddened. "I only meant…"

"Of course." Heather forced a smile. "Running a farm and helping out in the surgery keeps me very busy."

"Yes, yes, for certain sure." The woman, obviously glad to have been eased out of her blunder, handed the basket to Heather. "A few scones, some of my blueberry jam, and a bit of friendship starter…if you've a mind to make bread."

"Oh, thank you! I've been longing for some starter. I want to try that oven over there. That's most kind."

"What's most kind?" Heather's heart skipped a beat as she saw the doctor coming out of the barn. *Please, please, don't let whole story of yesterday come out, please.*

"I've brought a few things by way of thanks for…" She glanced at Heather.

"My name is Heather, but the doctor prefers to call me Lass." She hoped she didn't look as apprehensive as she felt.

"It was great good fortune your helper was about, the other day." Becky Johnson brought Heather's trepidations to life. "If she hadn't returned from the forest when Richard arrived seeking a drop of this wonderful elixir, he might not have made it home."

"What?" The doctor swung back on her. "Returned from the forest? What, may I ask, were you doing in the bush, after I specifically warned you…" He was looming over her, glaring down upon her.

"I went for a short walk, nothing more. I was not neglecting my duties." She had to battle to pull herself up, to boldly face the angry man looming over her.

"Did I not tell you there were hungry bears about, some of them with young which they'd defend to the death? Good God!"

"Go easy on the child, Doctor." Mrs. Johnson intervened. "Richard waited no more than a couple of minutes. And she was an angel sent, when my twins were born."

"Ah, well, then, Mrs. Johnson, we'll be thanking you for these fine offerings and bid you good day." He put an arm beneath her elbow to help her back onto the wagon seat. "Tell Richard to stop by when he has a minute. I'd like to check his heart."

"Of course, Doctor." Becky Johnson turned her team and headed back down the lane to the road.

"Now you, mistress." Once the woman was on the road and out of hearing, he swung on Heather. "Your job is to be available when I'm not, to take note of patients' conditions, and advise me upon my return. You are in no way qualified to go dispensing remedies, is that clear? And just where exactly were you, when Richard arrived complaining of chest pains? Having a romp with one of the local lads? Someone you met on your extravagant visit to the village? Sweet Jesus, perhaps I have won that stallion permanently!"

"What!" His words that had at first stung like a whiplash brought rage brimming to the surface. "Have I indeed been the centre of yet another nefarious wager between you and your scallywag brother? What was the bet this time, that I'd play the whore with one of the local lads? Well, let me tell you, Doctor, just because I worked in my brother's tavern does not make me any more a doxy than Lady Julia Thomas!"

"Not a convincing comparison, given that, from what I've observed of your friend, she's perfectly capable of being an entirely notorious woman."

"Then perhaps you'd best cast me out right now. I'm tired of being a pawn between two heartless, manipulating bastards!"

She swung about and strode in long, determined strides back toward the house, glad he couldn't see the tears streaking down her cheeks.

****

"Will, Will, where are ya, man? Come quick! Jewels is hurt!" His brother's yells broke his concentration an hour later and made him turn from the bowl of medicine he'd been mixing with Heather by his side. Through the door of the surgery he saw Jamie at the steps, lifting the limp body of Julia Thomas from his horse.

"Good God, man, what happened?" William strode outside to join his brother.

"She was riding like the wind on my gelding." The captain's face was ashen as he held her against his chest, her eyes closed. "And she tried to jump a great windfall. The dumb beast caught his hind leg in the branches and went down. Jewels flew through the air and hit her head against a tree. Dear God, Will, you have to save her!" Frantic, he swung on his brother as Heather came alongside.

"Bring her inside." Will took a quick look, then led the way. "Lass, bring ice from the ice house. Hurry, now!" The last two words were a sharp command, as Heather stood staring, ashen-faced, at her friend.

"Yes, yes, of course." She reached inside the surgery, grabbed up a basin, and set off at a run.

****

"Is she going to be all right?" Jamie MacTavish pressed against his brother's arm as he examined the woman on the table. "Sweet Jesus, Will, you have to save her! Save her, and anything I have will be yours...my house, my ship, Wings..."

"She won't be, if you continue to crowd me." William elbowed him aside. "From what I can see, she has a nasty bump on the head, but I won't know if she has any broken bones or other injuries until I examine her. Since you're proving to be an encumbrance, I'll be asking you to leave before I begin."

"But, Will..."

"You're nothing but a great nuisance, Jamie." He snapped out the words. "I'll inform you when it's acceptable for you to be with her again."

"Verrae well." With a huge intake of breath, he turned and headed for the door. "But, Will"—he turned back, his face filled with a desperation the doctor had not seen there since they'd found their parents dead— "If she won't make it, if these are to be her final hours, I want to be with her."

"I understand, and I'll not deprive you of such. Now I must work."

"Here is the ice." Heather brushed past the departing captain and rushed to stand beside the doctor, basin in hand.

"Take a length of cloth, wrap some in it, and place it on the bruise on her temple." He began to examine Julia's arms for breaks.

"Jewels." He heard her voice speaking her friend's name softly as she did his bidding, and he understood. This was her only friend in a strange land, and now she was in danger of losing her. Then, sharply, "Jewels!"

"What?" He glanced up from examining his patient's wrist.

Julia Thomas smiled up at him.

"What…?"

"Shhh!" She raised a finger to her lips and winked up at the pair. "I simply wanted to give the captain a small fright. Nothing like the specter of death to bring a man to his senses, to realize what he wants out of life."

"Jewels, that's awful!" Beside him the lass snapped at her. "Scaring the life out of me! I was having all kinds of awful visions…after the way your mother died and…"

"Bonny, Bonny, I'm sorry." She caught her friend's hand holding the ice to her forehead. "But I've grown weary of that great oaf chasing me around his kitchen table. I'm not about to let him catch me until he realizes he loves me and offers marriage."

"But surely you didn't deliberately fall off your horse, surely you didn't risk both the animal's safety and yours…" Heather was staring at her, eyes wide.

"Of course not!" Julia grinned. "But when I realized I was about to take a spill, I decided to make it work to my advantage. I only had the wind knocked out of me and got this nasty little bump on my forehead. When Jamie came rushing up and I saw the desperation in his face, I knew the time was right. Now will you put a serious-looking bandage on my wound before you let him see me again?"

"Jewels, how can you...?" Heather stared at her. "It's deceitful, it's..."

"It's exactly what my brother deserves." William chuckled as he fetched a length of cloth. "A woman who will always be at least two steps ahead of the bugger. Best wishes on snaring the wily creature, your ladyship. You have my blessing."

"Thank you, Doctor. Now, if you can just place me on that bed in the room yonder and give my intended an indefinite prognosis, I'll get on with my plan. And, incidentally, my name is Jewels."

"Certainly...Jewels." Chuckling, he wound the bandage around her head. Then he carried her to the bed, placed her on it, touched his forehead in salute, and went to fetch his brother. *Forgive me, Lord, but I'm enjoying this no end.*

"And how is the wee lass?" The captain caught William's arm as they met outside the surgery.

"You have to understand, brother, much as she puts up a great act of being wild and strong, she's still a lady, accustomed to being pampered. It will behoove you to do everything in your power to put her at ease, to make her happy."

"Aye, aye. Then you're saying she'll live? That she'll be right as rain again?"

"Medicine is an indefinite science at best." William forced a concerned frown to his forehead. "Sometimes care and affection can do more to effect a cure than the strongest treatments and potions. Go to her, keeping that in mind, brother."

"Aye, of course, for certain sure. Thank ye, brother."

****

"Bonny, I've something I must tell you." Three days later Julia sat down on an upturned bucket and watched as Heather milked the doctor's cow.

"What is it, Jewels?" She leaned her head against the animal's warm side and pulled on the teats. "Your tone says you're about to try to surprise me, but I've known you too long for you ever to be able to do such a thing. I put nothing beyond you."

"Ah-ha! Well, hold onto your bonnet this time, mistress. You're in for a treat. I'm going back to sea with Jamie."

"Ah-ha yourself. I already knew. The captain said as much on a recent visit to the farm. I must say, I consider it madness on your part, but then, you're an adventuress, so I can't say I was shocked. However..." She paused in her task and turned to face her friend. "I think it's a dangerous undertaking. You can only taunt and tease a man like Jamie MacTavish so long before he takes serious action."

"Do you think I'm not aware of the fact, Bonny? Good God, I love the man, and we're going to be married just as soon as Jamie can convince the minister to waive the banns. You and the doctor will be our witnesses."

Chapter 10

"Jewels, this is madness, even for you!" Heather scrambled to her feet and faced her friend. "You can't go roaming the seas with a man who's admitted he was little more than a pirate a dozen years ago. What do you know about him? How do you know he won't abandon you in some God-awful foreign port when he tires of you or gets you with child?"

"Bonny, he's a good man." Julia got up and went to place a placating hand on her friend's shoulder. "Didn't he prove he was honorable when he guided us to his ship? Didn't he treat us with the utmost respect during the voyage? Bonny, I love him, I love adventure, I love sailing. What more could I want? And anyhow"—she faced Heather defiantly—"your doctor sailed right along with him during the war, under the same letters of marque you now label piracy."

"He's not *my* doctor." The words snapped out. "He's my employer, nothing more. When I've saved enough money, I'll move on. Dr. William MacTavish isn't going to be my future."

"Move on to do what, my Bonny Lass? This is a wild, rugged country. A woman alone could encounter great difficulties."

"Well, then, perhaps I'll stay." She resumed her place on the stool at the cow's side. "At least I'll be free to decide my own future, not tied to some scallywag of a sailor."

"Bonny, for heaven's sake!" Julia caught her by the arm, forcing her to turn back to her and look up into her face. "We're sisters. Oh, I don't mean in blood." Heather had started up at her first sentence. "My father wasn't dallying with your mother. I mean we're sisters in spirit. We know each other to the core. Look at me, look into my eyes when I speak of Jamie, and you'll know that I love him now and always. And know he feels the same about me. Wish us happiness. Bonny. You're all the family I have now. I need your blessing."

Heather paused, looking up into her friend's furrowed face. Getting her approval meant the world to Julia Thomas.

"Of course you have my blessing, Jewels." She embraced her. "What can I do but wish you happiness?"

"Thank you, thank you, my Bonny Lass." When she released Heather and stepped back to look, smiling, into her face, her eyes were bright with tears. "And you'll ask Dr. MacTavish to be our witness with you?"

"Shouldn't your fiancé be doing that chore?" Heather grinned at her.

"Yes, he should, but he feels that you've more of a chance of getting him to agree."

"Me? Why ever would he think such a thing?"

"He feels that if he approaches the good doctor, the man will tell him he's mad to even consider marrying an aristocrat's daughter, a woman who is no doubt the object of a worldwide search by an outraged father. He's convinced he'll tell him he's making an alliance that could easily put a noose around his neck."

"Oh, and he'll think it's a perfectly sane idea if I

160

present it to him."

"Bonny, you're a disinterested party. He's not so likely to fly into a rage when you approach him with the plan."

"You think not?" Heather turned back to the cow and untied her lead rope. "I think I've relieved you enough for now, Molly. Let's go outdoors where I can get a breath of fresh air and clear my head of all this madness."

****

"They're going to do *what*?" Heather had all she could manage to avoid stepping back from the doctor's outrage as she faced him across the kitchen table. She'd thought it wisest to put some sort of barrier between them when she announced Jewels' and Jamie's plans. After breakfast, with the table separating them, with his belly full of good, hearty food, had seemed the best time. Now, as she looked into his reddened face, she wondered if there would ever have been a good moment.

"Marry. On Tuesday next. Captain MacTavish has managed to have the banns waived, since he must sail for the Caribbean as soon as possible. His ship is already loading timber for the voyage."

"Sweet Jesus, is the man daft?" He leaped to his feet and began to pace the kitchen in long, agitated strides. "It's bad enough he chose to kidnap a lord's daughter and bring her into his house, but now this! Bugger all, the man is bound and determined to get us both hanged."

"You exaggerate, sir." Heather tried to make light of the matter by beginning to clear the table. "Your brother did not kidnap Jewels...or me. Sir Robert

Thomas will long ago have given up the search for a daughter who has sullied herself by running off with a Scottish highwayman. Who'd have her now? No, he'll be too busy declaring her lost forever, dead perhaps."

"You can't know that for a certainty. Good God, woman, if my only child went missing, I'd move heaven and earth to find her."

"Ah, but you're not a peer of the realm. In Sir Robert's eyes, Julia is soiled goods, a disgrace to the family name. All he can be wishing at this point is that she never again darkens his doorway." *At least, I hope that's what he's wishing.* She sucked in a deep breath and continued, "Furthermore, I'd like your permission to hold a wedding party after the ceremony, here in the parlor. The captain's house is small, and…"

"Damnation, woman!" He stood in the centre of the room, feet planted firmly apart, hands on his hips, outrage darkening his face. "First you ask me to sanction this ridiculous match, and now you have the utter temerity to expect me to sponsor a celebration of it!"

"It would only be a small gathering." She paused, dishes in hand, in front of him. *Don't let his thundering deter you, Heather Grey. Jewels deserves as proper a wedding as possible.* "Ourselves, the vicar and his wife, and the happy couple. After the ceremony, I'll serve a small meal in the dining room. It won't take me long to rid the room of dust, and…"

"You're daft, woman. I'll not go having such an affair in this house. I'll stand as witness for them, but nothing more."

She placed the dishes on the sideboard and returned to confront him, this time with her own feet planted firmly apart, hands on her hips.

"Have I not proven satisfactory, Doctor?" Emerald eyes met sapphire ones without a flinch. "Have I not cleaned your house and barn, assisted with your patients, planted your crops, and done anything that might assist you in your work? Have I once complained or shirked my duties? And until now have I ever asked anything in return...not even payment beyond my keep? The captain is your brother. Isn't a decent wedding the least you can do for a blood relative?"

He glared down at her for a moment longer, then let out a long guffaw and headed for the door.

"No!"

"Well, then, might I at least be excused for a few hours that I may go to the village and give Jewels the glad news? I know she'll be delighted that you've agreed to stand witness."

"Argh!" His reply was a weak snarl. "Go. I have no patients that I must ride out to see this morning. But mind you're back in time to prepare the noon meal," he called after her as she headed outside.

"Never fear, sir." She paused in the doorway to flash him a smile. "I'll make you a meal fit for the benevolent gentleman you are. I'll leave Midnight in your care. It's too warm a day for him to gallop to the village beside my mare. Stay with the doctor, my boy," she ordered the dog.

The doctor's dark mutter as she skipped down the steps made her grin. Outwardly he might pretend to have scant caring for the dog, but she'd witnessed him petting the animal when he thought she wasn't watching. Midnight, with his easygoing, affable ways, had worked his way into the doctor's affection. Leaving them alone together could further form a bond between them.

****

"Bonny, what a wonderful surprise!" Jewels in trousers, knee-high boots, white shirt, and leather jerkin welcomed Heather at the door of the captain's cottage.

"Jewels, you look like a genuine buccaneer." Heather stared. "How on earth did you acquire such an outfit?"

"I had it especially made for me in the village, right down to the boots." She grinned at her friend. "Now that the truth of my gender is no longer a secret—I let it be known shortly after your revelation—I saw no need to go about in those rags we arrived here wearing."

"What did your intended think of your new attire?"

"At first, he was a wee bit appalled." She tossed her friend a saucy smirk. "Now he's getting accustomed to it, even admitting it will be practical and fitting when we return to sea. Now, on to more important concerns. I'm so glad you came, especially at this moment. Jamie has brought several bolts of material from Mr. Fowler's store. We're to choose cloth for my wedding dress, and yours as my attendant, as well." She drew Heather inside by an arm and indicated several rolls on the table.

"Oh, my!" Heather touched them. "Jewels, these must be the finest available. I can't allow the captain to go purchasing such for me."

"Phff!" Julia pulled an emerald-green bolt from the stack and held it up against her friend. "He and his brother are not poor men. He can well afford to attire not only his bride but her best friend as suits such a wonderful occasion."

"You're quite sure about this, are you?" Heather looked at her friend, who seemed engrossed in making a decision about the suitability of the color to Heather's complexion.

"About this shade? Quite. I've always thought you'd look beautiful in green. This matches your eyes."

"Don't go evading the issue. You know what I mean. About marrying Captain James MacTavish. He is a sailor, a former privateer, an adventurer."

"Exactly the kind of man I need." She dropped the cloth back on the table. "I couldn't wish for better or more suitable. Now…" She grasped a roll of bright blue silk. "What do you think of this…for the bride?"

A knock sounded at the door. As Jewels moved to answer it, Heather caught her by the arm.

"Ask who it is."

"Pshaw, Bonny." She brushed aside her friend's concern and went to open it.

"There they are, the pair of them!" Heather felt her breath suck inward with a force that all but choked her as the words burst in upon them.

The weird woman, the one she and the doctor had encountered on the road to his farm on the day of her arrival, stood framed in the threshold. Behind her, a young woman about Heather and Julia's own age scowled at them. She had waist-length silver hair, weird light eyes that matched those of the older woman, and was wasted to the point of emaciation. Her ragged dress hung from her gaunt shoulders like a shroud. *Witches.* Heather caught herself thinking. *Definitely witches.*

"What do you want?" Jewels thrust herself into the role of lady of the manor, drawing herself up to face the pair.

"We want the pair of you aboard the next ship bound for England." The old woman crouched close in front of Julia and glared up at her. "Women who have gone about disguised as men are a disgrace to their sex. And women who consort with such as the MacTavish brothers are nothing more than whores! Be gone, the pair of you!"

"On what authority do you base your demands?" Jewels stood her ground and glowered back.

"On the authority that Captain James MacTavish offered marriage to my daughter Miriah." She swept out a hand to indicate the young woman. "He defiled her, then denied he ever made any such promise. As for the other, the so-called doctor"—she crept around Jewels to confront Heather—"he's little more than a warlock, consorting with the savages and taking up their heathen ways."

"Get out!" Julia's hand shot out to seize a sword that hung in its scabbard by the door. Wrenching it from its covering, she confronted the crone with the drawn blade. "Get out of my house!"

Inspired, Heather snatched up one of the pistols that had been by the side of the sword and aimed it at the colorless girl, who'd begun to slink into the room behind Julia's back.

"Leave!" She took up a defensive stance to match her friend's. "Leave or, by God, we'll see you both in hell."

"A fine pair of gutter wenches, full of words befitting such trash!" the old woman cackled, but she began to back out of the house, her daughter following. "Perhaps you're well suited to the devil's spawn with which you've taken up. A curse on all four of you!"

With a swirl of her cape, she left the house, her daughter half running, half skipping behind her, casting apprehensive glances back over her shoulder at the two armed women standing on the threshold. The instant they'd disappeared into the trees behind the house, Jewels slammed the door and bolted it.

"Nothing good will come of your sinful laying with those two!" The old woman's cries came back into the room through an open window. "They've made you their whores. What need have they now to wed either of you?"

"Well!" Julia let the sword's point drop to the floor and, hands clasped on its hilt, leaned on the weapon. "So we're fornicating bitches mating with a pair of warlocks. Interesting." She grinned.

"Jewels, those women are insane." Heather allowed the pistol to drop to arm's length by her side. "And they're dangerous."

"Oh, come on, Bonny." Jewels stuck the sword back into its scabbard. "What could be a better part of an adventure than being cursed by a pair of witches? We're more than a match for an old crone and her ghastly daughter. And doesn't it give our men even more appeal? A rake and a shaman."

"Shaman?" Relieved to discover her heart rate was returning to normal, Heather put the pistol on the table beside the bolts of cloth.

"That's what Jamie told me the Indians call their healers…and William is regarded as one of them. Much more romantic than his being a doctor, isn't it? Now, let's get back to choosing our wedding finery. The event is only two weeks away, and we must give the seamstress Jamie has hired sufficient time to work."

"Aren't you concerned about what that weird woman said regarding the captain's defiling her daughter? The girl looked demented. Surely he wouldn't…"

"Jamie told me all about it. Last November, just before he sailed, he bought her a pair of moccasins at the mercantile in the village. She'd been running about barefoot in the cold, and he felt sorry for her. When the mother found out, she assumed he'd given them to her in order to seduce her. Since the girl is quite simple, cannot speak, and, according to Jamie, lives in fear of her mother, she went along with Hannah's accusation."

"And you believe him?"

"Bonny Lass, I know my captain. He would never take advantage of such a child."

"Jewels, how much do you really know about Captain James MacTavish?" Heather sat down on a chair and looked up at her friend.

"I know he's a good man, an exciting man, exactly the kind of man with whom I want to spend the rest of my life." She continued to peruse the material.

"No, I mean, really, Jewels." Heather caught her friend by a hand and stopped her. "About his past. Surely the captain must have told you something of it after he asked you to marry him."

"Oh, very well." Julia put the cloth aside and took a seat opposite her friend. "He and William are Highlanders, as you probably already know. Their family was routed during the Highland clearances. Their father was killed protesting; their mother died in the cold and snow after their home was burned. They were young lads at the time, with nowhere to go and no one to help them. Their friends and other family members had all died or been scattered. William, the elder, suggested they make their way to Edinburgh to an uncle, their mother's brother. He'd gone south years earlier and become a successful merchant.

"They did, and Callum Burns took them in. According to Jamie, he was a miserly creature, a bachelor who'd never married, being too much in love with accumulating wealth to allow for the possibility of anyone sharing it with him. He did, however, welcome the idea of a pair of hardy, nearly grown young lads to work for him. He sent Jamie to sea to learn the ways of trade and ships. William, who he discovered had healing ways after he cured one of Callum's horses, he sent off to the medical school in Edinburgh. He had plans to set the young man up in a practice and take the income from it."

"But that didn't happen." Heather urged her friend on when she paused.

"No, it didn't. William graduated just as the war came along. Jamie had been to New Brunswick and saw there were fortunes to be made privateering in the waters off the North American coast. He convinced William to join him. By that time Jamie was in command of one of his uncle's ships, so he and William took off across the Atlantic with it."

"You mean they stole it." Heather drew a deep breath. "Biting the hand that had fed them."

"I suppose, in a manner of speaking." Jewels stood and went to swing a pot of water over the languishing fire. "They fully planned to pay their uncle back with the spoils of war, but the old man died before the conflict ended. Thus, they were left with a ship named the *Misty Maid*, which Jamie considered no more than their rightful inheritance, since they had worked for Callum for years without pay. The *Misty Maid* suffered several injuries during the war, and afterwards Jamie was wealthy enough to buy a new ship, the *Highland Lass*. Bonny"—she swung on her friend in exasperation—"how in heaven's name does one get a fire going? I long for a cup of tea."

"Here, let me." Chuckling, Heather went to the hearth and bent to stir the fire to life. "Jewels, it's fortunate you're clever and beautiful. You're the worst housekeeper I've ever encountered. But why did William choose to leave the sea and settle here after the war?"

"Ah, now that's another story, and one best left for the good doctor to tell. Bonny, you're amazing! Look how quickly you got the fire going."

****

"Doctor, Doctor!" A lad of about ten years of age paused breathlessly in the door of the surgery where William and Heather were busy mixing potions.

"What is it, lad?" The doctor swung to face him.

"It's my dad, Doctor. He's taken a pain in his chest something awful! You have to come quick, Mama says!"

"Of course." He shoved the remaining bottles toward Heather. "Finish up here, lass." He headed for the door, then paused on the threshold. "Here." He pulled the key and its chain from about his neck. "Lock up the place when you finish." He dropped it on a sideboard, then strode outside and toward the barn. "Come along, lad. You can ride double with me. We've no time to spare."

Moments later, Heather stood in the doorway of the

surgery watching them leave, the child behind the doctor on Wings, arms clasped around his waist as they galloped up the lane. She was about to turn back to finish her work when she remembered the bread she'd left baking in the outdoor oven. Clutching up her skirts, she ran toward the house, Midnight at her heels. She dropped the key on its chain about her neck as she went.

****

She was placing the golden brown loaves on the kitchen sideboard when Midnight, standing in the open doorway barked.

"What is it, boy?" It wasn't his welcoming greeting. Going to join him, she saw Hannah Rob and the waif-like figure she recognized as her daughter slinking toward the surgery's open door.

"Oh, my God!" The words burst from her lips as she broke into a run toward them. "Mistress Rob, what can I do for you?" She hoped the normality of the request would be enough to snap the woman out of any sinister intent her skulking stance suggested.

Instead of responding, the woman, with amazing speed, flew into the surgery, leaving her companion abandoned. By the time Heather got to the door, the woman was flinging bottles and jars to the floor, screaming wild oaths.

"Stop it!" Heather grabbed the woman's upraised hand as she prepared to smash a full bottle of laudanum. "Stop it! Doctor MacTavish needs those supplies!"

"Needs! Needs! Tell him to go to those savages he calls his friends for his needs. I'll not have him stealing my patients with his pagan cures!" She smashed the bottle against the counter. Clutching its broken neck, she swung on the younger woman. In a single, vicious gesture she slashed it across Heather's forearm. Blood fountained from the wound. A blow from the woman's free hand sent her reeling backward into a sideboard.

A roar burst into the room. As Heather dropped to the floor, Midnight landed on Hannah Rob's back. Stunned by the impact, it took Heather a few seconds to come to her senses. When she did, she saw the big dog pinning the woman to the planks, teeth bared. The woman screamed obscenities at him.

"Midnight, stop!" Heather staggered forward on her knees and managed to grab the dog by its hackles. Pulling him to her, she fumbled to her feet, the blood from her wound making a puddle at her feet.

The girl stepped in at the door, stared for a moment at Heather and her wound, then grabbed her mother by an arm and fought to pull her to the door.

"Take this as fair warning!" the weird woman yelled as her daughter dragged her from the surgery. "I'll not rest until William MacTavish and his fornicating brother are laid in their graves!"

Clinging to a cupboard for support, Heather fought the whirling dizziness in her head and reached for a length of cloth. "I hope the doctor isn't too long away," she murmured to the dog that stood looking up at her with round, confused eyes as she wound it awkwardly around her arm. "I believe I'm in need of his services."

Consciousness deserted her and she sank to the floor.

****

Rankled to the core, Doctor William MacTavish rode down the lane toward his farmhouse. He'd never been called away on a false alarm until today, and he wasn't amused. He hadn't blamed the young lad who'd delivered the fake message, not after the child had confided that the weird woman had threatened to put a curse on him and his whole family if he refused. Yet when he'd ridden into Richard Johnson's dooryard to find him hale and hearty, and learned the truth, he'd been consumed by such a rush of anger toward Hannah Rob he could barely contain it. He'd whirled Wings about and headed back down the trail toward his farm at a full gallop.

He drew rein at the narrow footpath that led to Hannah's hovel, debating whether to ride to her door and confront her with her infamy or continue on home.

"Argh!" He made his decision and nudged his mount once more into motion toward his farm. Getting into an argument with the old witch would be pointless. Furthermore, there might be urgent cases waiting for him.

Riding down the lane toward his house, he saw the door of the surgery gaping open. More outrage surged through him. *Blast the girl, can't she even be trusted to lock a door?*

Then a sense of foreboding washed over him. When the dog Midnight started from the surgery, barking, it turned to fear clutching at his gut. Spurring his horse to the small building, he reined to a skidding halt, leaped to the ground, and bounded up the steps.

"Oh, dear God!" He dropped on one knee beside Heather. Blood soaked her clothing and smeared the floor. Her face was ashen, her lips blue, her eyes closed. A purpling lump and bruise dominated one side of her forehead. He patted her cheeks, and she slowly opened her eyes.

"It's about time you got home, Doctor." The words were a dry whisper.

"Sweet Jesus!" He didn't have to ask who her assailant had been as he gathered her up in his arms and laid her on the table. When he went to the sideboard for the supplies he'd need, he discovered his hands were shaking.

"I'll be needing to sew up that wound." He came back to stand beside her.

"Aye, doctor, I suspected as much." The trust he saw mirrored in her emerald eyes made something in his chest lurch.

"Here." He raised her head to the mug in his hand. "Laudanum to ease the discomfort."

"Surely a wee dram will do as well. Hannah Rob smashed two bottles of the drug. We'll be on short rations until we get another supply."

"Laudanum." He put the mug to her mouth. "Let me worry about supplies."

She hesitated only a moment longer before allowing him to pour the liquid into her mouth.

****

"Stay here and guard the place," he ordered the dog a half hour later as he gathered the unconscious Heather in his arms. "Don't let anyone inside."

Midnight had started to follow, but at the man's stern words, he hesitated, then, seeming to understand, lay down across the surgery's doorway with a mournful whine.

"Never fear, laddie. I'll take good care of her." He strode out of the building and across the field to the house, a cold wind from the river bringing charcoal clouds scudding over the landscape and forcing his hair back from his face. In his heart was a boiling mix of fear and outrage. Fear that he might not be able to prevent the death of this woman who'd become a part of his life and outrage against the hag who'd brought this terror upon him.

If she dies... He fought to clear the possibility from his mind. He was a good doctor. During the war he'd saved men far more severely wounded.

But she's just a wee lass, and she's lost so much blood. She didn't deserve any of this. If it weren't for me, that old witch never would have seen fit to lure me away, to attempt to destroy my drug supply, and the lass wouldn't have been injured defending it.

As he carried her through the kitchen, the smell of fresh bread made him feel even worse. She'd been baking when this misery had overtaken her, baking for them. He glanced at the golden brown loaves on the cupboard.

Once upstairs, he laid her on her narrow bed and began to remove the blood-soaked shirt. She muttered something in her semi-conscious state and made a weak attempt to still his hands on her clothing.

"Rest, lass," he said as he peeled the garment from her. "Remember I am a doctor."

But when he'd succeeded in fully divesting her of her bloody clothing, he had to keep reminding himself over and over again of the fact. Naked, she was a beautiful woman. Going into his own bedroom, he snatched up one of his new white shirts. He was relieved when he had her inside it and settled beneath the covers.

He took the key from about her neck and headed

back to relieve the dog of his lonely vigil.

****

He was dozing on a chair by her bed when she stirred and moaned. He jerked alert.

"Lass," he said, bending close. "You're safe now. The witch is gone."

"Doctor?" She blinked at him in the light of the candle burning on the washstand.

"Aye, lass, I'm here. I won't be leaving you."

"But…" She became more lucid and struggled to rise. "It's grown dark and I've not prepared your supper…nor done the barn work…"

"Not to worry." He held her to the bed. "I fed myself before you came back to consciousness, and took care of the stock. Dinnae fret yourself."

"I am feeling a bit weary." She slumped back against the pillows and mattress with a sigh.

Then, "Where's Midnight? He was with me when that woman attacked me. Is he well? He hasn't run off, has he?" Concern brightened her eyes.

"He's fine, never fear. He's in the kitchen, behind a securely bolted door, eating a bowl of food fit for a king. Since he probably helped save your life, he deserved no less."

"Thank you." A weak smile of relief lighted up her pale face, and her eyelids drooped. "I'm feeling sleepy at the moment. But"—she looked up him and he was amazed by the sharp determination that came into those beautiful green eyes—"never fear. By morning I'll be back at work. You'll not have a patient to tend in your own house."

"I've no doubt you will, lassie. I've no doubt you will." He settled back on his chair, crossed his arms on his chest, and shortly slept there beside her.

****

He lurched awake. Something was bumping his hand. Blinking sleep from his eyes, he looked down to see Midnight by his side, butting him with his large black head. Coming to full consciousness, he realized something else—the bed beside him was empty, its covers thrown back.

"Damn it, where is she?" He bolted from his chair and headed for the stairs.

"Lass!" he bellowed. "Lass, where are you?"

Bursting into the kitchen, he saw her, still garbed in the shirt he'd wrapped her in the previous evening, her lad's trousers showing below, her feet bare, standing at the sideboard attempting to slice a loaf of fresh bread.

"What do you think you're doing?" He strode across the room to take the knife from her hand.

"Getting your breakfast, of course, Doctor." Her face, sheet white, bore a stubborn, determined expression he was coming to know all too well.

"Of course you are not!" He caught her up in his arms. "You've lost quantities of blood. Today you rest. I'm taking you back to bed."

"No!" She struggled as best her weakened condition would allow. "No!"

She managed to swing her legs from over his arm and get them to the floor. There she stood, staring up at him, green eyes hard and determined. "No." This time the word came out more softly. "I cannot abide laying abed on such a beautiful morning."

"Verrae well." He put an arm about her and guided her to a chair at the table. "At least grant me the concession of resting for a time. Sit while I make our breakfast. Later, we'll decide what you're capable of."

She sat sulkily while he moved to the hearth and reached for the teapot hanging over the small fire crackling on it.

"No need to make tea." Her words sounded like those of a spoiled child. "I've already done that."

"Well, then, good. I'll just go down to the ice house and fetch butter. It won't be an elegant repast, but at least we'll have some nourishment in our bellies to start the day. And you're not to try to finish slicing that bread. I'll do it when I get back."

He went out, exasperated by her stubborn unwillingness to do his bidding as his patient, yet with a shaft of admiration brightening his annoyance.

****

"That was a decent repast, Doctor." She smiled over at him as they finished their meal of fresh bread, butter, blueberry jam, and tea. "That jam was delicious. Where do you keep it? And who made it? I must learn the recipe."

"Mrs. Johnson made me a supply last summer." He stood and began to gather up their dishes. Her smiles aroused something deep inside he wanted left untouched. "I keep it in a dark corner of the root cellar. And don't go making plans to put up preserves. You will not be here that long." He blurted out the last as he clattered their plates onto the sideboard and headed for the door. He didn't want to think that far ahead.

"As you wish." She leaned back in her chair and cast him an annoyed glance. "Then perhaps I'd best starting looking for another position. Perhaps I might even find a likely young lad who's looking for a wife to bring him comfort."

"As long as you're under my roof and eating my food, you'll not go throwing yourself at any young buck who happens to smile in your direction!" The words thundered out as he rounded on her. "I'll not have you making a mockery of your responsibilities to my medical practice by chasing all and sundry in the hopes of seducing some unsuspecting man into your clutches."

Hot with outrage, he nevertheless had the good grace to feel ashamed of his outburst as he strode out of the house and down to the barn. She was his apprentice, not his slave. As such she had a right to do as she chose.

****

By the time he'd attended the first couple of patients of his day, his anger had ebbed. The lass had nearly gotten herself killed defending his surgery, and what had he done? Threatened to throw her out of his bed and board before autumn. Small wonder she'd retaliated by saying she might well start looking for a husband to provide them for her.

As he heaved himself wearily into the saddle and headed into the village to put a fresh dressing on the arm of the blacksmith who'd burned himself the previous week, he decided a peace offering was in order. As soon as he'd seen to the man at the forge, he'd be stopping at George Fowler's shop.

Perhaps the merchant or his good wife could come with a suitable suggestion.

****

"What's this?" She stared at the package he'd thrown onto the kitchen table. Late afternoon sunlight slanted across the room over the wrapped bundle.

"Some things you may well use, now that the entire village is aware you're no a lad." He continued on across the room and took up the teapot hanging over the embers on the hearth. "I trust you've left me some tea?"

"Of course." The words came out in a bemused fashion as she continued to stare at the parcel.

"Well, go ahead. Open it." He carried the pot to the sideboard and took down a cup. Watching her out of the corner of his eye, he poured into it, then pretended to look out of the window toward the barn.

Slowly she unwrapped the burlap covering, a puzzled frown creasing her forehead.

"A dress!" Amazed delight colored the words as she took the soft, blue garment up in her hands.

"Aye, and there's more." He turned back to her, cupping the mug in both hands, his lips curling a bit in the enjoyment of her surprise.

"A length of cloth. Green cloth." Eyes widening with surprise, she held it against her and looked over at him.

"I thought you might like to make your own gown." He leaned back against the sideboard and tried not to feel the happiness her delight was giving him. "Mrs. Fowler in the village had a ready-made one on hand, as you can see, but a woman has her own ideas for a dress, she tells me. And…" He stopped abruptly.

"And?"

"And she thought green would match your eyes."

"She thought? I can't recall Mrs. Fowler being acquainted with the color of my eyes."

"Verrae well, damn it, woman, *I* thought green might match your eyes. Now are you satisfied?"

"Thank you." Instead of the teasing retort he'd

expected, the sincerity in those beautiful emerald eyes snatched at his chest as she gave the shy response. She gathered the package's contents and hugged them in her arms. Then she fled toward the stairs. He listened to her light footfalls as she scampered up to her room.

"Here, now," he called after her. "Remember you're less than a day from a serious injury. Take your time, or I'll be ordering you back to bed."

"Aye, sir."

You've been a fool, William MacTavish, bringing her gifts. He turned away from her happy response. *Already you can see it's given her the wrong idea. The fact that she was wounded protecting your chattels has weakened your resolve.*

****

"Well?" she stepped into the kitchen and swirled about in front of him. "What do you think?"

His breath knotted in his throat. She'd let her hair down. Golden brown curls cascaded over her shoulders and onto the back of the blue dress that fitted her like a glove about the breast, then draped over her hips. Even with that nasty bruise discoloring her forehead and her arm swathed in bandages, she was a beautiful woman, a very beautiful woman.

"You look...like a woman." He stifled compliments with his gruff words.

"Is that the best you have to offer, Doctor?" She stopped in front of him. "Then I fear you must be a great failure when it comes to courting."

"I'm not courting you, woman." He bolted to his feet and headed for the door. Grasping the handle, he paused. "But let me tell you, any lass who had the good fortune to catch my eye would find me a most charming lover. And no more dancing about. You're still weak and you'll make yourself dizzy."

"Have you considered the possibility, Doctor? Of courting me, that is?"

"Hardly. Now since you're feeling so spry, perhaps you might see fit to get a semblance of supper on the table."

Damn her! Damn Jamie MacTavish! Damn the pair of them for getting me into this mess.

His thoughts were broken by the sound of a wagon barreling down the lane. He drew himself up and felt relieved. Another emergency. It would take his mind off the provoking lass.

****

"He got his hand caught under a keel in the shipyard!" one of the two men on the seat of the wagon yelled as his partner drew rein to the sweating team at the kitchen door. "He's bad hurt, Doctor."

Doctor MacTavish was already outside, Heather close behind him. Someone inside the conveyance moaned. He strode to look over the boards into the wagon's bed, and she saw his jaw clench.

"Get him down to the surgery at once." He turned in that direction with long, determined strides. "Lass, come along and get water boiling. I'll need bandages, and lots of them."

"Yes, of course."

At the surgery she watched in horror as the two men carried a groaning young man inside. His left hand had been smashed to a bloody pulp. Sandy curls and a face that had probably only begun to need shaving made him look so innocent and childlike she felt her stomach churn.

Inside the surgery they laid him on the table, and the doctor began his examination.

"Laudanum," he ordered her, and she marveled at how he managed to keep his voice so calm and level under the circumstances.

Struggling to still the trembling in her body and soul, she obeyed. Once she'd handed him the bottle, he raised the young man's head and poured a generous quantity down his throat. The lad sputtered and belched, but she believed he'd swallowed most of it.

"Now," he said to the two men who stood near the door, gaping, "help me strap him to the table. The hand will have to be amputated."

"No!" the young lad came out of his suffering to interpret the words. "No! Not my hand! No!"

But the two workmen were already holding him down, fastening the straps about him.

"Lad, I'm sorry." William bent over him, and Heather saw deep compassion in the doctor's face. "But it's the only way I can save your life."

He turned to the workers who'd brought him. "You'd best go now. Does he have any family who can care for him after the surgery?"

"He lives with a married brother upriver," one of them said. "We'll get in touch with him."

"Good, good. But perhaps wait a few hours before informing him." Heather caught the meaningful glance he gave the pair. *Wait until we see if he'll survive.*

"Aye, Doctor. We'll come back directly for your instructions." The pair left, faces grey with concern.

"Now." Doctor MacTavish turned back to her. "Get to boiling that water. We've no time to waste."

****

"Here." Doctor MacTavish handed her the basin with the crushed, severed hand inside. "You'll find a shovel against the back of the surgery. Take it, go into the woods, and bury it deep, at least four feet, beyond the scent of bears or foxes. On your way, you may tell those two men who brought the lad that chances appear good for his survival." He looked down at the unconscious boy in front of him, his face furrowed.

Heather accepted the basin mechanically. All through the surgery and even yet, she reacted without emotion, obeying his commands as he worked like a creature without personal feelings. Somewhere in the back of her brain was the real Heather Grey, not this automaton who did this man's bidding without fainting or getting sick or revolting at the horror of it. Sometime during that awful day she'd become capable of being his assistant, God help her.

"Well, go!" he snapped when she stood for a moment, holding the basin. "I need you back here to help me clean up." He indicated the blood-stained table, the unconscious lad still upon it, the stump where his hand had once been swathed in bandages. She refused to think deeper, to how the doctor had closed the wound. She couldn't revisit those moments, not yet.

He turned his attention back to his patient. With shaking hands, she went out into the muggy heat of the July twilight. Automatically she brushed away the flies attracted by her burden.

The two workers met her with anxious eyes that asked a silent, fearful question.

"The doctor says his chances appear good," she said. Then one looked down into the basin, and his face turned a greenish grey. He stumbled off to be sick a few yards away.

"Good, good." The second man managed to hold his ground but swallowed hard. "Now we'd best let you get on with your work. We'll inform the lad's family. Come along, Jasper. We've travelling to do."

At the back of the surgery, she found the shovel and, dragging it behind her, headed for the trees beyond the ice house.

When she finished her gruesome task, she stood, holding the basin and the shovel, and stared toward the river, deadly calm in the dull heat. She needed to wash her hands and face in its cool waters. She couldn't return to the surgery with its ugly, murky smell and bloody ambience, not until she'd refreshed herself.

Throwing aside the shovel, she ran, occasionally stumbling, down the grassy slope to the river. On the bank, she stopped to remove her footwear. Then, heedless of her new dress trailing in the water, she waded to her knees. There she washed out the basin, flung it back to shore, then bent to splash water over her burning face until she felt a revival beginning to come over her.

She waded back to shore, picked up the basin, pulled on her stockings and boots, and headed back toward the surgery. *I've faced the worst. I can be his assistant. I can help him save lives. What more could a woman want out of life?*

But even as she had the thought she knew it wasn't true. She wanted so much more.

****

She re-entered the surgery to find him straightening from placing the unconscious boy on the cot she'd made up fresh the previous day in the small recovery room. He'd removed the lad's clothing down to his undertrousers and had opened all the windows to let in any breezes that might arise in the sultry day. The unpleasant remains of the surgery were still in the main room.

Heather drew a deep breath and headed for the hearth, where a pot of lukewarm water remained over the dying fire. The heat in the room was stifling, but she knew she had to scrub table and floor before the blood attracted flies or vermin.

"I'll fetch more water." He turned to her, and she was startled at how weary and grey he looked. Surely this was all in a day's work for him.

"Yes."

As he moved to pass her, she caught his arm. "Doctor, are you all right?"

"He's only a boy." The words sounded as if they were catching in his throat. "Like so many I worked on during the war. Their lives are never the same after an amputation."

He wet his lips, caught up a bucket, and headed outside. Heather watched for a moment as he walked toward the well, his broad shoulders stooped for the first time in her knowing him. She understood. Even though a doctor might do such an operation many times, if he was a good doctor, he never lost his compassion.

Chapter 11

He returned to the surgery, where she was scrubbing the operating table clean. Her sleeves were rolled up above her elbows, a few errant curls straying from the bun into which she'd had them gathered. Her face was pale as she rinsed the bloody rag in the basin of clean water, but otherwise she showed no signs of the stress and fatigue under which she must be laboring.

An amazing lass, if ever there was one. The thought invaded his mind. Quickly he tried to remedy it. *I have to see about ridding myself of her before I begin to depend on the wench. But why?*

The question startled him, coming close on the heels of his previous plan. *Why, indeed. She's proven excellent in every way, from farm hand to housemaid to cook to assistant. Getting rid of the best help you could hope for because she's a woman makes no sense, man. She keeps her distance. All I have to do is keep mine. God knows that shouldn't be all that difficult with my heart in a grave...and her a tavern wench.*

"You're staring, Doctor." She looked over at him and paused to shove a strand of hair from her face with the back of her hand. "Am I doing something wrong?"

"No." He moved to the end of the table opposite her. "You acquitted yourself well today, lass. I'm thinking I might recant my statement about sending you packing."

"Oh?" She straightened up and faced him. "And what makes you think I'd choose to stay, given the manner in which you've treated me?"

"Where else have you to go?" He didn't disguise the surprise her words had given him. He'd assumed she'd be only too glad to have a permanent position with him.

"Oh, I don't know." She picked up the basin and swaggered to the door to throw the contents outside. "As you've discovered, I have any number of skills. I could become a cook or a housemaid or a teacher or maybe even a healer on my own." She glanced back tauntingly over her shoulder. "Maybe I'll find myself a husband. There seems to be a dreadful shortage of marriageable women in this settlement."

"Don't talk daft, woman." He rounded the table to come up close behind her as she wiped out the basin. "It would no be safe, a lass wandering about alone looking for sustenance. Any manner of unscrupulous man might accost you. Any manner of unscrupulous man might..."

"Might find me pretty, might fall in love with me, might want to make me his wife?" The words were a saucy taunt.

"Damn you, woman!" He caught her by the arm and swung her to face him. The basin clattered to the floor as he swept her into his arms and kissed her, kissed her long and hard. A gush of feelings he'd never experienced flooded through every vein in his body. It brought a wild sense of release, a sensation of uninhibited pleasure. When she responded, his senses swirl.

Damn it, man, what are you doing?

With a muttered oath, he released her and strode out the door, slamming it behind him.

****

He was finishing his noon hour meal the next day when her scream from the barn brought him to his feet, crashing his chair over backwards.

"Lass!" In three long strides he was out the door and running toward the stable, heart pounding.

Dear God, what has happened? Did a horse kick her? Did...

At the open door he paused. She stood huddled against the door of Charlie's stall, her fist stuffed against her mouth, her face blanched and contorted.

"Lass, what is...?" He started to advance toward her, but she muttered a cry and pointed to the floor in front of him.

He followed her indication and saw a brown rock snake, coiled, sunning itself in the bright doorway.

"Lass, it's all right." He stepped over the reptile and went to her side. Something had happened he'd never expected from the self-sufficient, previously unflappable woman, and she huddled up against his chest like a terrified child.

"Lass, lass." As his astonishment lessened, he put his arms around her. "It's but a rock snake, taking a little sun. There's no poisonous snakes in this country, and definitely no constrictors. You've nothing to fear from Sam."

"Sam?" She looked up at him, wide-eyed. "The creature has a name?"

"Well, he does tend to hang around the farm, helping out by eating insects and slugs, so I thought he deserved a name."

"I don't like him." As if suddenly realizing what she was doing, she pulled away from him and brushed her hair back from her face. "He'll have to go."

"Verra well." With a sigh, William strode to where the snake lay, bent, and picked him up. He heard her gasp as Sam wound his length around his arm.

"See? Friendly as that great dog of yours." He turned to grin at her. "However, if you object to his presence, I'll take him down to the swamp and let him go. He'll find lots to eat there and probably won't come back. Are you quite sure you'd not like to meet him and maybe let him stay around?"

"No, no, no." The shudder that ran through her made him sorry he'd chosen to joke about her fear. He had no right, when she'd been courageous in all other aspects of the work and new environment she'd shared with him.

"Verrae well." He headed for the door. "Sam, you and I will have to take a wee walk."

"Doctor." Her voice, sounding weak and shaky for the first time since he'd known her, stopped him.

"Aye?"

"Thank you."

He glanced back at her and nodded. "It's the least I can do for a worthy assistant. But…" He paused again. "Why are you wearing your lad's clothing again? I noticed when I came down to breakfast this morning you weren't wearing your new gown."

"Aren't you aware? It has a goodly number of bloodstains from the surgery yesterday. I've put it to soak, but I doubt it will ever be the same again." Tears filled those remarkable green eyes.

"What is it?" Her response startled him. "It's only

a bit of cloth."

"That dress… It was the finest garment I've had since I was a little girl and my mother sewed one for me. I…I thought it made me look…pretty." The last came out in a gulping sob, and she covered her face with her hands.

"Lass." He made a move to go to her, but she shied away, and he remembered the snake resting comfortably around his arm.

"I'll just put Sam in the swamp." Feeling awkward, he wet his lips and backed out of the barn, then swung to head for the wetland in long, determined strides. He had to get back to her, to take her into his arms again.

But when he returned, he found her calmly filling the cow's manger with hay.

"Will you be riding out this afternoon, Doctor?" she asked as impersonally as if nothing had happened. "Will you be back by dark?"

"Aye." An unaccountable sense of disappointment overwhelmed him. She didn't need comforting, tough little tavern wench that she was. With a grunt, he headed into Wings' stall and led the stallion out to be saddled.

Or maybe, a nagging little voice suggested, *she's just returning the reaction, from when you kissed her and then slammed out of the room.*

The thing that plagued him most was the fact that her fear of the snake had endeared her to him more than he would have believed possible. Up until then, she'd been self-sufficient, apparently well able to take care of herself. Now, in at least one area of her life, she'd demonstrated she needed him.

****

He galloped down the lane toward the farmhouse as thunder rolled, heavy and intimidating, from the black clouds overhead. A bad storm brewing, and no mistake. He'd have to get the animals under cover before it broke.

As he turned Wings toward the barn, he saw her. In the pasture behind the building, the lass was endeavoring to lead a prancing, resisting Charlie inside.

"Sweet Jesus!" He galloped up to the barn door, released the stallion inside, and ran to join her.

"Lass, stay away from that animal!" he yelled. "He goes mad in lightning storms! Leave him to me!" At that moment, a great chain of electricity cracked the dark clouds over the river, thunder crashed, and Charlie reared, throwing Heather up and against the fence as if she were no more than a child's doll. As she collapsed to the ground, the big horse bolted into the barn through the open door.

"Lass!" He dropped to one knee beside her, heart banging. "Lass!"

Giant drops of rain spattered onto her face, and she opened her eyes, blinked, then stared up at him.

"Doctor…" The word mirrored confusion but brought joy racing through every inch of his body. He gathered her up in his arms and, through the ensuing downpour, ran as fast as he could to the house.

Once inside, he carried her up to her room and laid her on her bed. Relieved to see that her color was returning, he started to remove her wet clothing.

"What do you think you're doing?" She tried to sit up.

"I'm getting you out of wet clothing and into a dry bed." He shoved aside her protesting hands. "You've had a great shock. You need warmth. Now lie still and remember I am a doctor."

For a moment she glared up at him, then with a sigh, began to unbutton her shirt. "Very well. But I'll undress myself while you fetch me some hot, sweet tea."

He looked at her for a few moments, long and hard. Then he burst out laughing. "Aye, nurse. Get yourself to bed and I'll fetch the tea."

Relief made his legs weak as he went back downstairs. If she'd been killed, if he'd lost her... The thought pounded around in his head until he managed to shove it aside. He couldn't bear to host it any longer.

****

Jewels' wedding day. Heather could hardly believe it. She came down the stairs slowly, careful not to let the railings catch the green silk of her gown or any of the fine lace that trimmed it. The storekeeper's wife had proven herself a skilled seamstress. It fitted perfectly. Heather had never had such a beautiful garment, and she meant to take good care of it.

She heard the doctor moving about in the kitchen and paused to draw a deep breath. What would he think when he saw her? Would all the time and care she'd taken about her toilet, arranging her hair to take best advantage of its curls, prove worth the effort? Or would he simply see her as the lass, his servant and assistant?

"Good morning, sir." She stepped into the room, her heart beating so hard she feared he might overhear. Her breath caught in her throat as he turned from pouring whiskey from a flask into a cup, incredibly handsome in a perfectly cut coat, white shirt, neatly tied silk cravat, tan breeches, and polished knee-high boots.

"Well, sir, what do you think?" Begging her fluttering heart to be easy, she rounded for his inspection, then paused, cocking her head to one side. "Shall I pass muster as a witness at your brother's wedding and as attendant to my friend Jewels?"

For a moment he didn't reply, and she felt a sinking sensation. Though she berated herself for it, she realized she wanted his approval, maybe even a bit of his admiration.

"Well?" she forced herself to repeat.

"You look right...bonny." The words came out in a cracked tone she'd never heard from him before, the Highland accent heavy on his tongue. "Right bonny, indeed."

"Thank you, kind sir." She placed the bonnet trimmed to match her gown on her head and tied the ribbons beneath her chin. "May I say, you don't look too shabby, either. Now we'd best be off. But aren't you starting the celebrations a bit early?" She gestured at the flask and mug.

"Weddings are not among my favorite celebrations." He took a swig from the mug. "A little fortification is in order."

"You're the doctor." She walked up to him with what she hoped was ladylike dignity. "Now we must go. Charlie will be weary of waiting. I harnessed him before I dressed."

"There was no need." His tone softened as he looked down at her. "On a day such as this, I could have done the deed."

"Aye, I've no doubt. Still, it is my duty." She headed for the door. "Swill down the rest and get a move on. It's late."

Behind her, she heard him mutter something, a short silence, then the sound of the mug banging down on the table. *Bloody hell, why did I say that? Why did I have to come off sounding like a tavern wench?* She blinked and jutted out her chin. *You are what you are, Heather Grey, and it will take more than a fancy gown to make you anything more. Don't go getting expectations beyond your station.*

****

"Oh, Jewels, you take my breath away!" Heather gasped as she entered the captain's house. Her friend, arrayed in a gown fashioned from the bright blue silk now trimmed with layers of snowy lace, cocked her head at her and grinned. "It's not you I want to leave breathless, Bonny, although your compliment is most kind. What about my hair? Do you think the coiffure too extreme?" She touched the mass of raven curls piled artistically about her head. Interwoven into the coiffure were bits of lace that matched the trim on her dress.

"No, it's perfect. Jewels, the captain hasn't seen you, has he? My mother used to say it was bad luck for the groom to see the bride before the ceremony on the wedding day."

"No, most definitely not. Do you think I'd risk losing Jamie, perchance a silly superstition proves true? While I was preparing, he's gone to the vicar's to dress in his finery and await the bride and her entourage."

"Entourage?" Heather frowned. "But there's just myself and Dr. MacTavish."

"You're the very best entourage I could wish for." She bent forward and planted a kiss on Heather's cheek. "Now it's nearly time. We must go. I trust you have that elegant conveyance you use as a farm wagon waiting?"

Laughing, the pair went outside to where William waited, holding Charlie's bridle. On seeing them, he stepped smartly to assist the bride and her attendant.

"You are a beautiful sight, Lady Julia," he surprised Heather by saying to her friend as he swept her a deep bow. "My brother is one lucky man."

"I consider myself a lucky woman, Doctor." She smiled at him. "Captain James MacTavish is the man I've dreamed of marrying. And, if you please, my name is plain Jewels, soon to be Jewels MacTavish, your sister-in-law."

"Then let's not waste any time." He caught her about the slim waist and hoisted her up onto the wagon seat. "I'm sure my brother is champing at the bit. Lass?" He turned to Heather, caught her up in his arms, and swung her into the cargo space behind Jewels. "You'll have to stand and hold tight up there. It's not fit to sit in, especially in your finery, and there's only room for two on the seat."

"Never fear, Doctor. It won't be the first bumpy drive I've had."

"I little doubt it." He climbed onto the seat beside the bride and turned the horse toward the road. "Get along there, Charlie. We mustn't keep the captain waiting any longer."

****

The vicar and his wife met them at the door of the small church.

"Good morning, William." The Reverend Malcolm Scott greeted the wagon's driver with a familiarity and alacrity that surprised Heather. "You've brought the bride just in time. The groom has been pacing with such vehemence I feared he'd wear the floor through."

"I can well imagine." The doctor jumped to the ground and reached up to swing Julia down to join him, then Heather.

"William, it is so very good to see you again." The vicar's wife came down the steps to touch his sleeve and then, to Heather's astonishment, to gather him gently into her arms. "You must come by to visit, my dear. We would enjoy your company."

"I will try, Mrs. Scott, but the needs of my patients…"

"Of course. Your patients must come first. But when you have time…" She released him and stepped back, her face bearing a fond expression that puzzled Heather still more. What was his relationship to the vicar and his wife?

"Now, William, you go inside and stand up with your brother at the front of the church. Janet and I will bring the ladies directly."

"Aye, just as soon as I tie Charlie in the shade. I trust this won't be a long ceremony?"

"At the request of the groom, no, it won't."

Ten minutes later, when they entered the small village church, Julia on the vicar's arm and Heather behind beside Mrs. Scott, she caught her breath. She'd never seen an expression of first astonishment quickly followed by utter joy on any countenance such as there came over the captain's face when he saw his bride coming toward him. His jaw twitched and something suspiciously like tears brightened his eyes. It brought a catch to Heather's throat.

Will a man ever gaze at me with such blatant love

and rapture? What a precious moment!

She looked at the tall, handsome man standing beside the captain and something inside her chest lurched. Suddenly she knew she didn't want just any man to look at her as Jamie MacTavish was gazing at her friend. She wanted it to be the captain's brother.

The knowledge shocked her, sent a warm flush washing from head to toe. No. It was ridiculous. She couldn't be falling in love with him. She was a servant who washed his clothes and cooked his food and cleaned his barn. Educated men, rich men, like Doctor William MacTavish, did not fall in love with tavern wenches. She bit her lip and tried not to think about it.

The vicar was lining them up for the ceremony, and she found herself beside the doctor. Swallowing hard, she fought to ignore his nearness and focus on the words the vicar was saying, on Julia and her soon-to-be husband.

"Who gives this woman to be married to this man?" The vicar asked, and before anyone else could reply, Heather stepped forward. "As her best friend, I do," she startled the small assemblage by declaring.

"Good God, woman!" She felt a tug at her arm and saw the doctor's chagrined expression hovering over her.

"Thank you, Bonny." The bride winked at her. "I'd forgotten to attend to that part of the proceedings."

The vicar, recovering from his surprise, continued, "Captain James MacTavish, do you take this woman to be your lawful wife for better or for worse, for richer, for poorer, in sickness and health as long as you both shall live?"

"I do, aye, I most certainly do." The captain

beamed down at his bride. "And I can only hope she'll reply in like fashion."

Moments later, it was over. Heather fancied she sensed Reverend Scott's relief at the conclusion of this unorthodox ceremony and had to stifle a grin as the minister granted Jamie permission to kiss the bride.

The captain gathered her into his arms with an eagerness that crushed the silk of the gown and brought a gasp from Julia. Then they parted, both laughing.

"Congratulations, brother." William shook the captain's hand and slapped him on the back. "Now before you depart for your honeymoon, I invite you to a small celebration at the farm. Toasts must be offered to the bride."

"That's right kind of you, Will." Jamie turned to him, grinning.

"I'm afraid I've no better means of transport than my wagon." William said. "But there's ample room for you and your good wife, Reverend."

"Thank you, William, but we'll take our own. It will save your driving us home later." Reverend Scott smiled.

"As for us," Jamie took his bride by the hand and drew her toward the door. "I've purchased a new conveyance, one that will take us to your farm in style. Come and see."

He led the group outside and around to the back of the church, where Jamie's gelding stood harnessed to a buggy.

"The first of its kind in the valley." Jamie stood back proudly. "I had it specially made stronger than its counterparts in the Old Country, to withstand our rough roads. Now, come." He snatched Julia up in his arms, whirled her into the seat, jumped up beside her, and swung the horse toward the road.

"We'll just be taking a few minutes respite at our house," he called back over his shoulder. "We'll be along directly."

And then they were gone, Jamie urging the horse to a gallop and Julia laughing.

"You must forgive my brother, Reverend." William turned to the clergyman and his wife. "He is a tad anxious to be alone with his bride, and not always the most subtle about his intentions."

"The man's in love." Reverend smiled fondly at his wife who blushed and looked down at her hands. "I'd expect no less. I remember…"

"Malcolm." His wife's admonition was so quick and sharp, so out of character with the woman Heather had observed during the past hour it startled her. What had she feared her husband was about to say that had brought such an abrupt response?

"I was simply going to remark that I remembered our wedding day, my sweet. Remember it as if it were yesterday."

At his response, Mrs. Scott appeared to relax. She even managed to smile as she took his arm.

"I'll go and roust Charlie out of his dreams." William turned away and headed to where the Clydesdale stood dozing in the shade of a huge maple.

Was it her imagination or had the doctor, too, appeared relieved by the source of the minister's memories? Heather could only wonder, as she followed him toward his horse and wagon.

****

As they drove back toward the farm in the warmth

of the afternoon, Heather glanced at the silent man beside her and decided to venture a few of the questions that had been plaguing her curiosity.

"You seem to know the Scotts very well. Have you been friends for a long time?"

"I was married to their daughter." The wagon jounced over a large tree root, and Heather clutched at the seat, her heart jolting with it. "She died."

Married. The man had been married. Good Lord, this certainly wasn't any of the responses she'd thought possible. *And to the Scotts' daughter.* Her gaze stayed riveted on him, but his attention appeared focused on the road ahead, his features firm as granite.

She turned to follow his gaze and stare at the trail ahead. Suddenly so much became clear. He'd bought that land with the beautiful view of the river and built that excellently equipped farm for the vicar's daughter. The room at the top of the stairs had been theirs. Now the innuendoes the Reverend had made about being in love and remembering made sense. Doctor William MacTavish had been married to a woman he'd loved passionately, an absolutely respectable woman, a vicar's daughter. He'd never consider a tavern wench to take her place. Her heart plummeted. Dead women and their memories were perfect.

****

"What is all this?" Heather half rose from her seat as they turned into the lane to the farm.

The yard near the barn was filled with wagons, the pasture alive with a number of unfamiliar horses.

"Since you were so dead set on giving my brother and his bride a proper send-off, I decided we must do it up right."

They'd reached the house. Heather could see around to the front, where tables had been set up overlooking the river and piled with food and drink. People milled about, dressed in what she suspected was their best clothing. When they saw William, a cheer went up.

"Where's the happy couple, Will?" Arthur Weatherspoon came forward to greet them, grinning. "We're all set up for a party."

"They've taken a few wee moments to be alone." William swung down from the wagon and held up his hands to lift Heather to the ground. "You know my brother and women. This time it's worse. He's in love."

Guffaws of laughter went up from the men in the crowd, while some of the women demurred at such talk.

"Oh, aye." The man moved to take Charlie's bridle. "You two join the party. I'll put this fine fellow out into pasture with the rest of the horses."

****

"She dances well, Will." Jamie came to take a seat on the bench beside his brother in the warm summer night. He was watching Heather dancing a jig, to the accompaniment of a trio of fiddlers, with Jordon Fowler, son of the village shopkeeper. Laughing, they cavorted around the bonfire that had been lighted at dusk, after the remains of the huge wedding supper had been cleared away.

"Aye, that she does. And flirts with the young bucks right good, as well." William took a swig from his mug. "But then, she's a tavern wench."

"Damn you for a bastard, brother!" Jamie swung on him. "She's a fine woman. You'd do well to put your petty prejudices aside and look at her as such. It's high time you thought of marrying again."

"I married once, and that's enough."

The dance ended, but, as the brothers watched, twenty-year-old Jordon Fowler caught Heather by a hand and led her over to where his parents sat watching. The faces of all three family members were bright with welcome as George stood to acknowledge the young woman.

"See? Young Jordie isn't blind to the lass's charms." Jamie shot his brother a taunting glance. "He'd make a good match for her. He's a strong, decent lad who'll be taking over his father's business one day and able to provide a secure life. This past winter he's been working in the logging camps in the bush, and he's filled out. Last summer he was a skinny young lad. Now he's got muscles and broad shoulders and has turned into a right fine-looking bit of a man. The lass could do worse. Aye, the lass could do worse."

"Dunnae try to torment me, Jamie. You'll no goad me into taking a personal interest in Mistress Heather Grey."

"Then, for God's sake, Will, give her a chance for happiness elsewhere. She's young, she's beautiful, she deserves a chance to live her life to the fullest. I know you loved Kathleen. I can only imagine how it hurt when she and the babe died. But it's been years. It's time you got on with your life. Heather Grey is just the woman to help you do it."

"Because you found her, because you chose her for me?" He swilled the last of his whiskey, set aside his mug, and stood. "Verrae well, if it's courting you want from me, watch this."

He strode over to the fiddlers as they came to the

end of their tune and said something. At first they looked a bit apprehensive, then nodded and put bows to strings.

The strains of the new and sensuous kind of music called a waltz wafted out into the summer's night as Doctor William MacTavish walked over to the Fowler group, grasped a surprised Heather by the hand, excused them to the surprised family, and swung her out beside the fire. Within seconds they were whirling around the fire, the tall, handsome, elegantly dressed man and the pretty young woman in the emerald green gown making such an eye-catching couple the wedding guests moved aside to watch and admire. As Will led her firmly and confidently through dance steps she'd never before attempted, Jamie let out a war whoop and seized his bride to join them.

For a time their neighbors and friends were content to watch, unfamiliar with this new form of dancing. Then, couple by couple, they joined in.

Sparks from the fire flashed up into the soft black velvet of the summer night as dancers dipped and turned to the strains of the fiddles. And Doctor William MacTavish found himself looking down into the sparkling eyes of a woman he was determined not to love.

****

"It's been quite a day." Heather sat on a bench overlooking the river and stretched her legs out in front of her. The debris of the party littered tables and grounds down to the river. The guests had departed, promising to return on the morrow to help clean up.

"Aye." William sat down beside her. "A fitting send-off for a man who's finally been cured of his wenching and gambling, all in one fell swoop."

"You sound confident." She turned to face him.

"Aye, well, I know a thing or two about women, and if anyone can tame my brother, it's that friend of yours. She's more than a handful, I'd say."

"Oh, aye." She cocked her head to one side and shot him an impudent glance. "And just how do you rate me...in your expert opinion? Am I handful, as well?"

He could stand no more. He stood, pulled her to her feet, and crushed her into his arms to kiss her long and hard. Then he moved back to look down into those emerald orbs to gauge her reaction. What he saw there made him suck in his breath. He caught her up into his arms and headed inside.

In his room, he let her feet fall to the floor.

"Well." His word was a soft breath in the shadowy darkness.

"Well, indeed." She slipped her arms up and around his neck. "Very well indeed, Doctor."

****

He awoke to a wonderful sensation he hadn't enjoyed in years...that of a warm, curvaceous female body pressed against him. Kathleen. Her name billowed across his senses. But the curls on the pillow beside him were golden brown, not yellow. Remembrance broke over him like a dash of ice water. *Dear God, what have I done!*

Easing himself away from her, he slid from the bed. He was as naked as she. *Sweet Jesus, what have I done!* Cursing himself, he began a frantic effort to gather up his clothing from the floor in the grey morning light struggling into the room. Rain hammered at the roof. He looked back at her sleeping so innocently, it appeared, and branded himself a despicable cur. She wasn't his wife, he didn't plan to make her his wife, yet he'd defiled her without a second thought of what it would mean to her life, her future.

Naked and filled with self-loathing, he headed downstairs. Leaving the dog Midnight shut in the kitchen, he strode to the river and dove into the water as lightning cracked the sky and thunder rolled.

He swam under the angry sky until exhaustion began to haunt his limbs. Turning back, he struggled to shore to pull on the clothing he'd left there, now drenched in the downpour. The exercise hadn't helped the mixture of miserable feeling roiling in his gut. He needed to talk to someone…someone he could trust and who would understand.

****

"William?" Her voice startled him as he crouched at the hearth, checking the teapot, water from his clothing making a puddle about his feet.

He stood and turned to face her.

She wore one of his shirts wrapped around her nakedness. It hung to her knees. In the pause that followed her single word, he felt his chest constrict. So beautiful. He wanted to sweep her into his arms and carry her back upstairs to bed.

A bolt of lightning brightened the room for an instant, and thunder boomed like cannon. Was this the Almighty's way of reminding him not to repeat his transgressions of the night?

"William?" she asked again, her expression changing from expectation to one so blank he couldn't read it. "Or is it back to Dr. MacTavish this morning?"

"I…I don't know." He hated the dithering words that he heard himself voice. In another bolt of lightning he saw the hurt they sent into her expression. A knifelike pain hit his chest.

For a few moments they stood looking at each other. Then she turned back toward the stairs.

"In that case, I'd best dress and start breakfast. I'd be grateful if you put another log on the fire, Doctor."

No tears, no recriminations. What manner of woman was she? A tavern wench. He tried to use the description to harden his heart. Yes, a tavern wench. To such women, a night in bed with a man meant little…even, apparently if it was the first time. Next week, next month, she'd find another, and that would be that. As casual as one of the affairs he'd so often chastised his brother for indulging in, as he himself had, before he'd met Kathleen.

She came to your bed a virgin, a voice in his head and heart reminded him. *Hardly the whore you'd branded her, yet you had no qualms about taking her, taking her as fully and enjoyably as you took women in bawdy houses during the war.*

As he reached for a log, another sharp pain shot across his chest. Was he having a heart attack? No, definitely not. He was fit as a fiddle. Just a hunger pang. He hadn't eaten anything at the wedding party the previous evening, being too involved with guests and in watching Heather cavort about with Jordon Fowler. Curse the lad! He'd made him stupidly jealous, stupidly possessive of what he thought was rightfully his. *Argh!* He had to put it all behind him. He'd made a mistake, and that was that. A bowl of hot porridge and he'd be right as rain.

Thunder rolled into the kitchen. Fitting. A damn good storm would wash everything away.

****

"I'm coming, I'm coming!" His brother's annoyed words sounded from behind the barred door of his house as William pounded on it. Emotions that wrenched at his gut like a life-threatening illness roiled within him.

"Sweet Jesus, Will!" Jamie pulled open the door, clad only in trousers, chest and feet bare, his hair a tangle of curls. "What do you want? It's my wedding night, man."

"Jamie, I have to talk to you." Rain trickled down his face and neck, his shirt clung to his body as he faced his brother. "And it's morning, if you haven't noticed."

Jamie hesitated, then nodded. "I reckon it can be no small matter to send you here in this weather without either hat or coat. Come in."

"Jamie, dearest, who is it? Please tell them to go away and come back to bed." Julia's soft voice from the bedroom made her husband turn toward it.

"In a minute, darlin'. It's Will." He faced his brother. "Talk."

"Not here. Down at the barn."

"Bloody Hell, Will, this had better be life-and-death important." Jamie bent to pull on a pair of boots and grabbed a jacket and hat before he ducked outside, shutting the door behind him. Together they made a dash through the storm to the stable.

Wings, wet and saddled, whickered a soft greeting as the two men he knew dashed inside and closed the door on the inhospitable morning.

"Talk." Jamie pulled off his hat and slapped it

against his leg, sending beads of moisture flying.

"I slept with the lass," he blurted, his eyes searching his brother's face in the dimness of the storm-surrounded barn for a reaction.

"Well, then, good, excellent." Jamie reached out to slap him on the back. "Now I hope you've done the honorable thing and asked her to marry you straightaway. She's a fine young woman and deserves no less."

"I can't." William turned and walked deeper into the darkness of the stable.

"Why ever not? Neither of you is married. I can see no impediment…"

"Damn it, Jamie, you found her in a tavern! She's a tavern wench!"

"Not in the sense you mean. She worked for her brother. I saw only a woman playing hostess to a group of people far beneath her both in mind and spirit. And as for Jordie Fowler chasing after her, well, she is one of the few unwed women of marriageable age in this valley, and a beautiful one, at that. It's only natural for men to flock after her. And how did you find her? Were you her first?"

"Aye. Still…"

"Then all the more reason for you to do the right thing and do it as soon as possible. I've not the patience to discuss your foolish prejudices any further. There's an eager young bride awaiting me, and I'm finding your arguments against the lass ridiculous. Never mind asking my opinion. Let your heart tell you what is right."

"Jamie, she pleasured me, pleasured me as could only a woman with such knowledge of men as is not right for her to possess." He stopped the captain with a hand on his arm as he turned to leave. "How could she know of such things and still be a virgin?"

"Will, she's spent her life, the latest years of it at least, in company of a bastard of a brother and his barfly companions. Do you not think she might have overheard a great deal of their raucous talk?"

"But how can I ask her to take Kathleen's place, to be mistress of Kathleen's house? A woman of her upbringing, her background?"

"Look, Will, I know you worshipped Kathleen." Jamie MacTavish's voice softened as he put a hand on his brother's shoulder. "She was a beautiful woman with a snow-white background and reputation. But she was delicate, ill-suited to the way of life you're determined to live. You need someone like the lass…strong and clever and willing to partner you in all things. Someone who can love you with every ounce of body and soul. And dunnae tell me you didnae enjoy your night." He quirked a knowing grin at the doctor. "You've the look of a man who's finally unwound after months of being tight as a steel trap. Go back to her, ask her to marry you, and take her back to that nice warm bed as you're longing to."

He slapped his hat back onto his head, turned, and dashed back out into the storm.

Chapter 12

"Your breakfast is ready." She didn't avert her attention from the hearth she was kneeling in front of, stirring a pot of porridge, as he stepped into the kitchen. She was once again dressed in her lad's attire.

"Good. I'll get out of these wet things and be down directly."

He's treating me like a servant, like someone who's little more than an acquaintance. Heather stood and looked at the doorway through which he'd vanished. *Perhaps he'll even begin to treat me as a whore, something to use at his pleasure.*

They ate their breakfast in silence, the rain drumming hard against the windows, the wind picking up to a howling gale. *Somewhere upriver, Jewels and her new husband are no doubt passing the day making love, while I sit here, judged and condemned by the man I love.*

"You left early this morning." She could stand the tension between them no longer. She had to know what he was thinking, where he'd gone.

"Aye. I went to see my brother."

"You went to visit Captain MacTavish on the morning after his wedding?"

Her tone reflected her surprise.

"Aye."

"Didn't you think that perhaps he and his bride might not welcome company at such a time?"

"I had an important matter to discuss with him."

"Oh."

"I think you might well be able to guess what that might have been."

"I hope not." She looked over at him, a hot flush rising up her cheeks. "I hope you have more discretion than to discuss what transpired between us in the night with Captain MacTavish."

"Well, I don't." He got to his feet, shoving the chair back with a loud scraping. "And I hardly think you should be looking so outraged. It's not as if you were an innocent girl. You grew up in a tavern."

"So that gives you the right to take me to your bed, then cast me aside and rush off to give the details to your brother?"

"I'm a man who's been celibate far too long, who was once married and enjoyed the company of a woman in his bed each night..."

"Oh, and that excuses you, does it?" Her chair flew back, upsetting as she leaped to her feet. "A man is allowed to satisfy his needs, to take comfort and enjoyment where he may, but a woman who's been forced to work under deplorable conditions is not good enough for the high and mighty doctor!"

She headed out the door, out into the bucketing rain and wind. She'd try to lose some of her hurt and anger in the barn work.

****

"William, I was coming to see you." The Reverend Scott halted his shambling grey mare as the doctor rode up to meet his wagon on the road to the village.

"Good morning to you, Reverend." William touched his hat brim. "A fine morning after that deluge yesterday, is it not? Excellent growing weather."

"Indeed." The Reverend removed his shabby black hat to mop his brow with a handkerchief. "And promising to be a warm one. Will, might we step down and have a word?"

"Oh, aye." William dismounted. "Not a dying parishioner, I hope." He took both horses' bridles and led them to the side of the road.

"No, no." The minister got down stiffly from his wagon seat as William tied up the pair. "It's...ah...a rather delicate matter. Perhaps we might walk down to the river while we chat."

"Of course." With a feeling that he wasn't going to like what he was about to hear, William joined the clergyman on a path that led down the gentle slope through the trees.

"William, your brother has been to see me. He mentioned your involvement with that dear girl who works with you."

"Ah, sweet Jesus!" William stopped short and threw up his hands. "Excuse me, Reverend, but the man had no right to go discussing such matters with you."

"Oh, but I believe you're wrong, William." Squinting in the shaft of sunlight that broke through the trees into his face, the little clergyman looked up at the doctor. "Since it involves a matter of morals, it is my province."

"So are you about to seek a confession and a bid for forgiveness?" William tried to keep the annoyance and exasperation from his tone—and failed. "Because I'll give you both, but that's as far as I'll go. I won't discuss the lass. I owe her that much respect."

"It's neither." Reverend Scott held his ground. "I simply want to reinforce what your brother told me he already advised, that you marry the girl if you have feelings for her. And if you have not, you must vow never to let such a thing happen again. Do you have feelings for her, William?"

William sank down on the stump of what had once been a mighty white pine. "I dunnae know what I feel, anymore. Reverend, she's a tavern girl. She's grown up under rough conditions. She—"

"And you feel you cannot marry such a woman?"

"God, is there nothing my big-mouthed brother did not tell you?" Lowering his head, William shook it in dismay.

"He had to tell me the entire story for it to make sense."

The Reverend waited while William struggled to find an appropriate response. Only the chirping of birds broke the silence of the forest brightened with beams of sunlight penetrating its canopy.

"But there's still Kathleen..." When he finally looked up at Malcolm Scott, confusion mixed with hope roiled in his gut.

"Kathleen and your son are in heaven, my dear boy." The Reverend Scott placed a hand on William's shoulder, tears in his eyes. "And neither of them would want you to spend the rest of your life alone. This girl you call the lass, she's a good woman, a kind, hard-working woman, from your brother's account as well as from others who've come to know her. She's much more suited to your way of life than Kathleen ever was."

"How can you say such a thing? Kathleen was your daughter."

"I'm not denying she was a beautiful young woman who loved you with all her heart. But she was delicate, and you knew that when you married her. As ethereal as an angel, entirely ill fitted for the rigors of life as a backwoods doctor's helpmate."

"You're saying I cast her into a life that was too harsh, that probably killed her." William had to fight to keep his voice from breaking over the words.

"No, no, my boy. She wanted to marry you, to be with you, more than anything in this world. She would have been miserable without you. You made her happy in the days you were privileged to share. You must accept them as precious memories and move on."

"But this girl's past..."

"Ask her about it...calmly and fairly. Let her explain. And if, afterwards, you find you cannot accept her, then, as I've said, leave her free to find someone who can. She's young and deserves to have happiness in a marriage with a man with whom she can genuinely share her life."

****

He rode back to his farm in the sunshine of late morning, his mind roiling with thoughts of the young woman he called the lass and what he was to do about her. She seemed his perfect helpmate in every way, and in bed she'd more than proven she could satisfy him sexually. She'd even somehow managed to make her way into his feelings, his very soul, with her strength and kindness and thoughtfulness. What was he to do?

As he turned off the road and down the lane to his house, he saw Jamie's wedding buggy, with a nice little bay mare attached, tied up at the hitching post by his kitchen door.

"Argh!" Annoyance rubbed over his thoughts. *Two days married, and my brother has nothing better to do than come visiting. No doubt he'll be dropping hints as to what I should do about the lass.*

His initial impression was thrown asunder as the lass stepped from the door. She wore the blue dress, from which she'd managed to scrub away the bloodstains, and was followed by Jordan Fowler, looking young and virile and handsome in white shirt and well fitted tan trousers and black boots.

"Doctor." Her face bright with a wide smile, she looked up at him as he stopped beside them. "I'm glad you're back. Jordon has invited me on a buggy ride and picnic. Your brother has kindly offered to lend him his conveyance while he and his bride are off on a brief trip to Halifax before they leave for the Caribbean, and Jordon's mother has prepared a lovely feast for us. You'll find your meal on the table and tea on the hob. I'm trusting you'll give me leave for an hour or so?" She canted him a cat-in-the-cream smile and stuck the hat she'd worn for the wedding on her head.

"Ya cannae go wearin' that thing on a buggy ride." Where did that inane remark come from, when there was so much more he was burning to say? "It's not fitting."

"Well, it must be." She let Jordan help her into the buggy. "I've no other hat, and a lady cannot allow herself to become bronzed and freckled by the sun. Good day to you, Doctor. I'll be back shortly. Let's go, Mr. Fowler. I can't wait to see what delights you have in store."

"I'll take good care of her, sir, never fear." The tall, good-looking young man addressed him, grey eyes sincere and honest. "I'll have her back directly."

"You're damn right you will." *Sir, indeed. How old does this young bugger think I am?* "She has duties, and I'll not be taking them over so she can go gallivanting for half a day."

"Of course, sir. Thank you, sir." He swung up into the seat beside the lass with a young man's strength and suppleness.

Was I ever that young and agile? He stopped his thoughts from further pursuing the abilities of twenty-year-old men. The saucy look she cast back at him, as the contentedly grinning young man turned the horse about and urged it to a trot up the lane, made his body pound with outrage. Bold, shameless wench! Taking it for granted she could have leave to go cavorting with that young whippersnapper, a mere boy.

But looking at Jordan Fowler's broad shoulders as the pair drove up the lane, he knew the truth. Jordan Fowler was a man, with a man's wishes and desires.

He went into the house to find a meal neatly laid out for him on the table and tea steeping in the pot. Muttering his discontent, he took the drink to the table and heard an answering murmur of discontent. Midnight lay beneath the table.

"So she left you behind, too, did she, my lad? Well, no point in wasting energy over it. I trust you'll share my meal with me? I'd rather not eat alone…just now."

****

He was working in the orchard two hours later, pruning back an apple tree, when he saw the buggy turn in at the gate. Even at a distance he could see the lass's laughing face and the young man's broad grin. *What in God's name have they been up to?* With the dog at his heels, he strode toward the house as Jordan Fowler halted the horse at the kitchen door.

As the younger man jumped down and held up his hands to assist her, William noted that her dress appeared unwrinkled, and her hat atop the curls looked much as it had when the couple left the farm. A sense of relief flooded over him before he was able to brush it aside and tell himself he couldn't care less what they'd been up to.

"I've brought her back safe and sound, sir." Young Fowler turned to him and smiled. "And, Miss Grey, I'll be thanking you for a lovely time. Perhaps we can do it again sometime soon."

"I'd enjoy that." She favored him with a glowing smile. "Please thank your mother for a delicious repast. She's a wonderful cook, and"—she smoothed the skirts of her gown—"a fine dressmaker."

"She'll be pleased." He smiled, then turned to nod to William. "I'll be bidding you both good day. I must be getting the buggy back to the captain's stable."

William stood beside her, watching as the young lad climbed back aboard and drove off. At the road, he waved back to her, and she returned the gesture with an alacrity that made the doctor grind his teeth.

"I'll change into my working clothes and get down to the barn," she said, the words cold, her smile dissolving, as she turned to face him. "I hope your meal proved satisfactory, Doctor."

****

He rode into the village early the next morning. He had a mind to see if George Fowler had any of his wife's homemade candy. It might sweeten the lass's disposition when he next tried to talk to her. Since that buggy ride with young Fowler, she'd been aloof and impersonal. Now he had to talk to her, tell her about his past, his reluctance to engage in another relationship, how he felt about her. Otherwise, God only knew what she might agree to, with that young lad's urging.

"'Mornin', Will." George Fowler grinned a welcome from behind the counter. "Just the man I wanted to see. I'd like a private word with you."

"Certainly, George." He knew all about these private words, generally something a man was embarrassed to speak about.

"Come into my office." The merchant led the way to the rear of the store and opened a plank door.

Once they were inside with George seated behind the rough pine table that served as his desk, Will on a stool in front, the man wet his lips and looked down at his hands.

"This is a delicate matter, Will."

"George, I've been a doctor for a goodly number of years. There are few 'delicate' matters I haven't been privy to." He quirked a grin.

"It's like this, Will." The man looked up to meet his gaze. "My boy Jordon has taken a shine to young Heather. As you know, he's already invited her on a picnic in your brother's buggy. Jordie has asked me to speak for him in getting your permission to court her."

"Court her?" William couldn't have been more astonished if a white crow had fluttered into the room. "Court the lass?"

"Aye, I know it must come as a surprise to you, Will, but the lad is twenty now, and he has a decent future—he'll one day inherit this store. He's hardworking and a teetotaler, never touched a drop in his life. Furthermore, he's a decent-looking young fellow who'd be kind and loyal to a woman. After he danced with her at the wedding party, he was smitten. Well, maybe 'smitten' isn't a strong enough word. 'Wild about her' would better describe it. All he talks about is Heather Grey and how wonderful she is. So what do you say? Will you give your permission as her guardian for my boy to call on her?"

"Guardian? Good God, man." William was on his feet, his entire body hot with outrage. "How old do you think I am? Furthermore, the lass is not about to entertain any ideas of marriage. She came to this country to be my assistant, not run off with the first randy lad who takes a fancy to her. No, I'll not give my permission. You tell your son to stay well away from her or he'll have my boot up his backside."

"Will, Will, there's no need to get hostile." The storekeeper stood to face him. "I only asked to please the boy. I had no idea you had designs on her yourself. I never thought…"

"Designs, is that what you call it? Designs?" Will's rage spiked. "She's a hard-working, decent young woman for whom I have all the respect in the world. Now if you'll excuse me, I'll be getting back to my farm."

As the two men emerged from the shopkeeper's office, a man entered the store. Big and burly, with a corpulent red face, he strode across the room to lean on the counter with large, beefy hands, red hairs covering their backs.

"What can I do for you, sir?" George Fowler went

behind the counter as Will headed for the door.

"I'm looking for two women." The man spoke, his beady, bearlike glance roaming about the premises. "Two women with a big black mutt of a dog. They're wanted back in England, one of them to be charged with murder, the other the daughter of a high and mighty milord with a sizeable reward for her return."

Sweet Jesus! Will froze at the door and listened. *George, think, think. And by all that's holy, keep a wise counsel.*

"Two women?" George Fowler's words, after a slight pause, took on a jesting tone. "You must be new in this country, sir, or you'd realize it's difficult enough to find even one woman."

"Then you've not seen such a pair? They embarked from England aboard a ship named the *Highland Lass*, bound for this river valley, in early April."

"Aye, the *Highland Lass* did stop here, but she's sailed again. She brought me a supply of goods for my store, but no women or dogs."

"Then Captain James MacTavish must have taken them further afield. Do you know where the vessel was headed?"

"Halifax, I do believe. There's a ship about to cast off for that destination at the wharf this very day. If you hurry, you can catch her."

"Thank ye, storekeeper." The big man turned and strode out the door.

"God in heaven, Will." George Fowler pulled a large white handkerchief from his pocket and wiped his perspiring face. "You never told me Heather was wanted for murder and her friend a lord's daughter."

"I saw no reason to, George. Both have put their

pasts behind them. After all, didn't we all leave the old country for reasons that would not always square with the law?" He knew George had been a rebel in the Highlands as a young lad, that there'd never be any safe going back for him.

"Oh, aye." The shopkeeper shook his head and looked down at his hands, fingers splayed out on the counter. "But murder?"

"Untrue, trust me. Think no more about it." Will headed for the door. "And thank you, George. I'll be owing you all the medical care you and your family might be needing for several years to come."

****

"I've got something to talk to you about." He paused inside the barn door.

"Yes?" She paused in forking manure from her mare's stall.

"Put that thing down and come out here." He advanced into the shadows of the stable, out of the slanting rays of the afternoon sun.

"Aye, sir." She leaned the fork against the wall and advanced into the walkway to face him squarely. "Is it something about my work? Something displeases you?"

Damn her, she isn't about to make this easy, acting as if nothing has happened between us, as if we're still master and servant.

"It's about what occurred between us on the night of my brother's wedding, and your behavior with the young Fowler lad." Five feet apart, they faced each other as she came to a stop and placed her hands on her hips.

Bold, brazen hussy. Not so much as a batted eyelid or a blush. He tried to build up his resentment for the

222

confrontation ahead.

"Ah." She cocked her head to one side. "Is it an apology you'll be giving for running off without so much as a 'thank you, mistress' or a request for a repeat performance? Or are you about to deny me the right to go for buggy drives with Jordon?"

"Dear God, woman, have you no shame, have you no…?"

"Shame for acting as my heart dictated, no."

Her words ambushed him. *Sweet Jesus, how to proceed...* He fought for a response and blurted out what he'd planned to introduce carefully later, much later, in their conversation.

"As your heart dictated? And what would a lass such as you know about hearts? A girl raised in a tavern?"

"Ah, so that's the reason for your bolting like a spring colt." She turned away, took up her fork, and returned to the stall. "The former privateer, the previously married man, cannot countenance a woman who has known something of the world."

"Damn you!" In two long strides he was beside her in the stall, making her mare flinch and cavort back from the couple as he grabbed her by an arm. "Don't you dare go comparing my life with yours. A man…"

"'Tis acceptable for a man to have been a buccaneer, to have laid with all manner of whores, but a *respectable* woman must not even have knowledge of such matters." She glared up at him. "A *respectable* woman must be pure in both mind and body. I shall not live to see it, but I sincerely hope that someday it will not be the case. It's too bloody unfair."

She flung the fork aside, shoved past him, and

marched out of the barn.

"Argh!" He watched her go, then strode into Wings' stall. "Come along, laddie. We're going to the village and a fresh tankard of ale."

****

A hush fell over the tavern. Raising his tankard to take another drink, Doctor William MacTavish paused and turned to see its cause. He choked as he saw his sister-in-law, dressed in trousers, knee-high boots, shirt, and leather jerkin striding across the room toward him. Her face was dark as a thundercloud.

"I wish to speak to you, Doctor." She halted at his table, feet planted firmly apart, hands on shapely hips. "In private."

"I thought you and my brother were gone to Halifax."

"We have returned, several hours ago. I'll be awaiting you at our house." She swung about and strode back out of the room amid the blank stares of an astonished group of men.

"Fireball, what, Will?" One of them finally broke the silence, adding a chuckle. "Jamie has met his match in that one."

"I believe he may have." William polished off his ale and stood. "He just may have."

As he followed her from the tavern, he overheard someone snort. "That pair the captain brought from England have those MacTavish brothers trotting along behind them like a pair of puppies."

****

"Well, and just what is so all-fired important that you saw fit to drag me away from the first moments of rest I've had all day?" William entered the neat little house where a servant girl was busily sweeping the hearth. Galled by the parting remark in the tavern, he had no patience for whatever it was Jewels MacTavish had to say.

"Sit down." She indicated a place at the table. "Rose, you might like to take a few minutes' rest outdoors. You've done a fine job."

"Thank you, mistress." Glancing at the doctor, she bobbed a curtsey and went out.

"She probably thinks I wish to consult you about a pregnancy begun before the wedding." Julia went to the sideboard and took down a bottle of Jamie's whiskey. "As my darling husband would say, fancy a wee dram?" She held it up to him.

"From the tone of your voice and your expression, I think I will be needing it. Where's Jamie?"

"My husband is overseeing the loading of his ship. We're to sail again shortly, this time for the Caribbean. Therefore, this might well be the last opportunity I'll get to have a word with you for some time."

"Oh, aye." He accepted the mug and watched as she poured a smaller measure into another.

She took a sip, seated herself opposite him, and drew a deep breath.

"Bonny would have my head if she knew I was talking to you." She looked him squarely into the eyes. "But it's necessary...for both your sakes. During our excursion to Halifax Jamie has told me of your aversion to my dear friend, and your reason."

"Ah, sweet Jesus!" He leaped to his feet, mug in hand, and strode across the room to stare out a window. "Is there not a single person in this valley who does not know?"

"Jamie told only those whom he thought could help repair the situation. Like myself, he believes it a shame for two people to waste their lives because of a stupid prejudice on the part of one."

"And I suppose you're about to enlighten me." He turned back to her.

"Yes, I am." She took another drink from her mug, this time a larger one that made her grimace.

"I trust it's quite a tale, seeing as how you have to shore up your courage with drink before you can proceed."

"It is. It's the truth about Bonny's past."

"Sweet Jesus, woman! Is there no topic you feel uncomfortable discussing?"

"Very few. I'm not a shy woman, as you may have observed. However, I would never discuss my best friend's intimate life details unless I thought it absolutely necessary to her future happiness…and yours, Doctor." She took another drink from her mug, drew a deep breath, then continued. "It's true Bonny has lived most of her life in a tavern, that she may know what excites and pleases men from being exposed to indecorous talk. But that in no way renders her unsuitable to make you an excellent wife. You might view her as a tavern wench, but she's no whore…as I'm sure you discovered when you decided to take her to your bed. I can only imagine that you were sufficiently gentle and caring to make her trust you and be dedicated to pleasing you in the ways she'd heard described most of her life."

"Bloody hell, woman!" The words were a bellow. "You know only half the facts, and yet there you stand in judgment on my relationship with the lass! I've been married, and my wife died having our child while I was off tending another patient. Kathleen was a saint, a beautiful, pure-as-the-driven-snow saint. I let her down. How can I put another woman in her place, in the home I built for Kathy?"

"Ah, yes, Kathleen." Jewels narrowed her eyes and gave him the most penetrating stare he'd ever experienced. "My husband has described her as an ethereally beautiful woman, the perfect picture of virginity and respectability. But he's also told me she was delicate, like the bloom on a rose, fragile, not suited to life as wife to a wilderness doctor and farmer, or perhaps even to childbearing. William…" She moved to put a hand gently on his tense arm. "You have to move on. In Bonny you've found a mate, a partner such as Jamie has found in me. Don't let a stupid prejudice ruin your chance at happiness, at a life fulfilled. Be wise. The decision is yours."

Silence. Her words made sense, but still… *Dear God, give me a sign. Tell me it's time to move on.*

When he became able to voice a response, the words came out harsh and prosaic. Words he hadn't intended to say, words the confusion caused by his sister-in-law's reasonable argument had elicited.

"Aye, that it is, Mrs. MacTavish. And I'll be making it on my own, thank you very much. Now there's something you must know. A man arrived seeking a lady and a tavern girl travelling with a big black dog. He was big and burly and red-haired, with a bushy beard."

"Dear God!" For the first time since he'd known her, William saw Jewels MacTavish staggered by a statement. She sank onto a chair at the table, her drink clutched in her hand. "Where is Liam Jones now?"

"At George Fowler's direction, he caught a ship bound for Halifax, where he's been led to believe you and the lass disembarked. He'll be back once he finds out he's been sent on a wild goose chase. But you gave him a name. How is it you recognize the man?"

"He's the man who won Bonny in a card game and is, in all probability, the man who killed her brother."

"Hell and high water!"

"Well, thanks to Mr. Fowler, we're safe for a while." Julia regained her control. "And since Jamie and I will shortly be off to the Caribbean, I'll be out of his reach. But what about you and Bonny?" She looked up at him, eyes wide with concern. "When he comes back from Halifax, not everyone will know enough to lie like Mr. Fowler. Bonny and Midnight are a readily identifiable pair."

"Not to worry." He hoped he sounded more confident than he felt. "I did my share of fighting during the war. I'm not exactly helpless."

"Are you saying you'd fight for Bonny?" She stood, a slow grin lighting up her face.

"Aye, that I would." He struggled for a reason beyond what he guessed she was thinking. "Her mother was a Highlander. We Highlanders stick together against the English."

"Oh, aye." Casting him a smug grin, she sauntered over to the sideboard, then whirled to face him. "Well, then, go and care for her, you great fool. Guard her, keep her safe, and realize how you truly feel about her."

He slammed down his mug and strode out of the house, not certain whether he was more angry or confused. Damnation, why was everyone hell-bent on making him realize things about the lass they assumed he was too stupid to recognize on his own?

"Doctor MacTavish!" Ida Weatherspoon hailed him as he strode back toward the village so rapidly that Wings, at the end of his reins behind him, had to trot to keep pace. "Doctor, you must do something!"

"What is it, Mrs. Weatherspoon?" He tried to keep the annoyance out of his voice, but he'd had about all the interference he could handle for one day. "Arthur got the trots again?"

"No, no!" She caught him by the arm. "This is very serious. I stopped by Hannah Rob's hovel on my way to the village—I do on occasion, to see how that poor girl of hers is faring—and found the child lying among the bunch of dirty rags that serves as a bed. She was gasping for breath. That witch of a mother is once again feeding her field mice fried in butter as a cure! I tried to stop her, to make her listen to reason, to let me fetch you, but she took up a stick and chased me from the shack. In spite of her threats of what will happen to me and my family if I interfere further, I wouldn't be doing my Christian duty unless I informed you."

"She'll kill that child yet." Will mounted in a single, fluid gesture. "Thank you for coming to me, Mrs. Weatherspoon. You may have saved that girl's life."

"God speed, Doctor." The woman waved as he rode off.

Ten minutes later he dismounted in front of the canted log shack deep in the bush that served as Hannah Rob's home.

"Hannah," he called, dismounting and beginning to untie his medical bag from behind his saddle. "Hannah, it's Doctor MacTavish."

The woman ducked out of the small, crooked doorway and glared at him, a heavy stick clutched in her bony hand.

"I don't need the help of anyone who uses the cures of savages." She advanced toward him, wielding the weapon. "My daughter and I are doing very well. Now get away."

"No." He pulled his bag from the horse and headed past her into the hovel. "I cannot allow another human being to suffer when I might possibly ease her pain."

He'd barely gotten inside the door, had just focused his eyes in the gloom to see the gaunt figure lying on the bed of rags, when he was struck from behind. Pain danced in wild colors about him, and he knew no more.

****

"I'm afraid I've put the doctor in danger." Ida Weatherspoon looked down at Heather from the seat of her wagon, her sunburned face crinkled into lines of concern. "I tried to find his brother to get him to follow him, but I couldn't. So I thought I'd tell you on my way home and see if you think there's any need to worry."

"What are you talking about?" A rush of fear caught at Heather.

"I told him Hannah Rob's daughter is very ill. I'd stopped in on my way to the village to see if I could help, but that crazy woman drove me away. The doctor headed for her shack."

"Oh." Heather felt a surge of relief. Doctor William MacTavish could handle one angry old woman. After all, he'd been a privateer. "I'm sure he'll manage, Mrs. Weatherspoon, but I thank you for your concern and stopping by to advise me."

"Well, if you're certain." Frowning, the woman gathered up the reins of her team. "But she is quite mad, you know. I wouldn't put anything past her. She protects that daughter of hers like a wildcat. Go along there, Brownie, move yourself, Lou." She urged the horses forward and turned back toward the road. "Good day to you, miss."

"Good day to you, Mrs. Weatherspoon. And again, thank you."

Heather started back into the house, but the woman's words had made her uneasy. She'd met Hannah Rob, heard her violent curses on anyone she perceived as a threat to her daughter.

Quickening her steps, she crossed the kitchen, then dashed up the stairs to her room to change into her trousers, shirt, and boots.

"Midnight, you're to stay here to guard the place," she called to the dog as she ran to the barn to get her horse.

****

She smelled smoke as she rode down the narrow, muddy trail toward Hannah Rob's cabin. Its acrid scent was more than that created by a mere cooking fire.

"Hah!" she urged her mare forward at a full gallop, but before she reached the clearing from which the billowing cloud emanated, the animal slid to a halt, snorting and struggling to turn back.

"I don't have time for your antics." Heather leaped to the ground, looped her mount's reins to a tree limb, and ran toward the source of the burning. Bursting into the clearing, she saw Wings tied to a tree but frantically trying to free himself, while the cabin in the clearing's centre erupted in flames.

"William!" she screamed, racing toward the door hanging open on a single hinge. The heat nearly drove her back, but she managed to look inside. The doctor lay face down beside a ragged bed on which a girl she recognized as Hannah's daughter lay staring blankly upward.

"William!" His name was a shriek as she stumbled inside and grabbed his feet. It took all her strength to drag him toward the door. Sweat coursed down her face and between her breasts. Flames leaped to the bed and began to devour both it and its occupant. Feeling she was justified in assuming the girl was dead, she kept at her task, pulling, fighting with every ounce of her strength to save the living occupant from the inferno.

Just when she thought she couldn't move him any farther, she stumbled backwards out the door and a few feet more, dragging him after her. As she dropped panting beside him, the roof collapsed, sending out a shower of sparks and a blast of heat so intense her senses spun. Choking and gasping, she resumed her struggles, pulling him foot by desperate foot across the clearing until they were in the edge of the trees, out of immediate danger.

She fell down beside him, shaking. With the last of her flagging strength, she managed to turn him over and look down into his face. Placing a soot-blackened hand on his neck, she searched for a pulse as he'd taught her. And found one.

A wave of relief greater than anything she'd ever experienced washed over her. Then, as she stared back at the blazing cabin, a new terror engulfed her. The blazing building could trigger a full-fledged forest fire she would be powerless to stop. One that she and the doctor could be trapped in if she didn't get them out of its way, and quickly.

His moan brought her attention back to him. He'd opened his eyes and was struggling to blink back to reality.

"Doctor!" She raised his head in her lap. Hysterical laughter threatened to engulf her, but she fought it off. "Doctor, you're alive."

"Aye." He grimaced, baring even white teeth. "Lass, what happened? Argh, my head hurts."

He struggled up on one elbow, his face contorting with pain.

"Sweet Jesus!" he stared at the cabin engulfed in the flames. "The girl…"

"She died before the fire." Heather tried to still the trembling that seemed to have infected every inch of her body. "When I found you, her eyes were open and she wasn't moving. I've seen the stare of death before."

"Poor wee lass." He closed his eyes tight, contorting his features with the effort.

"Her mother must have bludgeoned you and then, when she knew her daughter was dead, set the place on fire." Heather drew a dirty hand across her face. "The woman is insane."

"Aye, aye." He started to get to his feet but staggered and would have fallen if Heather hadn't caught him. "You pulled me out of that inferno, didn't you, lass?"

"Dragged you a wee bit." She tried to make light of the situation. If it got too serious, she knew she'd burst into tears. "You appeared a might under the weather."

"Thank you, lassie." Blue eyes mirrored such sincerity it took her breath away. For a moment she could only stand locked within it.

"Now." He broke the spell. "We'd best see if we can quiet our horses sufficiently to mount them and get out of here. You did ride here, didn't you?"

"Of course. Oh, God, look! The trees beyond the cabin! They're aflame!"

"Bloody hell!" He turned to follow her horrified gaze. "With the bush as dry as tinder— Lass, catch up your mount and ride back to the farm. We're about to have a full-fledged forest fire on our hands. I'll head upriver to warn the village. With the wind blowing in its direction, the community will need to be ready to evacuate."

"I'll go with you. Two sentinels will be able to warn more people."

"No, no, lass!" Already he was releasing the stallion's reins from their moorings as he attempted to quiet the terrified animal. "You must go to the farm and make ready for any burned or injured victims. I'll warn the villagers. Wings is much faster than your mare."

Holding the stallion's reins in one hand, he caught her with his free arm and pulled her to him into a kiss so filled with passion her breath left her body, her spirit soared, and her mind cried, *I love you, I love you with all my heart and soul, William MacTavish.*

As quickly as he'd grasped her against his chest, he released her. For a moment, he looked down at her, blue eyes seething with emotion.

"Go," he said hoarsely. "Ride hard. I'll be back with you soon."

Recognizing the wisdom in his words, she ran to her mount and battled the animal's terror until she was able to scramble aboard. Then she and the doctor set off at a gallop, each to their own assigned destinations.

****

They kept coming and coming, stumbling wild-eyed and gasping out of the smoke that had engulfed the valley since the previous day. Heather, her hair straggling out of its queue at the nape of her neck, struggled to find places for them in the house and barn. Glancing up at the thick clouds of smoke blotting out the sky, feeling the sharp pain of wood smoke in her lungs, Heather Grey fought to control her rising terror and remain in command of the situation.

Doctor, please come back, I need you! The thought was a silent cry for help that, looking upriver at the dense billows enveloping the valley, she feared might never be answered. It had been over twenty-four hours since they'd parted in the road to the village, twenty-four hours since he'd kissed her and promised to return to her.

He will come back, he has to come back.

Shoving damp curls back from her face, she wouldn't think the word "if." Doctor William MacTavish was clever and tough and resourceful. There could be no doubt he would return.

"Miss?" A woman, her face smeared with charcoal, her dress ripped and blackened, came to join her. "Do you think the fire will reach this far? Should we start downriver along the bank?"

"Not yet." Heather looked into the woman's pleading expression. With a shock of horror, she realized she, at nineteen years of age, was in charge of this camp of refugees, that they were looking to her for guidance and reassurance. "We can't see the flames, and the wind is not in our direction...yet. But be ready to go."

She started toward the house, through a throng of people, all turning to her as she passed, all looking for leadership. *God, give me wisdom and strength.* She paused at the kitchen door, looked out over the smoke-choked river, and saw it…a ship, most of its sails furled, moving slowly toward the farm. The *Highland Lass*. Captain MacTavish and Jewels!

Catching up her skirts, she ran toward the river, waving and shouting.

****

"Bonny!" Julia leaped into the water and caught her friend in her arms as the longboat from the ship reached the shallows. "Oh, dear God, Bonny Lass! We were at the bay's entrance and headed for the Caribbean when an outbound schooner overtook us with news that the entire valley was aflame."

"Jewels!" Heather clung to her friend for a moment, then held her out at arm's length. "Jewels, that was brave of you and Captain MacTavish, but foolhardy. You shouldn't have returned. These people tell tales of dozens of ships ablaze further upriver. If the fire reaches us, the *Highland Lass* could well suffer a similar fate."

"We'd have been sniveling cowards if we'd turned tail and sailed for sea." Captain James MacTavish jumped from the long boat, leaving the two sailors who'd rowed them ashore to pull it onto the beach. "Now, how might we help?"

An hour later, the *Highland Lass*, her former cargo of Caribbean-bound lumber thrown overboard to make space, was moving back downriver, crowded with women and children. Captain MacTavish explained he'd dared not unfurl all their sails on the inward voyage, not knowing when he might encounter cinders. Now, beyond that danger, he had every inch of canvas to the wind in the effort to get his passengers to safety. He'd be back for a second cargo as soon as he delivered these beyond reach of the fire, he'd assured Heather. As he sailed away, his wife stood beside Heather on the shore and waved farewell.

"Jewels, you should have gone with him." Heather turned to her friend. "If things go wrong, there's no need for you to be caught here with me."

"There's every reason, my Bonny Lass." A look of grim determination Heather knew defied argument filled Jewels MacTavish's face. "We started this adventure together. We'll see it through together. Now, come. Let's get these people organized. The men who've sent their wives, sweethearts, and children away with Jamie need instructions. We can't have them moping about. I'll organize the farm work. You see to the food stocks and how to best ration them."

Inside the house, Heather was greeted by a crowd of women and children, huddled in corners, squatted on the floor. Some were suffering burns and cuts. She needed more room. Under such circumstances, Doctor MacTavish's secret room at the top of the stairs could no longer be respected.

She dashed up the stairs, then paused for a moment, her hand on the room's doorknob. What would she find inside? God only knew, but she couldn't stop now.

The door creaked open on hinges long unused. At first when she peered inside she saw little. The shutters were closed, and opening them would help little, since the darkness outside caused by the great clouds of smoke had blocked out most natural lighting. Advancing into the room, she closed her eyes for a moment to accustom them to the darkness. When she opened them, she gasped.

The room was outfitted as a luxurious master bedroom, a huge bed with hangings in its centre. But most astonishing was the lavish cradle by its side. Mounted on polished wooden hangings, it was level with the bed from which the occupants could reach out and make it sway. A rush of understanding flooded over her. William MacTavish's marriage to the minister's daughter had produced a child and something tragic had happened to both the baby and its mother. He'd maintained this beautiful big room as a shrine to them.

The dressing table held silver hair brushes and glass bottles and jars. The bedcovers were of the finest silk. Even the draperies on the shuttered windows were thick and luxurious. A large fireplace along one wall brought the image of intimate winter nights shared by the couple in that wonderful bed. The woman had been refined and probably very beautiful, with soft hands that had never milked a cow or shoveled manure or scrubbed down his surgery. Her heart plummeted. After having had a life with such a woman, he'd never be able to accept such as Heather Grey, tavern wench, into his life.

Chapter 13

"Mistress, where are you? We have a woman with a bad burn on her arm. We need your help."

"Coming." The summons from belowstairs brought her back to the moment. This was no time to go mooning about over a man who'd never seen her as anything more than a worker and perhaps a dalliance. Right now there was a disaster of catastrophic proportion on her doorstep, and she must deal with it as best she could.

****

The danger was over. That's what the latest messenger from upriver had said. Her face streaked with dirt, her hair straggling about her face, Heather Grey put her hands on her hips, drew a deep breath, and looked out over the encampment of refugees in her yard. House and barn were filled with other victims of the huge conflagration that had destroyed all in its path. The pasture was crowded with livestock they'd managed to save.

Overhead, vast charcoal clouds still drifted across a leaden sky. At the foot of the rise on which the farm was situated, the *Highland Lass* floated at anchor in the river, which had been brought to a near boil by the inferno but had now quieted to dark calm. The fire might be over, but the pain and devastation it had wrought hung over the valley like a giant pall. It would take years to recover, and the coming winter would be a hard one, with many crops destroyed and livestock lost, not to mention neighbors and relatives killed.

But what of the doctor? Not one of the messengers who came to the farm carrying news both good and bad had any intelligence of him. He'd last been seen helping families get to the relative safety of the river, but after that—nothing. Where was he?

Please, please, just send him back to me. The silent prayer came from her heart with all the passion of a plea. *He's a good man, a man this valley desperately needs. Please, please.*

"So there you are." Julia came to stand beside her. "Why don't you try to get some rest? I may not be as skilled a nurse as you, but I can manage for an hour or so. If anything serious comes up, I'll be sure to seek you out."

"Thank you, Jewels, but I couldn't sleep." She brushed a weary hand across her face. "Not until I know what has become of the doctor."

"You love him, don't you?" Julia put an arm around her friend's sagging shoulders.

"Yes." The word was barely above a whisper.

"So much in love with him you're afraid to say it out loud in case he doesn't return the feeling."

"Jewels, you know me so well." Heather turned to her, forcing a weak smile.

"Well, exhausting yourself won't help." She took her friend by the shoulders and turned her toward the house. "I've seen to it that your room is empty. Go and lie down."

"Very well." The words came out in a defeated

sigh. "But"—she rounded on her friend—"you will call me the moment there's news of the doctor...of William." The words were an order, not a request.

"Of course."

Then they saw the wagon turning in at the gate and recognized the driver. Benjamin Two Rivers drove a farm wagon slowly down the lane toward them, a bedraggled grey horse Heather barely recognized as Wings tied to its rear.

****

"Ah, Will. Sweet Jesus, Will." Captain Jamie MacTavish bent over the body of his brother lying prone on the boards in the back of the crude farm wagon driven by the shaman. Tears welled in his eyes as he looked down at the man, his clothes burned to rags, his face blackened almost beyond recognition. "Ya gave it your all, didn't you, laddie? And now they've brought you home like this."

"It happened while he was saving that great witch, Hannah Rob." Benjamin Two Rivers looked down at his cargo. "He shoved her into the river just as a great, fiery tree toppled toward them. The river swept her away to drown, while the doctor took the full brunt of the crash. I found him on the bank unconscious. His horse I discovered on the road to the farm, and caught him. I think the animal was trying to come home."

Although her heart banged a tattoo in her chest and her stomach roiled, Heather climbed into the wagon bed, knelt beside him, and searched for a pulse. And there it was. Faint, but still a pulse.

"He's not dead!" The words gushed out like a ray of hope. She pulled herself upright and looked at the group of men who'd come to surround the wagon.

"Carry him to his surgery. Now! Hurry!" Her words were orders cracked out like a drill sergeant's. "Benjamin, you must help me."

"Sweet merciful God! Alive!" Jamie MacTavish dragged a dirty hand across his eyes, then swung to the onlookers. "You heard the woman! Get the man to his surgery. There's no time to be gawking!"

Chapter 14

Doctor William MacTavish came back to reality with the sensation of searing pain in his back, down his arm, up his leg, into every portion of his anatomy of which he was conscious. His mouth, dried to dust, seemed unable to function. The place was dark. Or was he blind? The thought stirred him to move. And groan.

"You're back." Her voice welcomed him with soft, weary tones. "Thank God. Lie still. Rest."

"Lass." He croaked her name. He tried to move, and grunted at the additional pain it caused.

"Don't try to move." He felt her hand on his forehead, the backs of her fingers checking for fever as he'd taught her.

"Dark." He struggled to produce the word. "Am I…blind?"

"It's night."

"Candle…light." He had to know.

He heard her rise, move away, out of the room. *Relax, ease your body, ride with the pain, don't fight it.* He tried to follow the directions he'd so often given his patients.

A glorious light filled the doorway. A candle. He could see its halo. And at its centre stood an angel…an angel he called Lass.

"See…I can…see…you." He battled out the report.

"Of course you can." Placing the candle on the table beside it, she knelt beside his bed. In the flickering light, Doctor William MacTavish saw tears running down her face.

"Aw, lass, dunnae weep." He managed to raise his hand nearest her to touch her damp cheek. "It will take more than a wee fire to do in the likes of this stubborn Highlander."

"It was more than a wee fire." She sniffed and brightened the nimbus of the candle with her smile. "It burned most of this valley. It swung east several miles upriver and jumped the water to take a different direction, sparing this farm and all those who'd sought refuge here. But now you must rest. I have work to do. We've many souls who've lost everything, here in the house and barn. They must be fed and the injured tended. Don't fret." She stopped him with a hand on his shoulder as he made an effort to rise. "I have excellent help. Your friend Benjamin has given of his knowledge of medicines and natural cures. In fact, he treated most of your injuries. Jamie and Jewels are here, as well, and a number of neighbors whose farms have escaped the conflagration are most willing to assist."

She stood, blew out the candle, and then in the darkness he felt her lips on his forehead.

"Sleep, Doctor. This valley will be needing you more than ever. You must get well soon."

"William." He stopped her as she opened the door.

"What?"

"William…my name is William."

"And mine is Heather. Perhaps you'll begin to do me the honor of calling me such."

Her shadow gave a saucy swish, and then she was

gone. *Impudent little wench.* Her response engendered a grin that made him flinch as it tugged at his cracked lips. There could be no other woman quite like his lass.

****

"So he saved my life once again." William leaned back against the pillows she'd propped behind him and breathed a deep sigh as Heather finished her account of Ben's bringing him home and tending him.

"Again?" She looked at him in surprise.

"Aye." He drew a deep breath. "Now that you've told me you've uncovered the secret of the room at the top of the stairs, you may as well know all. After my wife and son died, I turned to drink. They passed in November, just after Jamie had sailed out of the river, not to return until spring. There was no one to stop me. I became useless, a great drunken lout living in squalor, hoping that instead of waking each morning to an attack of vomiting and raging head pain, I'd be dead. I ignored my patients, forgot my vows to help those in need of my services.

"In early April, Ben found me. He'd been gone on a mission for his band most of the winter. Without saying a single word, he attacked me, bound me, threw me over a horse, and headed for his village. There, against my will, he forced me into a sweat lodge. At first I could only choke and rage, but then the atmosphere, the chanting, the ethereal ambience began to soothe my soul. It took time and many sweats, massages, and other treatments chosen and administered by Ben, but by May I was well on my way to recovery. In June I returned to this house and took up my practice. Without Ben and his knowledge of natural cures, I wouldn't have survived."

Chapter 15

"My love is like a red, red rose that's newly sprung in spring."

Heather couldn't contain the happiness that was brimming in her heart as she sang and shook hay into Charlie's manger.

"My name is William," he'd said, in a voice that implied so much more than permission to call him by his Christian name.

"I'll make him a good wife…once he realizes that's what he wants and needs." She patted the massive horse as he nuzzled her. "I'll be a good doctor's wife. I've stood up to all the tests, haven't I?"

"But perhaps you won't measure up to the next one." The voice made her whirl, her heart plummeting as she faced the silhouette in the barn doorway.

No, it can't be. It can't possibly be…Liam Jones!

With a gut-wrenching sensation of nausea, she recognized the tangled, dirty curls, the wide, drink-reddened face, as the big man advanced into the barn. His right hand gripped a pistol held leveled at her.

"How did you find me?" Her words rasped from a dry throat.

"The dog." He pointed to Midnight standing by her side, a deep growl issuing from his throat. "An easily recognizable travelling companion if ever there was one. You should have left the cur chained in your brother's barn. And I had help. Just before the fire, I returned from Halifax, fuming with rage at being sent on a false trail. But I found help, in the person of the witch Hannah Rob. I'm told she drowned during the fire."

"Leave this farm at once." Her courage overcoming her shock, she drew herself up to face him. "The doctor will be coming down to the barn any minute. He won't be pleased to discover you've been threatening his assistant."

"Assistant, is that what you're calling yourself?" He advanced toward her, sneering. "More like his whore. Anyhow, I happen to know the good doctor lies abed recovering from his brush with the fire." He reached to grab her, but the dog, with a roar, leaped.

There was an explosion. Midnight howled and fell in mid leap, blood spurting from his side. Liam Jones stood with the smoking gun in hand.

Heather was too stunned to react. Then, as the dog lay unmoving at her feet, she came back to the moment. With a savage yell, she leaped at the man. He drew back the emptied gun and brought it down full force against her temple. Thrown against the boards of Charlie's stall, she slumped to the floor with a moan, unconscious. Her last memory was of the great horse roaring while massive hooves beat the barn floor.

****

Pain, pain, pain. It ravished her head, made her moan, and when she tried to open her eyes, the light brought more.

"Finally awake, are ye?"

His voice forced her to try to focus. At first all she

could see were his boots, as she lay on her side, but with an effort she managed to look up and recognize the brute looming over her. As more reality returned, she realized her hands and feet were bound and she was lying on the ground somewhere in the forest. Blackflies swarmed around her face in the sullen heat.

"Let me go." She choked the words from a throat that burned from thirst.

"Hardly, missy." He bent and jerked her to a sitting position, pushing her back against a tree trunk. "I didn't come all this way to chin-wag with you. I won you fair and square from your brother the night before you disappeared. I had to do murder for you, although it is not what I'd planned. If that fool Neil hadn't tried to prevent my claiming what was rightfully mine, all would have been well. I'll not be cheated.

"Now what I need from you is the whereabouts of your friend the Lady Julia Thomas. Her father has offered a hearty reward for her return. With it, you and me can set ourselves up for life. I'll have a fine farm and a tavern back in the Old Country. I'll be a man of means. Now, tell me, where is the wench?" He hunkered down beside her, grabbed a handful of her hair, and gave it a yank.

"There's a murder charge hanging over you in England. You can't go back." The pain of his brutality made her gasp, and her senses spun, but she masked it by speaking as normally as she could muster.

"Ah, but there you're wrong, missy. The authorities have become convinced that your brother was killed by a highwayman and that you were abducted by the same person, the man who came injured into his tavern, the man whose life you saved.

So you see, we're both free to return. Now tell me, where is your friend? She's worth enough gold to set us up for life."

"She's married and her husband is a powerful man who won't take kindly to anyone who threatens his wife."

"Oh, aye? Well, I don't believe you, and before I'm finished with you, you'll be begging to tell me the whereabouts of her ladyship."

He squatted in front of her, a huge bulk smelling worse than any farm animal she'd ever tended.

The stench, the possibility of being wife to such a creature, and the throbbing in her head combined to bring on an overwhelming bout of nausea. She retched, narrowly missing him as he jumped aside.

"Ah, nice." He stumbled to his feet. "Vomit on me, will you? Well, my fine lady, you'll have to do more than that to turn me away. I'll leave you to recover, but I'll be back. By then, I'm certain sure you'll tell me exactly where I might find your companion on this escapade."

He strode away, leaving her at the mercy of the night and the insects.

****

He awoke to the strange sensation that something was wrong. The room was dark and cold. He shivered and pulled the blankets more snugly about him. What had aroused him? Somewhere in his foggy state he seemed to recall a blast. A gun blast. Someone hunting on his land? Or had he imagined it? Had memories of the fire and trees exploding into flame been haunting him again? She'd given him opium mixed with milk to help him sleep. That concoction could have strange effects. But, no. He hadn't been dreaming. He pulled himself to a sitting position and rubbed his temples. What had he heard?

"Heather." He called her name softly at first, then when he got no response, louder. "Heather."

Damn, where was she? He stood and pulled on his pants and shirt. Since the fire, she'd always heard his slightest call.

Struggling to regain his equilibrium, he crossed the corridor to her room. In the moonlight he could see her bed had not been slept in. It must be the middle of the night. Where could she be?

Remembering the blast, he blew out the candle and headed barefoot and quiet to the stairs, then down their length. His heart banged against his chest. Something was very wrong, and it involved his lass.

He eased his way into the kitchen. Moonlight revealed its emptiness and the unbarred door.

"Heather!" Her name hissed from his lips as he strode across the room and outside. Just beyond the steps leading to the door lay a black mound.

"Midnight." He dropped to one knee beside the animal. "Midnight, wake up, lad. Where's Heather? What happened?"

The big dog moved slowly, languidly as he tried to get from his side to an upright position. Then Will saw the trail of blood from the direction of the barn.

"Dear God!" He examined the dog and found the raw area where shot had torn away a great section of his back and shoulder fur.

"I'll fix you up as best I can, laddie," he said softly. "Then you have to help me find the lass."

****

With bandages swathed around about his chest and shoulders, the dog wobbled to his feet, then, with a yelp of pain, shook itself and looked at William, dark eyes dull and heavy.

"Midnight." He took the dog's muzzle in both hands. "You have to find Heather. Now."

The dog licked dry lips and steadied himself.

"Water. You need water." He strode out to the well and dropped the bucket. Shortly the big dog was gobbling up the cold drink.

"Now, boy, go." William stood and ordered the dog. Midnight looked up at him for a moment, then with a whine, made his way unsteadily outdoors, put his nose to the ground, circled twice, then headed off at an unsteady trot toward the woods beyond the pasture.

"Good boy." William took off at a jog pace behind him, the night air clearing his head as he drew in deep breaths for the purpose.

They hadn't gone far when William glimpsed a flash of light ahead. A flame, he amended his initial observation.

His instinct was to rush forward, but intelligence overcame rashness as he caught the dog by the scruff and held his muzzle to stifle his whines.

"Quiet. Stay," he muttered and released the animal for the instant it took him to pull off his shirt. After making a loop from one sleeve, he pulled it about the dog's neck and managed to secure the animal to a tree using the other arm.

"Stay. Quiet." He ordered the restless dog again. So near his mistress, Midnight had to struggle to control himself. William understood his feelings, but rushing into the situation wasn't the way to help.

Inching forward, battling not to step on any snapping twigs, he made his way toward the wavering light. When he reached a point where he could see what was happening, joy mingled with fear washed over him.

To one side of a small clearing, Heather sat bound against a tree trunk, her head canted to one side, either asleep or unconscious. Laid out in a tangle of blankets near the fire was a man, the big lout he recognized as the same man who'd come inquiring after Heather and Jewels in George Fowler's store. Outrage and fear mingled in his gut to form a noxious rage.

He started forward, but a great roar made him whirl. The dog had broken free of his makeshift tether and leaped out of the darkness to land on Liam Jones. The man awoke with a scream and began to thrash at the animal that held him firmly by an arm.

"Midnight, no!" Heather, roused to consciousness by the outburst, shouted at the dog. "Stop!"

The dog, at the sound of his mistress's voice, paused but remained straddled over the cringing man, teeth bared, a deep growl rumbling in his throat.

"It's all right, laddie." Will moved forward into the firelight and took the dog by the shirt dangling from his neck. "He won't be hurting you again." Glancing at Heather, he saw such relief mirrored in her face he could barely look upon it.

Then her expression turned to one of horror.

"Will, look out!" He whirled to see the man had taken advantage of his momentary distraction to grab up a pistol and was pointing it at him. In the quickest move he'd made since he'd been injured in the fire, Will lunged. The two men struggled. The gun discharged. Liam Jones slumped against William's chest. As he slid to the ground, the doctor saw the dark hole in his chest at the level of his heart.

For a moment he stood over the body, the pistol clutched in his hand.

"William." Her voice brought him back to reality and he turned to her. Midnight was already by her side, solicitously licking her face. "William." The last was soft, a half sob. He dropped the weapon and forced rubbery legs to carry him to her side.

****

"He doesn't look much like a cupid." Heather leaned over the pasture fence and gazed at the silver stallion cavorting in the autumn sunshine. "Yet he managed to bring Jewels and your brother together, as well as you and me. Quite a feat for an animal, don't you agree, Doctor?"

"Aye, lass, indeed he did. He gave Jamie a jewel beyond compare and myself more Heather than any displaced Highlander has any right to expect."

"I just wish he and I hadn't been equal prizes in those wagers you made with your brother." She slanted him a sly grin.

"Will you never lay that to rest? They were only made that I might teach Jamie a lesson about gambling...and interfering in my life. I never expected him to bring me the likes of you."

He looked down at her, eyes twinkling.

"Oh, and are you saying you regret that bet?" she taunted.

"How could I? It served its purpose. It got Jamie to stop living a way of life that could only lead to disaster. The Lady Julia Thomas put an end to all his wild ways. And it brought me a partner beyond my greatest expectations. Now enough talk of the past. It's to the future we must be looking."

"Agreed."

"Blue sky." He leaned against the pasture fence and gazed out over the river sparkling in the sunshine. "Three weeks ago I didn't think I'd survive to see it again."

"It is beautiful." Heather stood beside him, hands on her hips, and joined his perusal.

"Perhaps that old reprobate Hannah was right." He drew a deep breath and coughed. His lungs still weren't back to normal.

"What do you mean?" She turned her head to look at him, emerald eyes sharp and piercing.

"Perhaps the fire was sent to punish the sins of Jamie and me. Perhaps…"

"Enough!" The word snapped at him, startled him. "It was a natural disaster, nothing more. One ridiculous old woman preaching fire and brimstone could not predict such an event. Things happen. Life happens. All we can do is live the best we can under the circumstances. Furthermore…" She turned back to look out over the river. "It's time you stopped laboring under a sense of guilt and remorse. What happened to your wife and son was a great tragedy, but there's no going back. You were in no way responsible."

"How can you say that? I was off tending other people when I should have been at home with a wife I knew to be delicate, that I suspected might go prematurely into labor. I should have been with them. I should have…" Anger at her presumptions made him whirl on her, grasp her by the shoulders.

"I can say that because I know Kathleen was a

good woman who loved you, who wouldn't want you to bury yourself under a burden of guilt." She met his heated expression, unflinching. "I can say it because I know she'd want you to get on with your life. I can say it because I love you."

He could only stare at the woman looking up at him, green eyes unblinking and honest. "There." After several moments of pregnant silence she shrugged away. "I've said my piece. Take it for what it's worth, Doctor MacTavish."

She headed for the house, her strides strong and determined. And suddenly he was running after her, limping a bit.

"Lass, lass." He caught up to her, swung her to face him. "Just now. Did you mean what you said?"

"Have you ever known me not to mean what I say, sir?" She stuck out her chin and squared her shoulders.

"No, no, that I haven't." He wet his lips and took a deep breath. "And have you ever known me not to mean what I say?"

"Never." She continued to meet his gaze steadily.

"Then you will believe me when I say I need you to stay, that I need you to share my life and work."

"You'll have to do better than that, Doctor." She pulled free and continued on toward the house.

"Ah, verra well, ya stubborn wench." He caught up to her again but, instead of laying hands on her, got in front of her, blocking her way, forcing her to stop. "I love ya. I suppose I must marry you...if I'm to have any peace on this earth."

"Hmmm. Not very romantic, William MacTavish." She cocked her head coquettishly to one side. "I think I'd like a bit of courting and a proper proposal before I decide if I'll have you."

She continued on toward the house, hips swaying, pausing only once, briefly, to cast a sly smile back at him over her shoulder.

"Damn and blast!" He kicked a dust hummock and sent dirt flying. Courting, indeed.

With a yell that would have done any young buck credit, he ran after her.

"Hold up, lass, just you hold up!" He caught up to her, spun her about and up into his arms. "If it's courting you want, it's courting you'll get. But first I'll be hearing that your intentions toward me are honorable, that you're willing to make an honest man of me. Heather Grey, will you be my wife?"

She looked deep into those bonny blue eyes and smiled.

"Yes, I believe I will, Doctor MacTavish, I do believe I will marry you."

****

"What's all this?" Will halted the buggy Jamie had lent them for their wedding travels from the farm to the church, then to Jamie and Jewel's deserted house to spend the night, and finally back to their own farm. Jamie and Jewels had declared the couple needed time alone without the interruptions of patients for at least twenty-four hours following their marriage. Captain MacTavish and his wife would stay at the farm and hand out rudimentary medicines, only contacting Will and Heather in the possibility of a life-or-death situation.

Now the newlyweds could only stare at their farmyard filled with wagons and people in the bright October sunlight. The river glistened, and the birches

256

and maples surrounding the property showed their best reds and golds.

"I think Jamie and Jewels may be returning the reception you gave them on their marriage." Heather hugged her new husband's arm and smiled up at him.

"Aye, that would explain it." A grin that she knew wouldn't have been possible that spring quirked the corners of his mouth. "Well, let's go, lass. No need to keep the guests waiting." He flapped the reins over the horse's back and sent it at a gallop down the lane.

As the couple arrived in the yard, a whoop went up from the assembled group. The gelding pranced and would have reared if Jamie hadn't caught it by the bridle and contained its excitement.

"Welcome, brother," he called. "We've been waiting. I won't ask what kept you, being a recently married man myself, but now that you're here, let's get on with the festivities."

A roar of laughter went up from the men in the crowd as Jordon Fowler came forward to lift Heather down.

"Congratulations, Mrs. MacTavish," he said. "I wish you all the best." And though she saw a wisp of sadness in his handsome face she knew he was sincere.

"Thank you, Jordan. That's most kind."

"Best wishes to you, sir, as well." He turned to William and extended his hand.

"Thank you, Jordon. You're a gentleman." The younger man lowered his head and blushed as he turned away.

"That was generous." Heather smiled up at William.

"Aye, considering he keeps making me feel old

enough to be your father by calling me sir." He grimaced down at her.

"Ladies and gentlemen." Jamie, his arm around a beaming Jewels, called for attention. "There'll be music and dancing here on the green later, but first *my* Mrs. MacTavish and I invite you inside to partake of a bit of food and drink and to toast the happy couple."

"What…?" William's face registered the surprise as his brother and his wife led him and Heather inside and into the centre of the house, where the wide doors of both the parlor and the dining room had been thrown open to form one large area filled with tables, chairs, food, and drink.

"Will, it's time you opened up this mausoleum to life and love again." Jamie put an arm around his brother's shoulders. "It's time to start anew."

For a moment Heather feared he'd be outraged at his brother's audacity. But it was only for a moment.

"You're right, brother." William turned to Jamie. "Yes, this time you're definitely right. Come along," he called the guests who were waiting in the kitchen and yard. "Come along, everyone. Tonight is for feasting and celebrating the happiness I've been so fortunate to find a second time."

****

The wedding guests were still dancing in the dooryard when William drew his bride aside and led her surreptitiously into the house and up the stairs. At the top he paused in front of the closed door, then reached to open it.

"William, you don't have to do this." Heather stopped him with his hand on the knob. "I used this room during the fire to house refugees. I know I shouldn't have, but we had so little space and so many homeless and hurt. As soon as I could, while you were recovering, I put everything back just as you'd left it. There's no need…"

"Oh, but I think there is." He shoved open the door, caught her up in his arms and carried her inside.

The bed had been made with fresh linen, the dressing table freed of his first wife's possessions, and the crib moved into a far corner. But, most amazingly, the new bedding and curtains had been embroidered with sprigs of heather.

"Oh, William!" she breathed as he put her feet on the floor. "It's wonderful. But how…?"

"I must admit I had a wee bit of assistance from the other Mrs. MacTavish and Mrs. Fowler." He grinned. "I must also admit I thought it a stroke of genius. Now." He went back to the door, closed it, and locked it. "Let us begin to enjoy this room and our lives together."

She gave no protest as he once again caught her up in his arms and carried her to the bed.

A word about the author...

Gail MacMillan is the award-winning author of over thirty published books, with numerous articles published in magazines throughout North America and Western Europe.

Visit her at:

macgail@nbnet.nb.ca